It's tough being a trophy.

Marla Maples has a lot to answer for. The world
thinks of second wives as hot little *pomme de terre*
who lure previously faithful but chronologically
susceptible husbands away from their virtuous
original mates with sexual practices that, while not
technically illegal, stretch the limits of respectability. Granted, such stereotypes exist for a reason.
But for every scheming sexpot dressed by Victoria's
Secret, somewhere there's a Mrs. DeWinter living
in the shadow of Rebecca, and harassed, to boot,
by a passel of antagonistic stepchildren.

SECRET LIVES OF SECOND WIVES

D0664329

ALSO BY CATHERINE TODD

EXIT STRATEGIES
MAKING WAVES
STAYING COOL

ATTENTION: ORGANIZATIONS AND CORPORATIONS
Most HarperTorch paperbacks are available at special quantity discounts for bulk purchases for sales promotions, premiums, or fund-raising. For information, please call or write:

Special Markets Department, HarperCollins Publishers, Inc., 10 East 53rd Street, New York, N.Y. 10022–5299.
Telephone: (212) 207–7528. Fax: (212) 207-7222.

CATHERINE TODD

SECRET LIVES OF SECOND WIVES

HarperTorch
An Imprint of HarperCollinsPublishers

This is a work of fiction. Names, characters, places, and incidents are products of the author's imagination or are used fictitiously and are not to be construed as real. Any resemblance to actual events, locales, organizations, or persons, living or dead, is entirely coincidental.

❦ HARPERTORCH
An Imprint of HarperCollins*Publishers*
10 East 53rd Street
New York, New York 10022-5299

Copyright © 2003 by Catherine Todd
ISBN: 0-06-095347-0

All rights reserved. No part of this book may be used or reproduced in any manner whatsoever without written permission, except in the case of brief quotations embodied in critical articles and reviews. For information address HarperTorch, an imprint of HarperCollins Publishers.

First HarperTorch paperback printing: June 2004
First William Morrow hardcover printing: July 2003

HarperCollins®, HarperTorch™, and ❦ ™ are trademarks of HarperCollins Publishers Inc.

Printed in the United States of America

Visit HarperTorch on the World Wide Web at www.harpercollins.com

10 9 8 7 6 5 4 3 2 1

If you purchased this book without a cover, you should be aware that this book is stolen property. It was reported as "unsold and destroyed" to the publisher, and neither the author nor the publisher has received any payment for this "stripped book."

For Maxine and Art

ACKNOWLEDGMENTS

Special thanks to Krista Stroever for helping me with excellent suggestions for improving this book, to Carrie Feron and Erika Tsang for seeing it through to publication, and to Larry Ashmead for believing in my work.

Thanks, too, to all the terrific people at Harper-Collins for their part in the production and publication of *Secret Lives of Second Wives,* including the production manager, Derek Gullino; my copy editor, Maureen Sugden; my publicist, Claire Greenspan; the jacket designer, Honi Werner; the sales and marketing departments; and the representatives on the road.

Finally, heartfelt thanks to my agent, Denise Marcil, for just about everything.

AUTHOR'S NOTE

Although the Immigration and Naturalization Service (INS) handled "extraordinary ability alien" processing at the time this book was written and set, the organization ceased to exist as of March 1, 2003. The immigration matters referred to in the novel are now handled by the Bureau of Citizenship and Immigration Services, part of the Department of Homeland Security. As of this writing, service centers and district offices retain their current names and locations, but administration and policies are obviously subject to change.

SECRET LIVES OF SECOND WIVES

CHAPTER 1

What is the opposite of premonition? There are people who "know" things in advance, or say they do. I am not one of them. In fact, I frequently don't "know" something even after it's already happened. I've always suspected that a penchant for portent is another form of Looking for Trouble, a selfish sort of instinct for misery. Still, it's hard to ignore people who are convinced something bad will happen, because life can change on you at a moment's notice. You listen, but deep down you don't really believe it.

All of which is a roundabout way of saying that when my well-ordered life started unraveling, despite ample hints and warnings, I didn't have a clue.

"OSCAR WILDE WAS DEAD BY MY AGE," Jack, my husband, said.

"So what?" I asked him, in what I hoped was an appropriately tender and sympathetic tone. "Your best years are still ahead." We'd been having this conversation in some form or other ever since the invitation to join AARP had arrived six weeks in advance of his fiftieth birthday, an event transpiring that very day. He'd dropped the envelope with a startled gasp, as if the impending birthday were a dreadful surprise, even though I'd been planning the party for weeks.

I had more or less run out of reassurances after "Grandma Moses didn't even start her best work until she was decades older than you" proved a flop.

"I feel like I've crossed over to the other side," he muttered darkly.

I didn't ask, *Of what?* "Oscar crossed over to the Other Side," I pointed out. "You haven't. You still have plenty of time for dissipation and frivolity. Want me to commission your portrait, Dorian?"

Normally this would elicit at least a rueful chuckle, but today he wasn't having any of it. "Did you know Wilde was only forty-one when he wrote that book?" he asked.

I didn't know. I was going to have to hide the Ellmann biography, at least until the party was over. I shook my head. "Do you think you could manage to enjoy yourself just a tiny bit this evening?"

Now he did smile, a little. "Sorry. Sure." He brushed his hair back from his forehead with his fingertips, a gesture that made him look about fifteen and adorable. It had worked on me the first time we ever met. "I'm looking forward to it, honestly."

It was my turn to smile. "Liar," I said. Although he

was far more gregarious than I was and the sort of person people gravitated to in a room, I'd discovered, belatedly, that he resisted being the center of attention, at least on this occasion.

He laughed. "Who wouldn't want two hundred of his most intimate friends to witness the beginning of his slide into senescence?"

I wanted tonight to be a success. After our wedding reception, it was the biggest party we'd given together, and it was supposed to be, in addition to a tribute to Jack, a kind of public statement of our partnership as a couple. Jack was popular and successful, and a birthday bash had seemed just the thing to honor him. I thought he'd warmed to the idea. Now I wasn't so sure.

"Maybe things did get a little out of hand with the guest list," I admitted. "Do you really mind?"

He raised his eyebrows in mock seriousness. "You promise there won't be any black balloons?"

"I promise."

"Not a single 'Over the Hill' banner?"

I nodded.

"I want to hear it out loud. It's binding that way."

"Banter maybe, but no banners. I can't control your friends," I said.

"I can," he said confidently. "Anyway, Lynn, the party is great. Really." The easy smile faded. "I'm sorry if I've seemed unappreciative."

"You haven't," I said. "I just want you to have fun. I don't want you to feel uncomfortable."

He shook his head. "It isn't that. It's just . . . there's some stuff you don't know."

"Worse than turning fifty?" I asked lightly, despite the inevitable frisson a statement like that evoked.

He shrugged. "Probably not," he said. "Never mind. We'll talk about it later. Okay?" He touched my arm affectionately. "I'll take my shower now, if you don't need me to do anything."

"No, that's fine," I told him. "Go ahead. I've called the hotel, and they seem to have everything under control." I sounded, even to myself, like the perfect Second Wife. Never be importunate. Don't push. Don't cling. Do not, in short, remind him of *her*.

Which didn't stop me thinking. *Cancer. Heart disease.* No, he didn't sound worried enough, and besides, he'd just had his annual checkup. Not an affair either; we'd only been married a year, and he *wouldn't*. Would he?

Something else, then. One of his children. My thoughts recoiled a little, withdrawing as they always did when they touched that topic. My stepchildren (if that's the right word for two fully grown adults with whom I had a relationship primarily characterized by its complexity) were Off-Limits.

I checked my watch. Whatever the "stuff" I didn't know was, it would have to wait. Maybe it was just the usual angst of acknowledging middle age, of swapping acid rock for acid reflux or discovering an unexpected enthusiasm for roughage. Nobody was immune. Certainly not me, although I had a few years to go before

I reached the milestone birthday. Women notice earlier anyway.

Besides, with the hotel handling the arrangements and the guest list consisting of reasonably sociable, well-intentioned adults, how could our party fail? All we had to do was show up and smile.

"THERE MIGHT BE A PROBLEM," the maître d' said, in my ear. Only about a quarter of the guests had arrived, my stepchildren were nowhere to be seen, and I was just about to sample a particularly elegant and delicious-looking crab puff. I never met a crab I didn't like.

"A problem?" I whispered back, catching the ominous tone. The puff stayed aloft, wedged between my fingers halfway to my mouth.

He nodded. "I'm afraid someone's attempted to . . . ah, pop a car, and the truck is stuck in the garage."

I looked at him without comprehension. "I beg your pardon?"

He affected a Gallic shrug, although he was no more French than I am. "Popped. You know. *Repo Man,*" he said urgently.

"You're saying somebody tried to repossess a car in the hotel garage and the tow truck is stuck in the entrance or something like that?" I translated.

He nodded. I studied the puff. I couldn't put it back, and if I bit into it my half of the conversation was likely to be severely limited. I grabbed a napkin and stuffed the hors d'oeuvre into the center.

A sudden, nasty thought occurred to me. "It's not the car of one of our guests?" I asked.

"Very possibly," he said. "I don't know. I'm afraid there's a rather . . . unpleasant scene. The hotel will sort it out," he said, folding his arms in a classic gesture of denial, "but until the truck is removed, your guests will be unable to get into the garage. I thought you should know."

Since this was Palo Alto—and not Manhattan—on a Saturday night, the parking problem didn't worry me as much as it might have. The streets were not chockablock with revelers, and there was more than one municipal lot. On the other hand, while the technology-stock bust had stranded a lot of newly impoverished Silicon Valley–ites with unaffordable car payments, repossession was supposed to be a private matter, like changing your underwear. Most took place in company parking lots or in the early-morning hours. You woke up one day and your car wasn't where it was the night before, like a visit from Santa Claus in reverse. After that, if anybody noticed that you were driving your wife's '95 Accord to work instead of the Lexus SUV, nobody would comment, much less gloat. Repossession meant failure, and failure, like the plague, might be contagious. The etiquette was to look the other way.

Still, it would be impossible to avert one's eyes with a repo man blocking the entrance, so I decided we should probably see what we could do to spare any of our guests the embarrassment. I didn't even want to speculate as to who it might be.

I looked around the room for Jack. "Have you seen my husband?" I asked the maître d'.

"I'm afraid not," he said.

"Okay," I said. "Then I'll go downstairs to the garage. When you see him, would you ask him to join me?"

I almost expected him to say, "Certainly, madam," but what he said was, "Yeah, okay."

THE GARAGE SMELLED LIKE EXPENSIVE GASOLINE.

"Repo Man" was about twenty-five and skinny, with an impressive collection of metallic facial adornments. "Oh, puhleeze," he was saying to another man, who was clinging to the driver's-side door of a BMW 740iL as if it were the life raft in *Cast Away*. The metal jaws of some contraption under the car had turned outward to lift the front wheels, but the turn was too tight for the truck to exit with its prey in tow. "Give me a break."

The driver was young, Asian, and looked near tears. "I'm this close to making the payment," he said. "This close." He made a gesture with the hand that wasn't gripping the door handle. "Can't you wait a few more days?"

"It's not up to me," said Repo Man. "I represent the legal owner. Which, unfortunately, is no longer you. Look," he said, in a slightly softer tone, "the easiest way to resolve this is for you to just let me take the car. If I leave now without it, we can get a judgment against you and come out with the sheriff's department. You don't want that, do you?"

"You bloodsucker," said the driver, wiping his eyes with the back of his hand. "Aren't you ashamed? What did you ever do for anybody? I *earned* this car!"

"I'm not ashamed," said Repo Man quietly. "*My* car is paid up. Old people, moms with kids—they make me feel bad. But you guys in high tech . . . Nah, I can sleep at night, no problem."

The driver was no one I knew, and I was unlikely to be of use in extricating the truck, since I had never even learned to parallel-park. I turned to go back up the stairs.

"I want a lawyer," the driver said.

"Oh, dude," said Repo Man. "What for? That's not going to do you any good. Your credit report sucks, you know that? It *sucks*."

The driver opened the car door and threw himself across both front seats, a posture that the gearshift must have made fairly uncomfortable. "I'm not getting out of this car until I at least talk to one. This is Silicon Valley. There must be a lawyer here somewhere. If you want this car so bad, go find me one."

"Oh, dude," Repo Man said again. Behind him, cars lined up to get into the garage were starting to honk.

I hitched up my velvet skirt so I wouldn't step on the hem navigating the stairs. I turned. "I'm a lawyer," I said, moving from the shadows into the bright fluorescent light.

This revelation generally has an effect similar to that of announcing "I'm a piranha" in a swimming pool. In this case, however, both of them looked at me with relief, particularly Repo Man, who believed, correctly, that the law was on his side. Neither of them appeared to question the theatrical emergence on cue of legal counsel dressed in formal attire and apparently given to lurking in dimly lit garages waiting for a summons. I give you the times.

They both started to speak at once. "Tell him—" "Can he do this?"

I looked at the driver, still sprawled over the palomino leather seats. "Are you behind in the payments?"

Repo Man rolled his eyes.

"Yeah," the kid said. "A couple of months."

"Seven months," Repo Man said.

"Well . . . ," I began.

"It's on private property," the kid said. "Aren't there laws against trespassing or something like that?"

"Look," I said, "I'm on shaky ground here. I'm not that kind of attorney. But I think it's okay to repossess on private property that isn't gated or locked."

Repo Man nodded vigorously.

"Isn't there some way to work this out?" I asked over the growing chorus of honking horns. "You can't stay wedged in here all night. The hotel will call the police. They probably already have."

"I got you the lawyer," Repo Man pointed out, inaccurately.

The kid sat up slowly. "I guess you have to take it," he said. "I can't pay. I'm going to get laid off."

Repo Man held out his hand. "I'll need the key to get the car straightened out."

The driver took the key off a key ring emblazoned with the BMW logo and handed it over slowly.

"If it's any consolation," Repo Man said, "you're not alone. You're the fifth car I've popped in two days."

"I'll get it back," the kid said.

"You do that," said Repo Man. "Buy yourself a lottery ticket."

"ASSHOLE," the kid muttered when the car was once more hooked up and towed away, a process accomplished with enviable dispatch.

"I'm sorry," I told him. I couldn't think of much to say to a stranger that wouldn't sound officious or trite, like "Money is not life's report card." Ha. Anyway, I needed to go back to my guests, who, I hoped, were finding places to park even as I stood there in the garage. "Are you going to be all right?" I asked him. "Do you have a ride home?"

He looked up as if he'd forgotten I was there. "What kind are you?" he asked.

"I beg your pardon?"

"Lawyer," he said. "What kind of lawyer are you?"

"Immigration," I told him.

His faced brightened noticeably, even in the garage's sickly light. "No kidding?"

I nodded, my heart sinking. I knew what was coming.

"Can you get me a green card?" he asked.

Probably not. The Immigration and Naturalization Service—the INS—tends to look with disfavor on granting permanent residence to the unemployed. "Are you on an H-1B?" I asked him.

"Lynn?" my husband called, from the top of the stairs. "Is everything all right?"

"Fine," I told him. "I'll be right there." I turned back to the kid.

"An H-1. Yeah," he said.

"Well, under the H-1B visa you are only allowed to be here while you're actively performing services for the employer. After that you lose your status, and you're technically illegal. Your best bet is to try to find another job right away, if you can, and file for another H-1. You can work on a green card after that."

He looked as if he might be near tears again, so I reached into my purse and handed him a couple of cards. "Here's my card. If you call my office on Monday, I'll talk to you for a few minutes. I won't charge you for that. But I don't think there's much I can do."

"Grady & Bartlett," he read. "Lynn Bartlett. That's you?"

"That's me. And you are?"

"David Peh," he said. "Thanks."

"I have to run," I said. "You can get home?" I asked again.

He shrugged. "I'll call my roommates. Somebody will come."

"I'm sorry about your car," I repeated.

He gave a half smile that made him look his age instead of the German-car-buying techno-tycoon obsessed with the oily excesses of sudden wealth. "E-holes," they called them in Silicon Valley. "It's okay. I will get it back, or one just like it."

His determined optimism reminded me why David and his ilk had transformed life as we knew it, for better or worse.

"I sure hope so," I told him.

CHAPTER 2

W hat was that all about?" Jack asked when I had joined him inside. Despite my reassurances, he still hovered protectively just inside the door. "Aren't you busy enough without trolling for business at my birthday party? And in the garage, no less?" He smiled.

"They find me everywhere," I told him. Which in a way was true. The high-tech boom had created such an incredible demand for skilled personnel that even the swollen immigrant stream—from China, India, and elsewhere—couldn't fill it fast enough. Now the boom had gone bust, and the visas were expiring or void, stranding a lot of talented people who had no desire to go Home. It was an interesting time to be an immigration attorney.

"Seriously," I said to Jack, "didn't the maître d' tell you?"

He shook his head. "He just said that someone called 'Madam' wanted me in the garage." He laughed. "I thought that had possibilities, so down I came."

"Sorry," I said. "It was just some poor kid getting his car repossessed. Another swiped-out techie. The maître d' thought it might be one of our guests. It wasn't."

Jack stopped smiling. Even in the dim light, I could see the color drain from his face. *Heart,* I thought again. I tried not to clutch at him. "Are you all right?" I asked.

"Fine," he said, a shade curtly.

"Are you sure?" I asked. "You look—"

"Don't *fuss,* Lynn. I'm okay."

Second wives, contrary to the popular stereotype of the buxom bimbo stealing away the man of some poor female more endowed with virtue than with appetite, do not have it easy. There are so many players from the past imposing on the future. You imagine experiencing your life together as something new, but instead it becomes a series of linked vignettes that are something to be compared to. Every word, every gesture, has a history. Or not. You can't *know*—that's the problem. It's like walking onto the stage in the middle of the play, when all the other actors know their lines except you.

Maybe his ex-wife used to nag him. Maybe he has a headache. Maybe he just wants you to shut up.

I dropped my hand from his arm.

"Harrison is here," he said after a moment. "He's talking to Kay. They were asking about you. I think somebody might need rescuing."

"No doubt," I said. Harrison was my law partner. He was sixty-four and courtly, but he always drank too much at parties and got sort of weepy about a week-long vacation he'd once had at Lake Garda with his ex-wife. Usually it wasn't Harrison who needed rescuing, but his conversational partners. Outside of social events, he was a good lawyer and my mentor besides, so I didn't mind.

Kay Burks was a real-estate agent, the hottest profession in the Bay Area after übergeek. We'd become friendly looking at houses from one end of the Peninsula to the other after Jack's business started to grow and we decided to find a bigger place that didn't have a History. Unfortunately, just about the time Jack's business took off, everybody else's did, too, resulting in a housing market whose prices reflected a constricted supply and an insatiable demand. "The sky's the limit" wasn't just a saying anymore. We were still looking. Meanwhile the appraisal on our own little tract house in Los Altos passed the million-dollar mark and was still climbing.

Like me, Kay was a second wife. I suppose that was part of the reason for our friendship; sometimes you like people better as club members than if you just meet them on your own. For Kay second-wifedom (-wifery?) was more an avocation than a happenstance; she collected aphorisms and anecdotes the way other people collected knickknacks. Still, she was very smart and very amusing. Her husband was an allegedly brilliant but somewhat humorless orthopedic surgeon. I couldn't see it, personally, but she seemed content enough.

"Lago di Garda," Harrison was saying, ominously.

Kay, backed up against a table with her wineglass in hand, was giving him her best real-estate's agent smile, the one you give the client who's insisting his house is really worth $50K more than it's listed for because of all the work he's done on the flower beds. Her mind was obviously elsewhere.

Harrison hadn't noticed. "We had dinner on the terrace every night," he was saying, awash in a tide of nostalgia augmented by a steady flow of bourbon. How had he gotten to this state so quickly? I'd been downstairs only a few minutes. He must have arrived half sloshed already.

"Hi," I said, opening my arms in a gesture meant to encompass them both. "Thank you for coming."

Kay's fixed smile turned genuine. "Lynn, you look fantastic," she said.

My outfit for this occasion was a collaborative effort, for which she deserved at least half the credit. "You need more *glamour*," she'd said, urging me away from the simple black dress I'd been planning to wear.

I do not generally favor a look with which the word "glamour" can comfortably be coupled. "I don't want to look like I'm trying too hard," I told her on a reconnoitering trip at Nordstrom's, waving away a velvet skirt-and-jacket ensemble whose price tag made me feel the need to breathe deeply into a paper bag.

She closed her eyes. "Possibly, but it isn't showing off to make *some* effort. Lynn, you have got to try this on. It's stunning."

Kay frequently spoke in superlatives, a habit, I have

noticed, not uncommon in her profession. "I don't know . . . ," I said doubtfully.

"Jack will love it," she said.

I wavered.

"It makes you look thin," she said when we were in front of the dressing-room mirror.

You don't have to be a marketing guru to appreciate the power of those five little words, the basis of more than one retail fortune. Glamour with an elasticized waistband.

"Cash or charge?" the salesclerk asked.

"You do look pretty nice, kiddo," said Harrison now. He glanced over at Jack, who was talking to some of his business associates in a circle. "But your husband looks like he's going to puke." He laughed a little unsteadily. *He* looked as if he needed to sit down.

Kay rolled her eyes at me. "If you'll excuse me, I need to freshen my drink," she said.

"I'll catch you later," I said. I turned back to Harrison. "Jack's a little depressed about turning fifty," I told him.

Harrison patted my arm. "He'll get over it. We all do," he said kindly.

"I hope so," I said, not wanting to confess any secret worries.

Harrison leaned very close. He was still a handsome man, with a full head of white hair, but the bourbon had given his blue eyes a slightly watery, unfocused cast. He had never looked that way at the office. "I'm past it, Lynn," he whispered.

Christ, not another one. Was there something in the air? "Nonsense," I said briskly.

"I mean it," he said. "I'm thinking of retiring."

"You're not serious," I said, genuinely surprised. Harrison and I had been partners for just a year. I'd counted myself incredibly fortunate when he'd taken me into his practice and offered me a stake in the firm. I'd had no clients to speak of in the Bay Area, and I'd closed my office in San Diego. I knew he wanted someone to turn the business over to eventually, but I never expected it would be anytime soon.

"I've been thinking about it," he said. "I'm just . . . tired."

"At the moment maybe, but not *tired* tired. You have more energy than most men half your age."

"You're a nice girl, Lynn," he mumbled.

I hadn't been a girl for about twenty-five years, but that was the way men his age talked. I wasn't offended. Still, I hoped he wasn't serious about retiring, at least not in the foreseeable future. Grady & Bartlett had far too much work for me to handle on my own, even with the associate and the paralegal Harrison had hired before he invited me into the firm. "You know we can't afford to lose you, Harrison," I told him. "The clients would all go to Elson." Elson Larimer was the biggest immigration law firm in the Bay Area, the General Motors to our Audi boutique practice. Because they had a lot of the major institutional clients—the investment banks, the biggest consulting firms, the large-scale businesses—locked up, most of our clients were individuals who heard about us by word of mouth. There were enough of those to prove a thorn in Elson's side, about the best we could hope for. Fortunately, for the moment there was plenty of work to go around.

He shook his head. "You can handle it, Lynn. I wouldn't consider it otherwise." He sighed.

"Well, we don't have to talk about this right now," I said. "Not immediately, right?"

In truth, a move like this would take a lot of preparation, something Harrison undoubtedly realized. I assumed it was just the liquor talking or what I now realized was the dolorous effect the mention of birthdays seemed to have on men of a certain age. A warning shot over the bow maybe, but not an imminent threat.

"Sure. Right," he said. "Well, I think I'm going to go home now," he said in the deliberate enunciation of the inebriated. "Wish your husband many happy returns for me, will you?"

"I'll do that," I said. "Right after I call you a cab."

He squeezed my hand. "Okay," he said sadly.

"DID HARRISON LEAVE?" Jack asked me as we were standing in the buffet line.

"He wasn't feeling well," I said succinctly. "He said to wish you many happy returns."

"Oh. That's a shame," he said. He understood perfectly well why Harrison had left, but he was going to be diplomatic and not mention it. Harrison was on my side of the guest list. I appreciated his discretion.

There is an art to drawing up the invitations for a party given by a couple when one of them has lived in the area his entire adult life—including grad school, marriage, children, and career—and the other is a relative newcomer. It was Jack's birthday party, but it would hardly do if all the invitees were people who used to be friends of Janet and Jack's when they were together—people who had known them from student housing or soccer or Jack's law firm before he left to start his own business. I'd been to some events like that, and it was like going to your spouse's high-school reunion when you were the only person there who didn't attend the school and get all the stories about lecherous Coach Snyder and what happened on Senior Ditch Day. The business of reinventing your life is a sticky one. It takes a surprising amount of careful planning, not to mention tact.

I twisted my wedding ring, little diamonds surrounding a larger one in an antique gold setting. It was lovely and original and entirely unostentatious. Inside, Jack had inscribed, LOVE AND FORBEARANCE. It was as good a motto for a second marriage as I could imagine.

"The food looks great," Jack remarked. It did, at least for a steam table—the right combination of grilled vegetables, a low-fat entree, and sinful offerings (prime rib, seafood pasta Alfredo) to appeal to every taste. He looked at his watch. "I wonder if we should go through the line yet. Patrick and Meredith aren't here."

Patrick and Meredith, my stepchildren, were an hour

late. "The problem is," I said carefully, "that if we don't go through the line, no one else will eat either, and then the food will just sit here and congeal."

"You're probably right," he said in a distracted tone. "Still, I wonder if something could have happened. . . ."

"Were they coming together?" I asked innocently. Meredith lived with her "significant other," Justin, a health-club instructor, and Patrick lived on his own. They didn't seem to like each other much, and so far the only nongenetic unifying factor I had noted in their relationship was their resentment of their father's second marriage.

"I'm not sure," he said.

I was beginning to feel somewhat less festive myself. I stepped forward and took a not insubstantial portion of seafood pasta. Despite my southern California roots, I held a decidedly Continental view of the consoling properties of nourishment.

Jack helped himself to grilled salmon, which he picked at. *No speeches,* he'd insisted when we made our plans for this event. *No toasts. And definitely no gifts.*

I studied him surreptitiously while we ate. I hoped it wasn't *No fun* either, but I was afraid he wasn't enjoying himself. He smiled and joked with everybody who came up to congratulate or commiserate, but when he thought nobody was watching, his expression was drawn. He was good-looking, rather than handsome, with curly, light brown hair going to gray. His eyes were hazel, flecked with brown. Thanks to an abstemious diet and a ruthless exercise schedule—the results of a belated realization that immortality was increasingly unlikely, to say the least—he hadn't gained an ounce over the last decade.

Or so he claimed. I'd never so much as seen him step on the scales. I envied that kind of confidence.

He caught me watching him and smiled. "I'm sorry, Lynn. The party's wonderful, really. I didn't mean to . . . I'm just a little preoccupied. It's business. It's not important right now. I promise I'll tell you about it later." He held out his hand. "Want to dance?"

"Sure," I said, somewhat relieved, although I felt a little like Michael Corleone's wife in *Godfather Part II.* "It's business" was usually a code for "none of yours." Still, it was an apology of sorts. I took his hand, wishing my skirt were fuller cut. I did not excel at dancing, any more than I did behind the wheel. In fact, before we were married, I hadn't danced since approximately 1978, which suited me just fine.

Jack, however, was a skillful dancer, as well as a tactful one. He apologized every time I stepped on his foot.

"You look great," he said. "I know I told you before, but you really look nice tonight."

"Thanks," I said, somewhat mollified. "So do you."

"Do you remember the first time we ever danced?" he asked.

Of course I did. It was the night we met.

"I'm not terribly good at it," I'd told him then. Usually I didn't apologize for my shortcomings in advance, but I figured he'd find out soon enough anyway.

He'd laughed. "I don't care. Neither am I." That was a lie, I discovered, but a kind one. He took my hand and led me onto the floor of the hotel ballroom. After our chaste dinner, the physical contact upped the ante quite a bit. He put his arms out, and I stepped into them. The beginning of the beginning.

"My lucky day," I told him now. "Happy birthday, Jack." I leaned forward to kiss him on the ear in a way that usually signaled that his present was coming later.

I missed, because he turned his head away at the last second, looking across the room. Patrick was waving his arm, signaling him from the door. Meredith leaned against the wall, her arms folded, her expression, as always, disapproving.

Jack waved back and propelled me over to where his son and daughter stood, his arm still around my waist.

My best stepmother smile froze on my face.

Jack's arm dropped to his side.

Between them, dressed to the nines, was their mother, Janet Katera Hughes Vivendi, her eyes alight with mischief.

"I hope it's okay," Patrick said, addressing his father rather than me, his usual habit. "Mom wanted to wish you happy birthday. She didn't want to crash your party, but—"

"But we promised her you wouldn't mind," Meredith said, putting her arm around Jack's waist and drawing

him into the circle, away from me. "It was a spur-of-
the-moment thing. You don't mind, do you, Dad?"

I looked at Janet's well-coiffed frosted hair. She'd
just had it done, or I'd eat my napkin.

"Well . . . ," Jack said.

"I won't stay long," said Janet gaily, sweeping into
the room. "I just wanted to say, *Bon anniversaire! Feliz
cumpleaños! Buon compleanno!*" Her eyes slid to
mine for the first time. "That means—"

"I know what it means," I said.

CHAPTER 3

So what did he say when you got home?" Kay asked me. It was Sunday morning, after the party, and we were having coffee and splitting a mango–passion-fruit–macadamia-nut scone at a bakery on the main street of Los Altos village. She'd called me at eight A.M. to tell me she had the perfect—*perfect!*—house to show me in Los Altos Hills, Los Altos's even more affluent neighbor, but it had to be today because another buyer was unmistakably interested. She'd made an arrangement to show it at 10:30, and why didn't we meet for coffee first?

I knew she was as interested in confession (mine) as commission (hers), but I didn't care. Despite the early hour, I definitely needed to get out of the house.

"Not much," I said, taking a bite of the scone. It was as big as a softball and about as heavy, but delicious. Pastry on hormones.

She looked at me inquiringly, waiting for me to swallow.

"Patrick came home with us," I explained, trying not to whine. "He had too much to drink. Jack thought he shouldn't drive."

Kay rolled her eyebrows. "Why didn't *she* take him home, then?" she asked.

I shrugged. "I didn't ask. As a matter of fact, I said as little to her as possible. Under the circumstances that seemed like the wisest course."

Kay shook her head. "That's just what she was counting on. You know that, don't you?"

I took a sip of coffee. "What difference does it make?" I asked. "I couldn't make a scene. It was Jack's birthday party. He wanted the kids there. They wanted their mother there. I couldn't spoil it for him. It wasn't his fault Janet showed up uninvited."

She leaned forward earnestly. Her diamond, whose size was somewhere between extra-large and ostentatious, caught the sun and sent a light beam straight into my eye. I blinked. "You've got to talk to Jack," she said earnestly. "He has to put his foot down with his children. Otherwise they'll make your life miserable. Mark my words."

I smiled. "Mark my words" was one of my mother's favorite expressions.

"I'm not kidding," Kay said.

"I know you're not," I told her. "It's just that I'm not ready to turn it into some apocalyptic struggle at this point."

"It already is an apocalyptic struggle," she said seriously. "You just don't realize it yet."

"Well, at least Meredith has stopped assessing my fertility," I told her. "Or at least I think she has. For the first few months, every time we met I could see her covertly looking for swelling under my clothes. I don't know whether to be relieved or insulted that she's given that up."

She laughed. "I know what you mean. My step-daughter was the same. It threatens them." She lowered her voice. "But what *really* gets them is the fear that you're going to get Daddy's money. That's what they absolutely can't stand."

"We have a pre-nup, Kay," I said.

She raised her eyebrows. "You're a lawyer," she said. "I can't believe you're that naive."

It was my turn to laugh. "Okay. Maybe you're right."

"You know I'm right. Tell me Meredith and Patrick haven't become more hostile since Jack's business took off."

"It's sort of hard to tell," I said. "It started doing really well right after we got married. Of course, times are rockier now. I don't know if that makes them feel better or worse."

She drummed her perfectly lacquered nails on the place mat. "You should come to my group," she said.

I hadn't known she was seeing a psychologist. "I didn't think that was allowed," I said.

She frowned. "What?"

"Outsiders. I thought . . . Isn't it important to protect your privacy, so people can say what's really on their minds?"

She looked at me with amusement and shook her head. "It's not that kind of group, Lynn. It's a support group for second wives. We call ourselves the Anne Boleyn Society," she added.

"Anne Boleyn?" I asked, choking on my last bite of scone. "Didn't she come to a pretty bad end?"

"Well, 'Second Wives Club' was already taken," she said seriously.

"I can't believe you never told me about this group," I said. This was hardly our first conversation on this topic.

She looked at me. "You weren't ready," she said.

That sounded ominous. "Am I ready now?" I asked, temporizing. I was afraid I'd give these issues too much weight by focusing on them so intensely.

She said slowly, as if explaining to a child, "You need to be prepared. We can help you. We've all been through it." She spread her hands on the edge of the table and studied her rings. Then she leaned forward conspiratorially, one club member to another. "That incident with Janet last night, that was just the opening salvo," she said. "You'll see. You mark my words—"

That expression again. This time I didn't feel like smiling.

"Yes?" I prompted her.

"It's war," she said.

PROMISES FROM A REAL-ESTATE AGENT, even one who's a friend, usually fall more into the category of wishful thinking, but this time the house really was perfect. Nothing much had been done to it since the original owners built it in the fifties, and the kitchen and bathrooms were so out of date they looked retro. The closets were built for the smaller wardrobes of the postwar era. But when I looked out the living room window at the view that encompassed everything from the Golden Gate Bridge to downtown San Jose, I thought, *I have to have it,* like a greedy child. A moment later my superego kicked in: *Jack would love this.*

"How much will they take for it?" I asked Kay.

"You can probably get it for five million. More or less," she said. "It needs some work."

"Christ," I said, although I'd been expecting something in that ballpark. Just hearing the number out loud made it seem worse. Much worse. I looked out at the view again and thought how I would enumerate the house's many amenities to Jack.

"I don't want to pressure you . . . ," Kay began.

I raised my eyebrows.

"Don't give me that look," she said. "This isn't real-estate hustle. The market's slowed a bit, but a house like this won't be available long. If you can, get Jack up here this afternoon to see it. I've got the key, and the owners are out all day."

"I'm not sure we can afford it," I said. "It's more than we talked about spending."

"Talk to Jack," she told me. "You'll be sorry if you pass this up."

*   *   *

THE BAY AREA REAL-ESTATE SITUATION has been described in horrifying detail throughout the national media, so I probably don't have to explain why two people of normal means (plus stock) could be contemplating the purchase of a $5 million fixer-upper. If you didn't get into the market before the dot-com explosion drove the prices up, you could find yourself commuting from Lodi or Los Banos, Central Valley communities not generally associated with urban affluence. Even though the market had softened by 15 or 20 percent since the peak, owning a house was now outside the grasp of anyone on a middle-class salary. Thanks to the astronomical rents, there were plenty of people fully employed in the service industries who were homeless. A number of them slept on buses every night, riding to the end of the route and back. University professors lived out of their offices. Teachers and firemen and social workers packed up their bags and moved out of the area. It was the same sort of division between haves and have-nots that had led to such an unhappy outcome for Nicholas and Alexandra, not to mention more than one monarch named Louis.

It was somewhat inconvenient to have a guilty conscience when you were living in a million-dollar tract house and had a couple more million dollars' worth of stock options burning a hole in your pocket. I mean, Silicon Valley was not exactly Calcutta, but—all the e-hole chest beating notwithstanding—an awful lot of what put you on the "have" side of the equation was attributable to nothing more than luck. Still, there was that zillion-dollar view, and an acre of land, and space for my own home office, and . . .

Thanks to Kay, I was armed with real-estate speak by the time I got home, not to mention brimming with passion. "Jack," I cried, throwing open the door, "you have to see this house." I almost lost it and shouted, *It's a steal,* but I was stopped in my tracks by Patrick, who was sitting with his father at the kitchen table. In my enthusiasm I'd forgotten he might still be there.

"Hi," I said.

Jack gave me a sheepish smile. "Join us?" he asked.

"Hi," Patrick said, not looking at me.

Jack put his hand on Patrick's arm. "It will all work out, son. You'll see."

Whatever it was, Patrick looked unconvinced. "You'll talk to her?" he said to his father.

Jack nodded.

Patrick got to his feet. "I've got to get going," he said. "Thanks for putting me up for the night, Dad." He turned in my direction but still didn't meet my eyes. "Bye," he said.

"Bye."

Jack was silent for a moment after he left. I had an uneasy feeling that I was about to hear something I wouldn't like. I wasn't wrong.

"What's up?" I asked, as cheerfully as I could manage. Blended families were like *Secrets and Lies;* everybody was hiding something.

"Sit down," Jack said.

Uh-oh. I sat.

"Patrick lost his job," he said.

Again. I mean, people had been laid off all over the Bay Area, some of them more than once, but I suspected that Patrick's dismal employment history had little to do with the economy and a lot to do with his talent for self-sabotage. "I'm really sorry," I said.

"There was some kind of misunderstanding with his boss," Jack said glumly. Patrick worked for an advertising agency. He was part of a copywriting team preparing print, radio, and TV ads for the youth market. I'd seen one of the ads for a portable video game— not something I'd ordinarily notice until Jack pointed it out. The creative director had wanted a soundtrack that was unique, and the team found a hip-hop song on an obscure dance label, traced the producer, and, after removing the vocals, reorchestrated the rhythm track itself to the finished commercial, Jack explained. He wasn't perfectly clear what Patrick's role had been, but teamwork is teamwork, after all. "He's better on visuals than with words," Jack observed. No kidding.

Before that, Patrick had had a misunderstanding with his boss at a brokerage house, and before that, he'd decided that high-school teaching, for which he'd spent a postgraduate year of preparation, was not for him. Jack had been subsidizing his rent for half a decade.

"That's too bad," I said neutrally. Biting your tongue comes naturally—though not effortlessly—when you have adult stepchildren.

"Yes." He rubbed his eye with the heel of his hand. He looked tired. And disappointed. Again. I reminded myself that his solicitude for his children was a quality I admired.

"The thing is . . . ," he said.

I could tell that the part I was really going to dislike was coming next. I refused to help him say whatever it was. I just sat there.

"I'm really sorry, Lynn," he said. "The thing is . . . Patrick wants to move back into the house."

CHAPTER 4

It wasn't supposed to be like this.

I'd met my husband, Jackson Hughes, at one of those continuing-education courses the California bar puts on to fend off regulation by the state government. There is a core suite of mandatory requirements, most of them having to do with the blunter side of practice ethics: how to dodge sexual-harassment lawsuits, how to avoid substance abuse, how not to get your ass in a crack by mishandling your client's money. For the rest of your required hours, you can pick and choose among varied offerings, so long as you do the time.

As you might imagine, a very lucrative business has arisen out of the need to provide these courses. For a while you could take Tibetan Bell Ringing or Interpersonal Office Dynamics Part II for credit, a grown-up version of what happened to university curricula in the seventies when the canon was thrown out. A former governor's bitter warfare with the state bar at length forced a retrenchment, so now some of the better programs come coupled with a resort package: learn how to behave yourself in the morning, play tennis in the afternoon.

I don't play tennis, but I was sitting in the ballroom of the Hotel del Coronado in San Diego listening to a videotaped lecture entitled "Innovative Prenuptial Agreements," surrounded by people who obviously did. Some had even brought their rackets to the lecture. It didn't matter; the video had no feelings to be hurt by lack of attention. Despite the proximity to the beach, it was hot and stuffy in the room. The speaker was reading from the program handbook, which was open right in front of me: " 'Although John has made no promises and shall be under no obligation to do so, he may, in his sole discretion, transfer to Mary from time to time, as her sole and separate property,' " etc., etc. Riveting stuff, that. And why do people have to read things to you that you can presumably read for yourself?

I caught myself listing forward, eyes closed, for the third time. I checked my watch. There was a half hour left in the session. I resigned myself to the fact that I had reached the end of my capacity for concentration, which, under the circumstances, wasn't all that large. I opened my attaché case and lifted the lid, balancing the case on my knees. Then I opened *Prodigal Summer* and started reading, the way I used to under the covers, after "lights-out."

I needn't have bothered with the subterfuge. No one else was listening either, with the exception of one or two people taking copious marginal notes in the program handbook. Either they were in the family-law and estate-planning field or they had a personal interest in a pre-nup, or maybe both. The rest of us were just marking time.

I was so lost in the book by the time the session ended, I didn't hear Jack's comment the first time out.

"Pardon me?" I said, looking up.

"That's a good book," he repeated, standing next to my chair.

"Have you read it?" I asked, surprised. I'd recently been to a Barbara Kingsolver book signing attended by 750 people. Approximately 725 of them were women.

He looked down, a little guiltily, and pushed his hair back from his face. "Actually, no. Not yet. My sister recommended it."

"Ah," I said neutrally. I recognized an opening gambit when I heard one, although lately they'd been a little thin on the ground. I didn't mind. It was a very public place, and I liked talking about books. Plus, the hair thing was definitely attractive. Besides, I didn't have anything much better to do than go home and share a can of tuna with Brewer, my cat. (Separate forks, naturally.)

"I liked *The Poisonwood Bible,* though," he said.

Much better. Points scored for that, for sure.

"What's this one about?" he asked.

I smiled. "Generally or specifically?"

"Generally, I guess." He sat down in the chair next to me. "Do you mind?"

He didn't sprawl all over the chair arm or lean

forward into my face, so I made a gesture: *Be my guest.* "I haven't finished, but so far I'd say it's about the interconnectedness of different life forms," I told him.

He made an involuntary face.

I laughed. "Sorry. I know that sounds sort of pretentious. You'll have to read it yourself and see what you think. I think it's great."

"I will. Thanks." He paused. "I'm Jack Hughes," he said.

"Lynn Bartlett."

"Are you practicing?"

I nodded. "Immigration. I'm a sole practitioner here in San Diego."

He swallowed. "Really? Well, I suppose San Diego must be a good place for that. Um, do you like it?"

I was used to this kind of response. Immigration is not the usual field of choice for top law-school graduates, most of whom choose to work themselves into neurasthenic fugue states at corporate law firms. "Immigration" conjures up visions of barefoot hordes carrying their worldly possessions in a cloth tied to the end of a stick, characters out of *El Norte.* I'd helped a few people like that, but in reality many of my clients were better educated than most of the lawyers I knew.

"I do, as a matter of fact," I said. "What about you?"

"Corporate. High tech, actually. Silicon Valley?" He said it almost sheepishly. This was the period when Silicon Valley was starting to make the news, gleeful reportage calculated to excite envy and lust, the era made famous by Po Bronson before he went off to interview failed techies starting a new life as sheep ranchers in Idaho.

"I've heard of it," I told him.

He looked as if he couldn't decide whether I was serious or not.

"I'm kidding," I said. "I went to Stanford, eons ago."

"Really?" he said again. "How did you end up here?"

I raised an eyebrow. "You mean where everybody surfs and smells like coconut suntan lotion?"

"Sorry," he said. "I didn't mean it like that." He probably did, though. That more or less summed up the view Northern Californians had of Southern California. That, and "They're stealing our water." It made for an interesting state government.

"It's a long story," I told him. "The brief summary is that my husband and I were living in New York, we got divorced, I couldn't afford to stay there, and my parents were living in Southern California, so I eventually settled here. I like it. There isn't a whole lot of culture, but it's much more livable than L.A." I smiled. "Plus, I like the smell of coconut."

"So do I," he said.

"Well," I said. The ballroom had more or less emptied out, and the vacuum cleaners would be brought in any second. I began to gather up my papers.

"Look, Lynn," he said, "if you're not doing anything tonight, would you like to have dinner? I don't know anyone in San Diego, and I was just going to get room service here. It would be much nicer to eat in the dining room and have someone to talk to."

I liked that he kept it low-key. I liked that he didn't touch me. I especially liked that he didn't try to flatter me or act too attentive, a modus operandi that always put me on my guard. This is making me sound as if I'm devastatingly attractive or catnip to men or something like that, and I'm not. I'm not bad-looking, but I was already over forty, and being treated like Jennifer Lopez smacked to me of insincerity, if not idiotic desperation.

It was just dinner and conversation. Still, I couldn't help checking for a tan line on his ring finger.

He caught me looking and smiled. "I'm divorced," he said.

As long as we were being candid, I thought I might as well go for broke. "How long ago?" I asked.

He laughed. "A long time ago. Years. You're very cautious, aren't you?"

I shook my head. "Just experienced," I told him.

A LONG TIME LATER, Jack told me, "You have no idea what you looked like, sitting in that big room with your nose in a book. You seemed so calm, so centered. You looked like the kind of person who would never 'settle.' I really liked that about you. I still like it," he added, and kissed me.

By then we had told each other our life stories, met each other's friends, and spent several weekends together, mostly in bed, in Los Altos or La Jolla. We'd gone hiking in the mountains, disagreed passionately over the merits of *All the Pretty Horses,* and developed a mutual affection for Bandar the binturong at the zoo. I had even met Meredith and Patrick, who seemed, in addition to safely grown and out of the house, politely uninterested in our relationship.

But I still thought he gave me too much credit. I wasn't calm; I was resigned. I would rather be alone than with the wrong man, so I was alone. I didn't really mind; I had friends, I had a reasonably successful practice, I had a condo in La Jolla, and Brewer the cat to come home to. I might have been picky and dismissive, but I'd found that too many men who say that what they really want is a relationship with an independent woman are not necessarily emotionally equipped to handle it.

Jack said, "My ex-wife, Janet, was very artistic and creative. She felt stifled in the marriage—I was building the firm, and I was working a lot—so she left me for an Italian professor at Stanford. The marriage hadn't been good for quite a while, but I didn't want it to end because the kids were still at home, and they were very upset. I don't hold it against her, though; we all get along now. She and Valerio moved to Florence for a couple of years, which the kids loved. Now they're back on the Peninsula." He looked at me. "Family is very important to me," he said. "My own parents didn't get along that well, and I was determined not to duplicate those hostilities in front of my kids."

When you're in a relationship with somebody, you listen to this sort of speech very carefully, even (or especially) when you're in love. Reading between the lines, I extracted mostly positive things: He didn't trash her character (I hate it when divorced people do that, however justified they think themselves), he'd taken a responsible attitude toward his children, he didn't seem to be pining, and the ex–Mrs. Hughes was securely remarried. What I didn't learn till later was that Janet had declared bankruptcy when it was time to send Patrick to college so she wouldn't have to fork over her portion of the tuition money. That Jack had been paying her psychiatrist bills for years because, according to Janet, "he owed her." That her second husband was spending more and more time in Italy, alone. That she called Jack at least once a week and sent him postcards of impressionist paintings with cryptic little messages, "just to keep in touch."

Anyway, we went on like this for some time. In many ways a long-distance relationship is just about perfect—there isn't enough proximity for those endearing little habits to become annoying, and you get to preserve a measure of privacy and "space." It takes work to sustain romance when you've seen somebody flossing his teeth, or worse. The next step—the one where you get to wash each other's dirty underwear and see each other first thing in the morning (no joke when you're over forty)—was one I wasn't in a big hurry to take.

Which is why, when Jack started his campaign to get me to marry him, I at first resisted.

"What's the rush?" I asked him. "Aren't we fine as we are?"

Also, I'd already been married, so I knew the downside, you might say.

I MARRIED MY FIRST HUSBAND, Jonathan, while I was still in law school. Law school is such a bleak and lonely experience that I made the stupid mistake of thinking that shared misery might make a sound basis for a successful marriage. It actually did, for a while; we were both too busy to disagree about anything. But then Jonathan graduated and took a job at a top-tier New York law firm, so I transferred to NYU to finish out my second and third years.

The life of a new associate is something like a medical intern's; perpetual exhaustion is de rigueur. Anxiety runs high, because you don't learn practical things in law school, so when you do land a real legal job, you don't have a clue what's going on. You compete with a lot of other smart, volcanically ambitious associates from good schools, all of whom have their eye on the mere handful of partnership slots seven years or so down the road. All this is not conducive to a stress-free life, and the spouse is expected to be Understanding.

I was, up to a point, but Jonathan was extreme even by new-associate standards. He worked nights. He worked weekends. He worked Thanksgiving Day and

Christmas Eve. He had a sleeping bag and an air mattress in his office, and on more than one occasion, he spent the night. He voluntarily passed up his vacation without consulting me, although he was entitled to at least three weeks. He brought work home when he wasn't at the office, muttering to himself and glaring at me when I made any noise. He lost weight and started to develop a hollow-eyed, fanatical look reminiscent of a young Savonarola.

"You don't understand," he told me after an entire year in which we went out to a movie together approximately three times and to cultural events virtually never.

"But what's the point of living in New York if you don't take advantage of it?" I'd complained. I did almost everything alone.

"This is what you have to do to succeed," he said fiercely. "This is what it takes to make partner."

I pointed out that this is what it took to be important enough to get your heart attack reported in the *Wall Street Journal,* which he did not appear to find amusing.

"Is this what life is going to be like for the next seven years?" I asked.

He didn't answer me, which of course was an answer in itself.

What did animate him was my apparent lack of interest in a corporate career similar to his own. "Did you sign up for the Tinker MacDonald interview?" he asked me.

I shook my head.

"It's the biggest firm on Wall Street," he said. "Do you have any idea of how much you'd make to start?"

I knew.

"You have good grades," he said more urgently. "You might get an offer."

I had already explained that I didn't want such an offer, information he appeared not to have absorbed. By the third or fourth missed opportunity, he started to panic. "Do you know what you're giving up?" he said.

I did not think it would be tactful to point out that I could see what I was giving up every day. To live the life Jonathan was living, or even an approximation of it, was unthinkable. I tried, once more, to explain: "I don't really want to practice corporate law," I told him. "I'm looking for something more low-key."

"Low-key?" he said in a horrified tone. He made it sound as if I'd confessed to a preference for necrophilia. Which, I suppose, is about as low-key as things can get. "Like what?"

"I don't know yet," I said. "I'd like a smaller firm and a practice that's less"—I searched for the right word—"intense. I'm looking around," I added, more confidently than I felt. "I'll know it when I see it."

"You'll be left behind," he said seriously. "I hope you know that."

"Left behind how?" I asked, although I could guess.

"Financially. Professionally. Socially. You name it."

He meant that he would be embarrassed to be married to someone who couldn't—or wouldn't—Compete. It would be okay if I made a living selling macramé plant hangers or herbal supplements, but if I was going to step into the arena, I had to play hardball.

"Think about it," he said.

"I will," I told him.

Three months later I accepted a job with a medium-size immigration law firm in Los Angeles, where my parents lived.

THE WORST THING ABOUT A BAD MARRIAGE is that it makes you doubt your own choices. Once I had failed rather dramatically to choose wisely, I'd lost confidence in my powers of discernment. Serial monogamy with a succession of glowering workaholics didn't appeal to me at all, but the truth is, I admired competence and dedication, and I might go on being attracted—at least initially—to Jonathan's type. Not only that, but "choosing" implies one selection from a range of possibilities. The range was narrowing, to say the least, and anyway, it seems to me that most relationships are the result of a series of benign and intriguing accidents. Choice might not have all that much to do with it, whatever Freud had to say on the subject.

All of which is a roundabout and probably inadequate explanation of why, despite his charms, I hesitated when Jack asked me to marry him. *He* was competent and dedicated and successful, all the qualities I'd once thought I admired in Jonathan. Maybe his virtues would turn out to be vices, too. Also, by then I'd been essentially alone for a long time and I craved a certain amount of solitude and privacy, which might have been another way of saying that I'd become crotchety and inflexible, depending on whom you asked.

Jack, on the other hand, was optimistic enough for two. "You'll love living in the Bay Area," he said cannily. "People don't start tax revolts every time there's some needed public expenditure. They support the public library. It's your kind of place. And professionally it couldn't be better," he said, warming to the topic. "There's a huge demand for immigrant technological workers. It's the perfect locale for an immigration practice. You'd have unlimited opportunities. Besides," he added, looking at me in a way that had an extremely positive effect on my anatomy, "I love you. I want to be with you all the time, not just now and then." He smiled. "I won't crowd you, I promise. I know you're independent. It's what I love about you. I wouldn't try to change that."

"What about Meredith and Patrick?" I asked.

"They love you already," he said firmly. Too firmly, probably, but I didn't know enough to be suspicious. "And anyway, they have their own lives now. They just want me to be happy."

Okay, anyone over the age of fifteen will probably recognize the naiveté on both sides of this conversation. But Jack's certainty was so convincing. Plus, he was leaving his law firm—cutting back, he said—to become a consultant at an Internet start-up. With *options*. With luck he could retire altogether in a couple of years. Plus—and this plus was a big plus—he wooed me with books. Not just any books, but books he thought I would like. Even better, I did like them, for the most part. It was very flattering and not a little erotic to be courted through your mind. I mean, how could you resist a man who sent you *Le Mariage* and *Le Divorce* because he *knew* you'd love Diane Johnson? Even if he hadn't read them himself?

Also, he was the only grown male I had ever met, dated, or heard of who did not scream at the set during televised sporting events involving some kind of ball. I mean, think about moving in with someone and discovering that a dialogue with the refs formed the backdrop of every weekend afternoon, not to mention Monday nights.

Not only that, he made me laugh. It's not always easy to remember that now, but he did. Not that I had to tot up a scorecard. I was in love with him, too. I think I had been ever since he fished a daddy longlegs out of the bathtub and, wearing only a towel, carried it outside on the edge of a Kleenex box and put it down in a flower bed outside my front door. I am not a big fan of spiders, and personally I probably would have squashed it, but I had never met a man so tenderhearted and affectionate.

So there was Jack—kind, gentle, smart, funny, well read, decent, and honorable—all the qualities you weren't supposed to be able to find outside the pages of a novel. And intent on getting me to marry him.

The outcome, as they say, was never really in doubt.

The clincher (if you discard Dear Abby's test: "Are you better off with him or without him?") was one of those moments of introspective clarity in which I realized that I'd become almost feline in my fondness for routine. I had a comfortable practice, a comfortable condo, and a comfortable life. I was wryly unmarried, but not unhappily so. I'd had my share of uninspiring dates. After more than a decade, I was ready for something more than nights curled up with Jane Austen and a truculent tomcat. There comes a point in your life when you finally internalize the fact that no one is given an eternity of looks and youth and options. You have to do something. You have to move on.

The Spanish explorer Cortés scuttled his ships on the coast of Mexico so there could be no going back. If I did marry Jack, I would have to sell my condo, close my practice, burn my bridges, sink my boats. Anything less would be cowardly, a failure of nerve. It was time to stop hedging my bets.

"Marry me?" Jack asked, for approximately the sixth time, as we were having black-bean soup, my favorite, at George's at the Cove terrace café in La Jolla. A half dozen proposals. Expecting more might be pressing my luck.

I would miss George's view, not to mention the soup, which was outstanding.

I put down my spoon decisively. "Yes," I said. "Yes, I will."

CHAPTER 5

"He wants to move in with us, just for a while," Jack repeated.

Various responses—ranging from the juvenile ("I'd rather be flayed alive") to the just ("But we agreed . . .")—came to mind. I opened my mouth to shriek . . . something . . . and then closed it again. Sometimes there is a tactical advantage in silence.

I looked at him.

"I know we talked about this before we were married . . . ," Jack said.

"We did a little more than talk," I pointed out. As a matter of fact, it was part of the pre-nup: *No other residents in the house except in the case of emergency and by mutual consent*. So far this didn't seemed to qualify on either basis.

"I know that," he acknowledged. "I'm sorry. I didn't think this would ever come up."

"Jack, I really don't think it would work out very well," I said. I didn't want to elaborate my reasons, so they hung there unspoken: *The house is small, your son dislikes me, I need my space. You promised. . . .*

"It would only be temporary," he said.

The universe was only temporary, when you put it into a large enough time frame. I didn't want to trust "temporary."

"Just till he finds another job," he added.

"Jack, he keeps getting fired or quitting. It's not going to be that easy to find something else." This was probably tactless, but sugarcoating the situation would have Patrick installed in the guest room by the end of the day.

"I have some contacts," he said, looking embarrassed. "I can probably help."

He'd helped far too much already, in my opinion. It's always a little too easy to analyze somebody else's family dysfunctions, but I thought that a big part of Patrick's problem was the fact that he'd never had to do much of anything on his own. Jack had told me how much the divorce had upset the children and how guilty he'd felt when he realized the extent to which his absence had changed things for the worse. It didn't matter that the divorce wasn't his idea; he'd been making it up to them ever since. I had to respect him for his feelings, but I couldn't really approve of the results, especially now that I was having to live with them in every sense of the word.

"Wouldn't it be better for him to live someplace else?" I asked. "It can't be very good for his self-esteem to move in with his dad." Usually I hate the term "self-esteem," but I was desperate.

"Who else would take him in?" Jack said. "I'm his father."

His friends. His mother.

I didn't have to say anything. Jack knew what I was thinking. "Janet's going through a really bad time right now," he said bleakly.

Right. She'd looked like it at the birthday party.

"Plus, they don't get along that well," he added.

This conversation was beginning to have "done deal" written all over it. "So what did you tell him?" I asked.

He looked grim.

"Please be honest," I said.

"I said I would check with you."

"And?"

He hesitated. Then he met my eyes. "And that I was sure you would agree."

Done deal, definitely. "So basically he's gone to pack up his stuff, right?"

"Probably," he said. "Look, if you really object, I'll call him right now. I'm trying to do the best thing for everybody. I didn't think I had any real choice, but I won't insist if you just can't live with it."

Oh, great. Then I could be the heavy and wreck their plans. "What I object to is not being consulted before you told him it would be okay," I said quietly. "I know this is hard for you, but this is my house and my life, too. We're supposed to make decisions that affect the two of us in concert, remember?"

"I know," he said. "I'm sorry." He looked at me.

"Don't think I don't understand that this isn't fair. I do. I wish he—" He stopped. I knew what he wished. I wished it, too, more than he did probably. "I really need your help with this," he said after a moment. I could almost see him searching, cannily, for the right approach. There were no flies on Jack. "We can help him together," he said.

I said nothing.

"So what do you want me to do, Lynn?"

Not put me in this situation, for one thing. I knew he didn't like having to ask permission regarding something concerning his children. Or anything else. But if I didn't protest now, what would the future hold? "Would there be a time limit?" I asked.

"To what?"

"To how long Patrick lives with us. Three months? Six months? A year? Or would it be open-ended?"

He looked horrified. "He's not moving in with us for good, Lynn. It's only temporary. I promise."

"It might be a good idea to define how long temporary is," I suggested.

"If that's what you want," he said coldly.

None of this was what I wanted. "It's what I'll agree to," I said.

"He'll probably think we don't trust him," he muttered.

I looked at him. I wasn't going to touch that one if my life depended on it.

"Six months, then," he said, lips tight. "Will that satisfy you?"

"Jack," I said, "I'm sorry to keep picking at this, but I think it's better—much better—that we lay our cards on the table now rather than after Patrick moves in. I know you don't want to hurt his feelings, but *I* have to know what happens if he hasn't found a place after six months." The muscles in my neck and shoulders were knotted and tense, and I could feel a headache starting at the base of my skull. The confrontation I'd always feared—the one with Patrick or Meredith on one side, me on the other, and Jack in the middle—was taking shape. I'd been fending it off ever since we'd been married. I sensed the ground rules shifting.

"I'll take care of it," he said. He looked at me. "Surely you can trust me as much as that."

Marriage, especially remarriage, is a continual balancing act. Sometimes you're a team, and sometimes it's just you in the outfield, all alone with the fly ball. Separate but equal. Figuring out exactly how to achieve that without degenerating into a nagfest on the one hand or a dictatorship on the other has fueled counseling sessions since Adam and Eve (who was, at least according to some versions of the annals of the First Family, a second wife herself).

There were a number of remonstrances I could make, a dozen points I could raise in negotiation. We could hammer out the details, get everything specific and nailed down. We could also end up thoroughly disliking each other. Sometimes the lawyers needed lawyers, so somebody else could be the bad guy.

Besides, I'd been around long enough to know that

"trust me" was a male thing, for better or worse. And also, I understood that what Jack wanted, more than anything else, was for Patrick to make a success of things. "Trust me" also meant "please don't destroy my illusions."

"Of course, I do," I said.

"Thank you," he said.

SOMETIME LATER, when we had sat reading the Sunday papers, thinking our separate thoughts, he said with determined cheerfulness, "There's coffee cake. I forgot to tell you. I got some this morning."

He meant he'd picked some up because Patrick was spending the night. No other reason would inspire him to admit a calorie-laden carbohydrate gut buster to his breakfast table.

"Was it good?" I asked.

The look on his face was comical. "Well . . . I didn't actually have any, and Patrick wasn't feeling well, so . . ."

I laughed. "If you didn't try it, why do you want me to dispose of it?" I asked. "Let's just throw it away."

"Did you get something?" he asked solicitously, domestic harmony, for the moment at least, apparently restored.

"Kay and I had coffee earlier," I said. I neglected to mention my own encounter with the scone.

"Oh, that's right. What were you talking about? I forgot to ask you."

"When?"

"When you came in. You sounded excited."

The house. Mentally I'd put it on hold, and I'd almost forgotten. I said carefully, "Kay's found us a house. It's practically perfect. I thought you might like to go see it this afternoon."

He looked away. "I can't. I'm sorry."

"That's it?" I said, more sharply than I intended.

He put down the paper. "How much is it?"

I tried not to wince. "Five million."

"Out of the question," he said. He started to pick up the paper again.

"Wait," I said. "I thought we'd discussed this, but we can rethink it. What price range were you thinking of?"

"I'm thinking now might not be the best time to move," he said.

"Jack, you know I've been looking at houses with Kay for months. Every month—every week—that we wait, the prices go up, even in this economy." I stopped. Experience had taught me that when Jack, ordinarily the most companionable of husbands, clammed up, something was wrong. Besides, he had the stricken look from the night before. "What is it?" I asked after a moment. "Is it the business?"

"Lynn—"

I waited.

"In a way," he said finally. "The business is okay, but I did something stupid."

"Tell me," I said.

He sighed and swirled the dregs of the coffee around

and around in his cup. "I exercised a lot of incentive options, and then I hung on to the shares," he said.

Uh-oh. "You didn't sell," I said. I thought he'd sold them already. He'd told me nothing.

"That's right," he said curtly.

"And, um, the stock price went down, right?"

He nodded.

"So," I said carefully, "we have a big tax liability and not enough to pay it off with if you sell the shares now."

"I thought the stock would keep going up," he said by way of confirmation.

All over the Valley, disillusioned workers were singing this sad refrain. If you used your incentive options to buy, say, a hundred thousand shares of stock—paying five to ten cents for each share—and the stock is trading between sixty and seventy dollars a share, the difference between the dollar price you paid and what the shares were worth (approximately seven million in this hypothetical) is taxable to you in profit, even if you never sell the shares. You can see what happens if the value of the shares goes down before you sell. A lot of naive techies had been caught in this trap, but Jack was an attorney and a businessman, and he was supposed to know better. Holding on to the shares without selling—which might be seen as a demonstration of loyalty to the company—was in reality the most blatant and dangerous kind of gambling.

"Anyway," he said, sounding very tired, "it's not your problem, it's mine. It's a good thing we've kept our assets separate, isn't it? Maybe I should have put the house in your name."

I was in no mood to celebrate my good fortune. "How much is it?"

"More than a million," he said. "The thing is, the business is solid, even though the stock has fallen, so I don't really want to sell. I have to figure out what to do."

"It isn't that much, but I have some stock, and the profits from my condo in La Jolla . . . ," I began.

"Absolutely not," he said. "I won't take your money."

I was, I must confess, a bit relieved, although I didn't see where else he was going to get it, unless he sold the house. My separate funds were my safety net. I didn't like to admit the second part of that sentence— *in case things didn't work out*—but it hung there nevertheless. "I'd still like to help," I said.

"I'll handle it," he insisted, picking up the paper again for emphasis, like some husband in a fifties sitcom.

Except no one was laughing.

"Jack—"

He looked at me. "Later, okay? Please, Lynn."

"Okay."

Don't shut me out, I thought, but I didn't say it.

CHAPTER 6

That was the weekend.

On Monday I went into the office early, in part because I had a lot of work to do and in part because of the oppressiveness of trying not to trip any verbal land mines at home. At least at the firm I was in charge. More or less.

Our administrative assistant, Adam Nguyen, was already at his desk when I opened the door.

"You're in early," I remarked.

He grinned. "I like the quiet," he said. He never said so, but I suspected he came in early to use the firm's computer to write his novel. I didn't mind; he was a great secretary and a cheeky presence around the firm, although of course he would probably go on to other things eventually. His parents, who were fairly traditional, had expected him to study engineering or computer science at Stanford, but he'd confounded their hopes and studied English literature at San Jose State. "I couldn't take all that money and go against their wishes," he'd told me. "Now that the dot-com world is collapsing, they're starting to forgive me." Still, he lived at home, and he didn't like to rub their noses in it.

I wanted to read whatever he ended up writing, because he was almost scarily observant. The only problem was, I was afraid he might be writing about the firm, and, despite the adage about not being able to recognize a description of yourself in print, it was possible that complete candor might put a strain on our employer-employee relationship. If that seems paranoid, think of Boswell and Johnson. Think *Survivor*. Rarely does exhaustive scrutiny result in a flattering portrait, even if the subject is Mother Teresa.

Anyway, instead of perusing some Generation Y cri de coeur, I locked myself in my office with a stack of H-1B visa applications that needed preparing or reviewing. H-1Bs were renewable (up to six years, plus extensions) visas for immigrant workers, and they were—or had been—the lifeblood of the high-technology industry. About half of all the H-1B visa holders in the United States were computer specialists of some sort, and about half of those wanted to stay on permanently after their visas expired. Not surprisingly, the program, although functioning reasonably well on the global level, was plagued with abuses, not to mention fraud. Employers sometimes used the visa to intimidate and underpay the H-1B workers, who couldn't squawk without getting fired and, possibly, sent home. Applicants had been known to fake their documents and submit phony résumés. The Immigration and Naturalization Service was overworked, understaffed, invariably chaotic, and occasionally cranky, particularly since immigration issues had become a matter of national security. Some INS officers got away with being downright mean. (One poor applicant waited three hours in line to be photographed and, observing the INS rule "no eyeglasses in the picture," put his glasses in his pocket. The INS agent rejected the developed picture with the explanation "no eyeglasses in the photograph" because the edge of the frames could be seen sticking out of the applicant's pocket. He had to stand in line all over again.)

Practicing in the immigration field required a mind for details, a high level of ambiguity tolerance, and a sort of creative response to problems that would probably make a securities lawyer's hair stand on end. Harrison's practice had grown exponentially because of the Silicon Valley's high-tech explosion, and a lot of what we did, in addition to securing temporary visas, was to find some way for the best-qualified temporary workers to stay on permanently. Most of our clients— computer scientists, financial experts, businesspeople—were better educated, more motivated, and a lot richer than we were. On the whole it was an interesting, satisfying job, and the clients were appreciative. So far I'd never regretted turning my back on a Wall Street practice and all-night orgies putting together S-1 Registration Statements or other equally riveting documents. I mean, my documents weren't all that fascinating either, but at least the clients were generally entertaining.

After an hour or so, our associate, Brooke Daly, tapped on my door. "Hi, Lynn," she said, her wide, insincere smile plastered on, "mind if I come in?"

I'm not sure why I had it in for Brooke, but I did. Maybe because she reminded me of the Reese Witherspoon character in *Election*. She was insanely perky, the sort of person who probably had three columns of activities under her name in her high-school yearbook, but no friends. The person the teacher picked to be the "safety" in fifth grade, the one who wore an arm badge and instructed other children not to run in the halls. The first kindergartner to learn to tie her shoes. You get the point. Brooke insisted that I was her "mentor," even though I hadn't hired her and she worked mostly with Harrison. She flattered me subtly and—when subtlety didn't work—overtly, but she treated Adam in a manner just far enough above rudeness to escape rebuke. And, as Dave Barry has said, the person who is nice to you but rude to the waiter is not a nice person.

Still, she was a competent—though inexperienced—lawyer, and in a small office (two partners, an associate, a paralegal, and Adam), no one has the luxury of avoiding someone she doesn't particularly like. So I said, with scrupulous civility, "Sure. What's up?"

She sat in the client chair, bouncing up and down a couple of times, as if she could barely contain her energy. "Harrison called," she said. "He wanted me to give you a message." There was just a hint of something self-important in her manner that made me grit my teeth.

"Great," I said toothily.

"He's not coming in," she said. "He's sick."

"That's too bad," I said. I hoped she didn't mean "hungover." "Did he say what was the matter?"

She shook her head. "But he said he probably wouldn't be in for a few days." She straightened in the chair. "He said, if it's all right with you, I could handle his work for him until he gets back." She looked at me expectantly.

"Okay," I told her, "but don't send anything out before I've looked at it, and ask me if you don't know the answer to something, no matter how small it is."

"I *know* that, Lynn," she said with a smirk, but she didn't, not really. I'd already caught her giving inaccurate advice to clients over the phone, and once someone who called for counsel was stuck at the Canadian border for three days before Harrison heard about it and figured out what to do. Brooke had sworn the client misunderstood her, and Harrison let it go. But good lawyers, the ones who reach the top of their fields, don't wing it. Ever. If you don't absolutely, positively know the answer to a question, you find it out before you open your mouth.

"Good," I told her. "I know you know it, but it never hurts to be reminded."

She looked as if she would have liked to say something snippy, but she swallowed it and left the room. I didn't think she'd ever get it, the internalized striving for perfection that characterizes a first-rate practice. She just thought I had it in for her (which was true) and wouldn't let her try her wings (which wasn't). She succeeded better with Harrison because he was, not to put too fine a point upon it, a man of advancing years and receding energy, far more susceptible to the allure of perkiness. Not to mention big tits.

Anyway, after she left, I called Harrison at home to commiserate. If he was going to be out for several days, it had to be something serious. His cell phone was turned off, and I got his home voice mail twice; the second time I left a sympathetic message and figured he was taking a nap. I was debating whether to return to work immediately or sift through the day's e-mails when Adam buzzed me. "It's Ms. Burks," he said. "She says it's urgent."

"Hi, Kay," I said, picking up. "What's wrong?"

"There's nothing wrong with *me*," she pointed out. "What's wrong with *you?* You didn't call me back. The house is going to get away."

It took me a moment to realize what she was talking about, which I hoped was more a problem of focus than of declining mental abilities. I'd already reached the age where people were starting to make little jokes about forgetting things. Ha, ha. "Sorry," I said when the synapses had connected enough for me to recall the perfect house that would indeed get away. "I should have called you. We're not going to make an offer."

"Why not?" she shrieked. "It was perfect for you. You said so yourself!"

There are times when it is not an advantage to have a friend as your real-estate agent. I was about to have to tell her that all the time she had spent with me in a professional capacity was likely to be uncompensated. "Jack . . . ," I began.

"Just take him up to see it," she said. "I bet he'll love it. In fact, I'm sure of it. You know I wouldn't push you, but we've been looking for *months,* and I don't think you're going to find anything closer to what you say you want than this."

"It's not that," I told her. "I know it's perfect. It's . . . it's just more than we can afford right now."

Her real-estate agent's ear was perfectly attuned to the ring of sincerity and regret. "Oh. Okay." She hesitated. "Do you want me to check out something in a lower price range?"

"Um . . . actually we might want to postpone the search for a while."

"That's a shame," she said after a moment.

"Yes," I agreed. "I'm so sorry. I know how hard you've worked on this." I sighed. "That seems so inadequate. Sorry," I said again.

"Do you want to talk about it?" she asked.

I saw that she was imagining some greater crisis than a tax obligation, so I gave her a brief summary of the change in our circumstances. "It's not so bad," I concluded. "It's not like I hate the house or the neighborhood. I would have liked something new, something *ours* together. It would have been like starting over. But now I guess we'll be lucky if we get to keep the one we're in."

"That bad?" Kay asked sympathetically.

"I'm not sure," I said. "Jack has this thing about how it isn't my problem, how he can handle it all himself. He wants to protect everybody—me, Patrick, everyone. I offered to contribute some of my own money, and he wouldn't hear of it." I tried not to sound aggrieved.

"Michael's the same," she said. "You might as well just let him do what he wants."

"It's not that," I told her. "It's more a sense of getting shut out. He's not telling me things. One day I'll come home from work and there'll be a big 'For Sale' sign in front of the house."

"And it won't even be my listing," she said.

I laughed. "Probably not. Maybe I'll be glad, if the time comes. It might be the only face-saving way of getting Patrick to move out of the house."

I could hear her sucking in her breath. "He's *not* moving in with you?"

"I haven't told you. I found out when I got home yesterday. He's lost his job, and he can't afford his apartment."

"You shouldn't have invited him to live with you," she said in a horrified tone. "It's a mistake. He'll cause problems between you and Jack."

Her apparent certainty on this topic was alarming. I didn't exactly feel like confessing that I'd more or less been presented with a fait accompli. "Jack says it's only temporary. We've agreed on six months."

"And what happens when he's still unemployed and

apartmentless in six months? Which one of you is going to kick him out?"

I was silent.

"Okay," she said. "I'm going to suggest something I've already suggested, but this time I really think you should listen. I want you to come to a meeting of the Anne Boleyn Society. You need the support. You'll get some good ideas about how to handle this sort of thing. You don't have to do anything—it's not like AA—and if you hate it, you don't have to come back."

"I guess it couldn't hurt," I told her. "I don't seem to be figuring this out on my own. When's the next meeting?"

"Thursday night. Pick you up at eight?"

"Thanks," I said, feeling furtive, as if I were embarking on a career of crime.

CHAPTER 7

Harrison didn't come back into the office the next day or the day after that. He didn't answer the phone either. I began to be concerned. Lawyers check in. There's always some loose end that needs tying up, someone who needs some information you've got that he doesn't. It's a big nuisance when you're in, say, Tahiti, trying to figure out the time difference so you can make your call when you'd rather be diving in to the pupu platter, but you do it anyway. And Harrison had never been one for shirking his responsibilities, at least not in the time I'd known him.

I wasn't frightened exactly, but I remembered his morose talk at Jack's birthday party and wondered if I shouldn't try to contact his daughter, who lived in New Jersey somewhere, or the police. I'd never met her, and I thought how overprotective I would sound, so I decided to let it go for a couple of days. After that I would start calling the hospitals.

On Wednesday, Ronnie Sanchez, our paralegal, came into my office with a sheaf of papers. "Can I run something by you?" she asked.

"Of course," I said encouragingly. I felt like adding, *my child.* She looked so absurdly young. "What's up?"

"Mind if I close the door?"

I gestured: *Go ahead.*

She sat in the client chair, still clutching the papers. "This is embarrassing," she said. "I hope I'm not out of line."

I smiled. "I doubt that very much," I said. I waited.

"Well," she said, still hesitant, "Brooke asked me to send in some paperwork to the INS for her, some work she was doing for Harrison, you know?"

I nodded.

She cleared her throat. "I noticed . . . I just thought . . . there's something . . . unusual about some of them. Brooke said it was okay and that I shouldn't bother you, but . . ."

Someone more devious might have been making a rather clever attempt at backstabbing, but Ronnie was straight-shooting and rather shy. I would have preferred one of her to ten Brookes, despite her inexperience.

"You did the right thing," I told her. "It's the integrity of the work that matters, nothing else. Don't ever hesitate to come to me or to Harrison with any question you might have, even if you think it's silly." I looked at the papers she was holding. "Are those what you had a question about?"

She handed them to me, her jaw tightening slightly as she watched my face.

I looked through them for something anomalous. There were several "approval notices" (technically an INS Notice of Action) for labor-certification I-140s, to be attached to the applications for adjustment of status (from temporary to permanent resident). I didn't see anything unusual. I looked at Ronnie.

"Look closer at Mehra and Govitsky," she suggested.

"Oh," I said, suddenly seeing what she meant. "They both have the same bar code, don't they? How odd. How old are these?" The INS had started putting bar codes on its Notices of Action a year or two before. I checked the dates. "Nope. Fairly recent. How odd," I said again.

"Also," she said, looking down at her hands for a moment, "also . . . the paperwork for the original labor-cert filings is not in the client files."

"Maybe the files are in Harrison's office?"

"I asked Brooke to check. She says they're not."

"Well, I don't know what to say. Clearly we need to check with Harrison before we act on any of these, so hold off on sending them in. In the meantime I'll talk to Brooke."

"Okay. Thanks."

"Thank you," I said. "It's probably just a misfiling or something like that, but you made the right call. Good work."

She smiled.

*   *   *

BROOKE WAS SLOUCHING BEHIND HARRISON'S DESK, her feet up on it in spirit, if not in fact. She straightened quickly as soon as I walked in, as if her ass had found its way into Harrison's chair purely by accident. "Hi," she said. "What can I do for you?"

I wondered why every phrase out of her mouth irritated me so much. Probably she was just no more than normally obnoxious, the effect of overdeveloped ambition and underdeveloped sincerity. Still, I found myself analyzing her every utterance for hidden malice. Once I realized it, I sometimes compensated by treating her with more friendliness than she probably deserved.

"I thought I'd check out these approval notices," I told her. "Ronnie says she can't find the original documentation in the client files."

"I told her it wasn't important," she said dismissively. "Harrison probably has them at home."

I closed my eyes and took a deep breath before I spoke. "Possibly," I said, "although I can't see why he would. But as long as we aren't certain about the documents, it doesn't make sense to file them, does it?" I sounded annoyed even to myself, but I couldn't help it.

She shrugged. "I guess not," she said. "If you think it's that important."

"I don't know how important it is," I said evenly. "That's the point. You know what the INS is like—if the documents are wrong somehow, they'll send them back. In the meantime someone's visa could have expired. Dates and accuracy are very, very important."

"Very important," she agreed, nodding. She looked

as if she were only half listening. "I wonder . . . ," she began.

"What?"

"Well, Harrison's been getting these calls from the INS all week. I wonder if it could be connected."

I blinked. "From whom?" I said.

"I wrote it *down,* Lynn. It's right here." She handed me three telephone memo slips.

I glanced at them, but since as a rule immigration lawyers rarely get called by anyone at the INS, it was not a name I recognized. "I'll check it out," I said. "It might be urgent."

"Would you like me to call?" she asked. Then, catching my look, she added, "I mean, since Harrison asked me to handle things while he was out . . ."

"No thank you," I said, with formal patience. "But if you could get me all the files for these clients, I'd like to look them over in my office."

"No problem," she said. Perkily.

AN HOUR LATER I LEFT A MESSAGE on Harrison's home voice mail. "Call me," I said. "You have to call me. No matter what. It's *urgent.*" I hung up quickly, checking to see that the door to my office was still tightly closed. I felt dizzy and a little sick. Despite my lack of affinity for premonitions, I had a big one now. The shit was going to hit the fan.

"There must be some mistake," I'd kept telling the INS legal officer when she told me that the Notices of Action were apparently counterfeit.

"They're not genuine," she insisted. "You can tell because they repeat the bar code. In some cases there's no code at all. Also . . ."

Also, the labor certifications and the H-1Bs for which the apparent approvals had been issued had never been filed.

"Are you sure?" I asked. I mean, it's not as if the INS hadn't been known to lose things, although of course I didn't bring that up.

"As sure as I can be," she said. "We do occasionally lose documents, but there's not even anything logged in to the computer."

"There must be some mistake," I said, realizing I sounded like a parrot with a chip on its shoulder, but unable to think, for the moment, of any other reply.

"I'm sure you'll want to check your own records," she said coolly.

"Yes, of course. Of course. It's just that I—"

"You understand that we will be following up on this, don't you?"

Boy, did I ever. "You'll have my—our—full cooperation," I told her.

"I certainly hope so," she said.

"I'M GOING TO BE LATE," I told Jack, when I reached him at his office. "I'm not sure how late. Something's come up." I didn't want to go into it on the phone, at least not until I knew for certain what had really happened. The parameters of disaster. "Um . . . I'm expecting a call from Harrison," I said. "I think he'll call me here, but just in case he calls the house, could you please tell him where I am and ask him—*tell* him—it's really important that I speak to him?"

"Okay. Sure," he said. He sounded just a little bit annoyed.

"Bad time?" I said.

"No, it's okay. I was hoping you'd be home for dinner tonight, that's all."

I smiled. "Did you have something special in mind?"

"Always," he said. "But actually this is Patrick's first night back in the house, remember?"

I hadn't. I stopped smiling. "Oh . . ."

"And I just thought it might make him feel more welcome if we were both there for dinner."

"I'm sorry, Jack, I really can't make it. We'll do it tomorrow— Oh, no, I can't tomorrow night either. Well, we'll work it out. I'm sure he doesn't mind. Get takeout."

"It's not the *food*, Lynn. If you can't make it, you can't."

I could hear in his voice that he thought I had concocted some excuse to keep from coming home. Although I was not guilty in fact, I might have been in principle, since I wasn't completely persuaded that I wouldn't have stooped to doing exactly that, if only I'd thought of it in time. Besides, how welcome did I really want Patrick to feel?

"Sorry," I said again, feeling guilty over my own ungenerous thoughts.

"We'll see you when we see you, then," Jack said curtly.

"Fine," I said. "Great."

IN THE END I DIDN'T GO HOME until well past midnight. I didn't want to go through the files while the others were still there—it was far too early for that sort of explanation—so I waited till after hours to start my sleuthing. Besides the documents flagged by the INS, I wasn't sure what I was really looking for. What I feared I might find was more of the same.

The problem with finding counterfeit documents for clients who were also missing genuine documentation is that it strongly suggested that the original applications were never filed. You might actually get away with it as long as the INS didn't notice. For example, you could file a bogus labor-certification approval with the INS with form I-140 requesting permanent resident status. INS approves the I-140. So you're home free. Or maybe you manufacture the I-140 approval, too, and attach it to the adjustment of status, and you get away with that. The clients wouldn't know the difference, as long as their visas or permanent residency was apparently approved.

The question was, *why?* And who?

Why is easy if it happened only once or twice. You forgot to file something, so you tell the client you've filed it, hoping to get it filed immediately to cover your tracks. If you can't file it on time, you get more desperate. Then you're stuck manufacturing the documents and hoping that the INS won't realize they're fake. The problem—in addition to the fact that what you're doing is fraudulent, illegal, and immoral—is that you have a lot of clients who have paid a lot of money to secure their immigration status, and now they're in this country illegally. Depending on the circumstances, they can be sent home immediately, have to pay a big fine, and/or forfeit the right to return for years. This was not a situation likely to make anyone very happy.

I prayed it was just the one or two cases, but after only a couple of hours' search, I turned up three more client files with suspicious-looking documents. All of them worked for Kojima Bank, one of our biggest and most important clients. There were also some older files predating the bar codes that looked fishy, too.

I was speechless with dread.

By midnight I was so upset and distracted I decided to postpone further investigations. I had no illusions about getting a good night's sleep, but I was just spinning my wheels, and until I got to Harrison, I couldn't know exactly how to proceed. I had my keys out and was locking the door to the office when I heard a phone ringing inside. I opened the door again, thinking it must be Jack.

Sure enough, my private line was ringing. I grabbed for the phone. "Hello?"

There was silence on the other end of the line.

"Hello?" I repeated. "Harrison?"

A long sigh, and then nothing. Did I hear a *clink* in the background?

"Harrison, is that you? Answer me, damn it!" I took a deep breath and let it out slowly.

"I'm your partner, Harrison. Don't—"

Before I could say *Don't hang up,* the line went dead.

I dialed his cell phone, which was still off. I called his home number.

The phone rang and rang.

CHAPTER 8

The porch light was off when I got home. I pulled into the driveway, but when the garage door rolled up, Patrick's Miata was parked next to Jack's Lexus, which left zero space for me. I lowered the garage door again, locked the car door, and walked up the path to the front door.

I almost stepped on Brewer, who responded with an aggrieved meow. I bent over and picked him up, putting his front legs over my shoulder in the "fireman's carry," which he loved. "What are you doing out, Brewer Man?" Okay, so I'm one of those people who talk baby talk to their pets. But he was twelve years old, it had been just the two of us for a long time, and on the whole he'd been a good sport about moving, so he probably deserved a little coddling.

I moved closer to the front door, fumbling with my keys. It was dark, and I recoiled jerkily when my foot touched something huge and soft on the porch. I bent over, still clutching the cat and my purse and the keys.

It was Brewer's foam bed, the one he slept on in the utility room.

I pushed open the door and set the cat down in the hall. I could hear the TV on in the family room. It was jarring, particularly so late. I knew it couldn't be Jack.

Patrick was sitting on the couch watching a *Seinfeld* rerun. An empty glass and an apple core, without benefit of plate, were sitting on the coffee table in front of him. He lifted his eyes. "Hi," he said.

"Hi," I said. "Welcome." I hoped I sounded wonderfully sincere. "Um . . . did you put the cat out?"

He nodded, his eyes drifting back to the set.

"Well, don't, please. We don't let him out at night. Probably it's better if you don't let him out at all."

"The thing is," he said, looking at me with a mixture of malice and triumph, "I can't sleep in the house with a cat. My eyes swell shut, and I sneeze. Dad said it would be okay if I put it out."

I noticed that "it." I also noticed that he had never sneezed once in the house in the entire year-plus his father and I had been married, though he'd been around the cat on many occasions. If he was allergic, this was the first I'd heard of it. After the day I'd had—my practice possibly in ruins, my partner acting suspiciously— I was not, to say the least, in a conciliatory mood. "Well, it's not okay," I said fiercely. "It's January, it's freezing at night, and he's a senior cat. Plus, there are"—I tried to think of the appropriate menace. Coyotes?—"predators," I emphasized. "Keep your bedroom door closed."

He looked at me blankly, his jaw dropping open a little. Then he shrugged. "Whatever," he said. His gaze returned pointedly to the screen.

"Good night," I said.

He didn't answer me.

I was going to put the cat in the utility room, but I wasn't sure I could trust Patrick not to put him out again after I'd gone to bed. I gathered up Brewer and the cat bed and took them into our bedroom. I considered the litter box, but it was already so late I thought I could leave it till morning. I didn't want to risk stepping in it in bare feet in the darkness.

Jack was asleep, but he woke up a little when I came in bearing burdens. "Hi," he mumbled. "What time is it?"

"Late," I said.

"Everything all right?" he asked.

Ha. "We'll talk in the morning," I said. "Listen, be careful if you get up in the night. Brewer's bed is on the floor at the foot of the bed."

"He snores," Jack remarked sleepily.

"I know, but it's nonnegotiable," I told him.

He made a sound that might have been a snort or a laugh, and went back to sleep.

I lay awake a long time, staring into the darkness. Even with the door closed, I could hear the television in the family room far into the night.

CHAPTER 9

I'd intended to get up early and get to the office before everyone else, but after an entire night of not sleeping, I finally drifted off around five and reawoke in a sort of stupor around eight-thirty. I could remember a time when I could shake off sleeplessness (and worse) with a hot shower, but I'd squandered my youthful energy on all-night bull sessions and other frivolities (and once I read ten Shakespeare plays in a single night for a final). Those days were gone with the bell-bottoms and Birkenstocks. I hauled myself out of bed, dreading the day. Jack had already left, and Patrick would sleep for hours yet, so there was nothing to distract me from the expectation of imminent disaster I dragged around like a soggy blanket.

RONNIE SANCHEZ WAS WAITING in my office when I got in. She looked pale. "Hi," she said softly.

"Hi," I said "What's up?"

She looked down at her notes. "Well, a Dr. Strela

called. He's Russian. He works at Stanford. He'd like to see you, right away."

"Good, a potential client." I needed—would need—every one I could get if word got out that the firm had falsified INS documents. "Have Adam pencil him in tomorrow, or whenever he can make it. Also," I said carefully, "we need to have a firm meeting. Today. The sooner the better." I was going to have to ask, in the most diplomatic possible terms, whether anyone had noticed anything odd about Harrison's behavior or legal work.

"Okay," she said. "But shouldn't we wait until—"

I cut her off. "It can't wait," I said.

Her eyes filled. Since she wasn't the type who got weepy over a curt answer, I realized that something was up. I looked around. "What's wrong? Where is Adam?" I asked. "And where's Brooke, for that matter?"

"Um . . . they went to the hospital." She looked away.

"Who's in the hospital?" I asked carefully.

"Harrison," she said, in the same quiet voice. She sounded almost embarrassed to confess it, which made me a little ashamed. Did they think I wouldn't care?

"What happened?" I asked. *Heart attack,* I thought, or even a stroke. Or a drunk-driving accident. After last night I'd believe anything.

She shook her head. "It's not clear. He's in intensive care, that's all I know. Since last night or early this morning. Brooke said she'd call when she found out anything."

"What hospital?" I asked.

"El Camino."

"Good," I said. El Camino was a "normal" hospital. Stanford Hospital was cutting-edge, but you had to put up with platoons of med students peeking into your orifices at all hours in the name of education. "I'm on my way," I said.

"Really?" she asked.

"Of course. If Brooke or Adam calls before I get there, tell—"

The phone cut me off.

Ronnie and I both looked at it. "I'll get it," I said.

"I don't know anything," Adam said, after I'd answered. "We're coming back to the office. His condition is described as 'guarded,' but they won't let us in to see him. No visitors."

"Did they say what happened?" I asked.

"Just that they won't release any information except to family. Does his daughter know he's in the hospital, do you think?"

"I'm sure the hospital will have called her." I did not add that he very well might be under investigation by the DOJ and not exactly unsupervised.

"Oh, okay," Adam said woodenly.

I sighed. "I'll give her a call, just in case," I told him.

"Thanks, Lynn."

WHILE RONNIE SEARCHED FOR THE PHONE NUMBER, I called Kay at work. "Did you change your mind about a house?" she asked, before I could say anything.

"Not until there's a change in our finances," I told her. "I'm sorry."

"I'm sorry, too," she said. "That was insensitive. I don't know what comes over me. It must be something in the air in this office. I keep hearing 'ask for the sale, ask for the sale' in my head, and the words just pop right out of my mouth. What can I do for you?"

I told her I wanted to find out about Harrison. "Can you ask Michael?" Her husband was a big deal in orthopedic surgery, so of course he could find out anything he wanted to, if he was willing to try. Managed care hadn't changed things that much.

She called me back in a few minutes. "Oh, Lynn, I'm really sorry to tell you this. Michael says they have him down as attempted suicide."

My throat closed. *Right after he called me.* As a confirmation of my worst fears and suspicions, it was pretty definitive. "How?" I asked, scarcely able to get the word out.

"Sleeping pills and booze, apparently," she said. "Oh, sorry—I guess that sounds callous. But it was obvious at Jack's party that he had a drinking problem."

"I guess so," I told her. "I'd just never thought it affected his work."

She made the noncommittal noise people do when they think you're a naive fool and don't want to say so.

"You sound exhausted," she said after a moment.

"Couldn't sleep," I told her. There was no point in going into why, at least not yet. I still needed to sort things out in my own mind. "Um, I may not make it to your group tonight. There's a lot going on here."

"Try," she said firmly. "There will always be a lot

going on. If you aren't positively at death's door from some communicable disease, I'm picking you up as we agreed."

I was silent.

"Please," she said.

"You're supposed to say, 'You'll thank me later,' " I said.

"You'll thank me later," she said. She laughed. "That actually happens to be true."

"Okay," I told her. "I'll try."

HARRISON'S DAUGHTER, Jennifer Grady, was a litigator in a big-time law firm. "Thank you for calling," she said when I had tracked her down at her office. "But the police called me last night."

I told her I hadn't seen him and didn't know anything concrete, but that in all events I was sure he would want her to know he was in the hospital.

"Are you?" she asked, somewhat curtly. "I'm not. I'm sure he would prefer no one knew. He tried to kill himself, did you know?"

"I did," I said, "but it isn't common knowledge here."

"Who did you say this was?" she asked.

I explained, again, my relationship to her father.

"Oh, right," she said. "I remember now. Are you under arrest, too?"

I gasped. I began to see why Harrison was not close to his only child. "Is Harrison under arrest?" I asked.

"He will be, if he recovers. He got the news last

night." She paused. "I see that you aren't asking me what he's under arrest *for,*" she observed.

I breathed out slowly. Some of the guilt I felt about being the last person to talk to him before he tried to off himself evaporated. "No," I said. In fact, I had a million questions, but not for her. *Be careful,* I told myself.

"Anyway," she said suspiciously, "if you are who you say you are, shouldn't you have known that?"

I pictured her sitting at her desk in an Armani suit, dressed for combat. I tried not to dislike her on the grounds that animosity ought to be conceived face-to-face, but I abandoned my principles. "Actually," I said, "if what *you* say is true, I'm the one your father left holding the bag."

"I thought as much," she said, although she could have fooled me. "I'm sorry about that." She didn't sound the least bit sincere. "Dad's been on a downward spiral ever since my mother left him. He can't seem to get it together. To tell you the truth, it's been rather embarrassing."

I thought that was putting it mildly, under the circumstances.

"In any case, I'm sure it's best we don't get into this further. I wouldn't want to jeopardize his defense in any way. I'm sure you understand."

"Well," I said, "I won't take more of your time. I'm not sure they'll let me in to see your father, but if they do—"

"You want to *see* him?" She sounded surprised.

"We have things to discuss. Eventually. For the moment I just want to see how he is. If I can get in, do you want me to tell him you'll be coming?"

"God, no," she said. "Don't do that. I've got a big trial coming up. I don't know when I'll be able to get away." I could hear a pen (or something else) tap-tapping against the phone. Maybe it was her fingernail. "He won't be expecting me," she said after a moment. "We haven't seen each other in three years."

"I see," I said. "Is there any message, then?"

She appeared to think this over.

"No, no message," she said finally.

CHAPTER 10

Intensive-care units are generic and interchangeable, like airport lounges. I went up to the nurses' station and asked for Harrison's room.

"Family only," said the nurse, with a hint of inquiry.

I nodded. I appreciated the way the exchange was phrased, giving me an out and the hospital an out, in case I proved to be something less than a blood relative. I didn't even have to lie. "Thank you," I said.

"He's probably sleeping," she added. She looked at me, the family (as she thought) of someone who'd attempted suicide. "Don't stay too long," she said. "Don't upset him."

"I won't," I promised, but as I walked toward his room, I wondered if I would. I'd thought only about Harrison, all alone in his despair and weakness, but then I realized that if it were me, I wouldn't have wanted anyone to see me in that condition, particularly not someone I'd injured. I wondered why I hadn't thought of it before. I hesitated in the doorway, suddenly certain that it would look as if I were coming to gloat. I turned around to go.

"Lynn?"

Harrison was pale and puffy as cotton, a featureless organic receptacle for bags and tubes and blinking monitors that pulsed and beeped and bubbled under their own steam.

"Hi," I said softly. "I'm sorry to wake you up. I just came by to see if you were okay."

He made a small sound that might have been a laugh. "I'm okay," he whispered.

"They were worried about you," I said. "Brooke and Adam and Ronnie."

"Do they know?" he said.

I wondered which he meant. *About the suicide attempt. About the faked documents.* I shook my head.

"Don't . . ."

Don't tell, he meant. "I won't," I said. "But they'll find out . . . everything . . . eventually."

"I know," he said. He sighed gently. "I botched it."

I wondered if he'd really meant to die or if it was a sort of dramatic apology gone wrong. I wondered if he knew himself. I certainly couldn't ask him. It was frustrating, because there was so much I needed to know.

"Lynn?"

"Yes?"

"Are you mad at me?" He sounded like an eight-year-old who'd forgotten to make his bed.

I didn't know what to say, under the circumstances.

"We don't have to talk about this. I'm going. I just wanted to be sure—" I stopped, not even certain myself what I meant.

"Are you?" he persisted.

"Yes, of course I am," I told him finally. "What did you expect?" I came closer and lowered my voice. "I'm not here to gloat, or to upset you. We shouldn't be talking about this. You have to get well first."

Harrison settled back into the pillow with the appearance of satisfaction. "Thank you," he said. "Thank you for not lying to me."

"*I* never lied to *you,*" I said, with less restraint than I probably should have.

"Come back . . . ," he said. "Come back . . . later. We'll talk."

"Harrison, do you even have a lawyer?"

He nodded. "Last night . . . before . . ."

"Well, if your lawyer permits, eventually I need to know what happened and why."

He turned his head. "Fuck my lawyer," he said. "I'm a dead man. I can do what I want."

"We'll see," I told him. "Get some rest."

"Promise you'll come back," he said weakly.

I nodded, but his eyes were closed. "All right," I said.

"Lynn?" he said again. "Are *you* okay?"

I didn't know how to answer that. Harrison wanted absolution, but I wouldn't grant it. It would have been so easy to lie, to tell him, *Yes, I'm okay,* when he was desperately sick and probably sorry for whatever he'd done. It would have been easy, and I'm not sure why I wouldn't say it, except that it wasn't true. I was discovering a certain hardness in myself I didn't entirely approve of, but I didn't altogether dislike it either.

"I'm not sure yet," I told him. "I'm still waiting to find out."

BROOKE AND ADAM WERE BACK AT THE OFFICE when I got there. "How was he?" Adam said when I walked in the door.

"Did you get to see him?" Brooke asked. "They wouldn't tell us anything."

"I didn't find out anything definite either," I said. "No visitors, they said, except for family. But I gather he's out of danger."

Adam looked at me quizzically but didn't say anything.

"I *told* you she wouldn't get in," Brooke said.

I ignored her. "Unfortunately, Harrison's health isn't the only issue," I said. "If you could all come into the office, we need to have a talk."

"Even me?" Adam asked. He was nonlegal staff and didn't usually attend firm meetings.

"Everybody," I said. "We're all in this together."

"Uh-oh," Adam said.

"Precisely," I told him.

AFTERWARD I CLOSED THE DOOR to my office. I wanted—needed—to talk to Jack. He still had no idea what was going on.

His cell phone was turned off.

"Oh, honey, he's in a meeting in San Jose," Doris, his secretary, said. "If it's important, we can have him paged." Doris always called me "honey," even though she was only ten years my senior. She was the dream secretary—motherly, kind, efficient, and happily married. I loved her.

"No, it's nothing that can't wait," I said reluctantly. "Do you know what time the meeting's over?"

"Umm, I think he said something about a dinner afterward. I thought he left you a message, honey. Did you check?"

"I've been out," I said.

"You're not working too hard, are you? I know how that husband of yours drives himself. I hope you two newlyweds are finding time for some fun."

I smiled. She made us sound like a couple of oversexed twenty-year-olds. "We manage, I guess," I told her.

"Good," she said. I wondered if she was trying to tell me something, but both of us were too discreet to pursue it further. There are rules for such conversations, and I didn't want to make her uncomfortable by breaking them.

"Anyway, how are you?" I asked her.

"Still employed," she said dryly.

"Me, too," I said. At least for the moment.

"You go, girl."

JACK'S MESSAGE said that since I had already said I "would be out," he'd arranged to have dinner with some potential clients in the City. Like Doris, I knew how hard he was pushing to get business for the company. Still, he shone on such occasions. He attracted people because he didn't flatter them or fake an interest—his enthusiasm was genuine. He could extract something to admire from the most dismally self-centered marketing type. I'd seen him do it. Since I myself tended to lapse into fruitless silences on such occasions, I admired his gift.

I picked up the phone and dialed Kay's number. "It looks like I'm definitely on for tonight," I told her. At least I wouldn't be home alone, brooding over my professional woes.

"You won't be sorry," she promised. "Oh, I said that already, didn't I?"

"Yes," I said, "but I don't mind hearing it again."

CHAPTER 11

The Anne Boleyn Society met in the private room of a local restaurant. Kay had told me they started out meeting in member homes, but nobody felt comfortable in an atmosphere in which the husband or the stepchildren might overhear. After I got there, I understood why.

It's tough being a trophy. Marla Maples has a lot to answer for. The world thinks of second wives as hot little *pommes de terre* who lure previously faithful but chronologically susceptible husbands away from their virtuous original mates with sexual practices that while not technically illegal, stretch the limits of respectability. Granted, such stereotypes exist for a reason. But for every scheming sexpot dressed by Victoria's Secret, somewhere there's a Mrs. de Winter living in the shadow of Rebecca and harassed, to boot, by a passel of antagonistic stepchildren.

Arm candy was not in evidence this evening. Kay handed me a name tag and an oversize glass of Ridge

Zinfandel, potent and dark as sin itself. "Relax," she said, reading my mind. "I'm driving."

The libations had already been flowing fairly freely, if appearances were any indication. By the time we sat around in a circle, sorority-house style, tongues were loosened. "Who wants to start?" Kay asked.

I stared down into my wineglass, reminded of school. I hoped nobody would call on me if I didn't make eye contact.

"I'd like to introduce my friend Lynn Bartlett," Kay said after a moment. "Her husband's ex-wife showed up uninvited at his fiftieth birthday party."

There was a chorus of sympathetic murmurs. I flashed Kay a look and she shrugged. *What did you expect?*

Now that Kay had established my bona fides, my marital history was apparently fair game. "What did you do?" asked Melanie, a very self-possessed-looking blonde of about my age. She was sporting a "look at me" tennis bracelet and a diamond that would not have been sneered at by the sultan of Brunei in his palmiest days.

"Not much," I said,

This was apparently the wrong answer. There was a reproachful silence.

"It didn't seem appropriate to make a scene," I added defensively.

Melanie shook her head sadly. "That's what she's counting on," she said.

"What did your husband do?" asked a worried-looking older woman. Her name tag was smeared, and I couldn't read it.

I swallowed. "He, um, kissed her on the cheek and asked her to dance," I said. "His children had brought her, and he was trying to put a good face on it."

"How did you feel about that?" someone asked me.

I squirmed. "I didn't like it, of course, but it seemed to me the only graceful way to behave."

"Does your husband's ex-wife send him letters?" Melanie asked after a moment.

I nodded. "Postcards. Occasionally."

"Does she call him up when something needs fixing?"

"She did that once," I admitted.

"Recently?"

I lowered my head.

They exchanged looks and nodded, even the elderly, worried-looking one. "She wants him back," Melanie said. "Or at least she doesn't want to let him go."

"She's married," I pointed out.

"Then she wants two," she said.

I laughed, but no one else did.

"And his children are probably in on it," said a woman whose name tag read DR. BILLINGS. She saw me look at it and said, "I'm sorry. I'm so used to writing it this way for staff meetings at the hospital. I'm Claire." She sighed. "My husband's first wife found something she needed to call about every single Friday night, particularly when it was our weekend with the kids. If she didn't call, the kids called her and left messages, so then she had an excuse for calling back. Sometimes she left nasty messages. The kids fought me tooth and nail about everything for three years. My husband . . ."

There was a sigh of expectation. Everyone but me seemed to know what was coming next.

"My husband just withdrew. . . ."

"They do that," Melanie said sagely.

"And let it happen," Claire said. "He refused to do anything about either the kids or his ex-wife."

"They feel guilty," the older woman said.

"That's right, Lorraine," said Claire. "Everybody wants to be first with everybody else, and children don't like it when their father's attention shifts away from them to somebody else. Wives don't like to be left. I don't blame them for that. But I did blame my husband for not putting our relationship first and for letting his ex-wife and children treat me rudely."

"So what did you do?" I couldn't help asking.

"I told the ex-wife that her venom was just fueling my vigilance," she said grimly. "And then I gave my husband an ultimatum."

I waited.

She spread her hands wide, an umpire signaling *You're out*. "And now he's my ex-husband," she said grimly.

How comforting. This was like one of those "Mrs. Lincoln" jokes. When were the helpful tips coming? "That's awful," I said.

She shrugged.

"I'm getting divorced," Lorraine said.

Attention shifted in her direction with a sudden, communal gasp.

"What happened?" someone asked, a shade too eagerly.

Lorraine sighed. "You know that Robert had a stroke?"

A few people nodded polite acknowledgment.

"Well, while he was in the nursing home for rehabilitation, Frederick—that's his son—came and checked him out. The staff told me Frederick said he was taking him home to Minnesota."

"Didn't anyone call you?" Kay asked.

Lorraine shrugged, with all the dignity and the passivity of the helpless elderly.

"Frederick had Robert's power of attorney. He told them not to tell me anything until he'd left. I got the divorce papers last week."

"You could fight it," I told her.

"Lynn's an attorney," Kay said.

"I don't know anything about that field," I added quickly. "But there are people who could help you. And in any case you need representation for the divorce."

"Truthfully, I don't know if I want to fight it or not," she said. "Do I want to sit in a courtroom in Minneapolis for weeks fighting over my husband's ruined body? I'm not sure I have the stamina for that. Besides, I don't even know that the divorce wasn't Robert's idea. They say that people change after a stroke. . . ." She shook her head. "It's a shame, though. I would have taken good care of him. . . ."

"At least make sure you're taken care of financially," I urged. "Does . . . Robert have any assets?"

She looked at me and smiled. "Of course," she said. "Why else do you think Frederick got him away so fast?"

The other women murmured assent.

"But I don't want his money," Lorraine said. "My first husband left me well enough off when he died. I wonder . . ." She looked at me. "My stepson asked me to send my wedding ring back," she said. "Do you think I should?"

"Was it a family heirloom or his mother's diamond or anything like that?" I asked.

She shook her head. "Robert and I picked it out together," she said, smiling at the memory.

"Then tell your stepson to go f—" I stopped, surprised at my own vehemence. "Tell him no," I said, more discreetly.

Lorraine smiled.

"Amen," said Melanie.

"ARE WE READY FOR THE CLOSING CEREMONY?" Kay asked. The glasses were empty, and the restaurant staff had once or twice poked their heads around the door. Since this was the Bay Area, not a single person had gone outside to smoke.

"Closing ceremony" sent a little shiver down my spine. I hoped it didn't involve smashing the wineglasses into the fireplace or a unity pledge or anything like that. I have always felt uncomfortable with coerced demonstrations of camaraderie, particularly if they involve broken glass.

I looked at Kay.

"For our new members and guests," she said, "the closing ceremony is just for each person to say a sentence or two. It's a saying you like, or what's on your mind right now. Something you'd like to share."

I wondered if I could get away with *Thank you for having me*. I'd found the evening interesting, in the way that automobile accidents and typhoons are interesting, but I'm not sure how helpful it was to uncover everyone else's misery. Still, I had to admit there was a lot of combined experience in the room, and it might have been useful to find out how other people handled problems like, for example, moving into your new husband's house, the one his kids had walked in and out of for years without keys, so that you felt like an interloper, a narcissist whose requests for privacy were met with uncomprehending stares. That sort of thing.

Maybe when I got the rest of my life straightened out, I'd come back.

"Who wants to start?" Kay asked. This was apparently rhetorical, a part of ritual, because a moment later she said, "I will, then. I haven't shared much tonight, but here's something I heard that I liked: 'Women mourn, men replace.' "

There was a curious murmur of assent among the Replacements.

"I saw this on a Web site," said a slender silver-blonde with celebrity hair, the kind of 'do that reflects better on the hairdresser than on the client. " 'Give me your tired, your poor . . .' "

"That's on the Statue of Liberty," Lorraine said.

The blonde shrugged. "Well, *something* like that. Anyway, it ends 'your angry children yearning to break me.' It was on a poster."

No one said anything.

Dr. Billings sat up straight. "In the animal kingdom, replacement mates will often dispose of their predecessor's young," she said. I couldn't tell if it was meant to be a joke or not.

"I just want to say," Lorraine offered quietly, "that no matter what it took, I would have taken care of him."

"Think about it. So much of remarriage has to be built from loss," Melanie said.

"Lynn?" Kay prompted me after a moment.

I opened my mouth to express some courteous platitude. They were all watching me.

"I wasn't prepared," I said, surprising myself. "I thought all I had to do was be nice to everybody and we'd all get along." I swallowed.

Lorraine reached over and patted my hand.

"I just never thought it would be this hard," I said.

"Welcome to the club," Kay said.

CHAPTER 12

I might have to close the firm," I said to Jack over the breakfast table. I kept my voice scarcely above a whisper—we usually had privacy at breakfast because Patrick slept in till nine or ten, but I wasn't taking any chances. Since the night I'd challenged him about the cat, Patrick had more or less stayed out of my way, so long as no one else wanted to watch TV in the family room at night. Every morning I picked up the remnants of his midnight snack and disposed of them before Jack could see, so it didn't become an issue. *It's only six months,* I told myself. Brewer returned reluctantly to his bed in the laundry room, and we all tiptoed around on little cat feet.

Jack looked up from the *Wall Street Journal.* "Oh, Lynn," he said. "It can't really be as bad as that? What did the INS say?" Since I'd told him the news about Harrison, he'd refused to believe that things were as bleak as I'd painted them.

"Which time? I've had conversations with four different people so far." I speared a bite of out-of-season melon, lifted my fork, then set it down again. "I think . . . I hope . . . they realize I didn't have any part of faking the documents, so they won't come after me with criminal charges."

"Good God," Jack said.

"But," I added, "I still have to go through the affected clients on a case-by-case basis. For some who obviously qualify, the INS will grant the visas or green cards anyway. But it's arbitrary, and they won't do it for everybody, so I'll have to start all over with the application process, and of course I can't charge for it. And I have to go to Kojima Bank and tell them that two of their top executives are de facto illegal, after they've already paid for their visas. How is the firm's reputation going to survive that?"

"Have you said anything to the rest of the firm?"

"There's just the three of them," I reminded him. "They know about the problem with the documents, of course, but none of them know exactly how serious it is yet. I was hoping to get more information from Harrison after he got out of the hospital, but he says his lawyer advises him not to speak with me. He's under house arrest, and I think they're working out a plea bargain," I added bitterly.

"I bet," Jack said. "Don't blame the lawyer for that. I'd advise the same. What I can't understand is, why'd he do it? It's not like the work's that difficult."

I ignored the insult, which was probably not intended. "The most charitable explanation," I said, "is that his drinking problem is worse than we thought. Maybe he had blackouts or something and forgot to file the paperwork, so he panicked and faked it." My worst fear, the one I didn't confide to Jack, was that the signs of slippage and alcohol abuse in the office had been there all along, and I'd missed them. I'd racked my brain, I'd discreetly queried the staff, but, on the whole, Harrison had covered his tracks well. At least until the very end. "It doesn't really matter why he did it, does it?" I asked Jack. "The only thing I wonder is if he brought me in as partner to cover for him in some way. I just feel so used, not to mention really, really angry."

"I doubt he set you up, Lynn. Harrison doesn't seem like that type somehow. Besides, he did try to kill himself. At least that shows some remorse."

"He didn't seem like the type to fake documents either," I pointed out. "Maybe he's just sorry he got caught." The truth is, I felt like a failure, too. Either I'd been duped and had failed to see it coming or Harrison had needed help and I'd failed to see that. One way or the other, there might have been something I could have done to have prevented disaster. I said, with more bravado than I felt, "I wish I could share your confidence, but I can't be sure of anything other than that he left me with a big mess to clean up, an indeterminate number of probable malpractice actions to handle, and a financial situation we can ill afford."

"Well," Jack said. His eyes drifted back to the newspaper. I had already learned that expressions of emotion were not something he was comfortable making, and the Financial Situation was practically off-limits.

Nevertheless, I needed to know. "Sorry. I've been going on and on," I said. "How's your business doing?" Jack's business was a software company that built navigation guides for consumers shopping on the Internet. It started with the recognition that as the number of Internet sites proliferated into the millions, there was a need for tools to help people navigate the World Wide Web more effectively. Unfortunately, since Internet commerce had suffered a setback, so had the company.

"Fine," he said.

"Really?"

He shrugged and looked pointedly down at the *Journal*.

"What about our tax liability?" I asked.

"I'm working on it," he said without lifting his eyes.

"Jack—"

"Lynn, please."

I felt like the nagging wife in some late-night sitcom. I opened my mouth to protest, then closed it again.

"Besides," Jack added, "haven't you got enough to worry about right now?" He grimaced. "Also—and I really regret the timing—but don't forget my mother's coming to visit this weekend."

My serotonin level was definitely plummeting. "You're right, that is this weekend. With all this going on, I'd forgotten. Of course." We'd invited her weeks before.

He looked at me. "If you think we have to, we can always postpone it for a bit," he said nobly and insincerely.

"Nonsense," I said. "She's probably got nonrefundable reservations."

"Probably," he agreed. He looked relieved. "If you're sure . . ."

I reminded myself that one of the things I'd admired about Jack was his loyalty to his family. I mean, would you really want to be a daughter like Jennifer Grady, who didn't even show up when her father tried to commit suicide? Jack had a highly developed notion of what was owed to one's relatives, whether they deserved it or not. I supposed I should be grateful.

Clearly I was a failure at Family. I did not tend to see it as something that brought a lot of joy just in principle, probably as much a result of my own upbringing (my parents appeared to view most of their relatives as messy and unpleasant) as anything else. My family home had not been the scene of tearful annual reunions. We had holidays alone, just the three of us, in quiet contentment. My mother now lived in a retirement community in Arizona and traveled almost incessantly with her widow friends. I talked to her once a week, when she could sandwich me in between her golf games and bridge club, and she usually spent a week with me at Christmas. This year she was planning a holiday cruise. Someday her needs would change, but right now she treasured her independence and resented interference, which was perfectly all right with me.

Moira Hughes, my mother-in-law, persisted in calling me "Janet," except when she called on the phone, in which case she called me "May-I-speak-to-Jackson-please" without benefit of further salutation. According to Jack, her affection for his first wife had postdated the end of their marriage and had arisen not so much out of conversation or contact (there being none) but at the onset of Jack's interest in me. Even so, I could easily have been cordial to her for a weekend, just not the one during which my entire professional career was threatening to disintegrate. But I didn't think I had any choice.

"Of course I'm sure," I said. "It will be lovely to have her."

"No, it won't," Jack said. "I know she's difficult." He sighed. "We'll have to have a family dinner," he added. "I think we ought to go out, don't you?"

"Don't be silly," I said.

THE TATTERED REMNANTS of Grady & Bartlett had taken the news on the chin, for the most part, and geared up to fight back. I kept buying doughnuts for our firm meetings (harder to find, now that the Bay Area had gotten so trendy) and coffee to ease the blow, and I set them in the middle of the conference table, as far out of my reach as possible.

"So how bad is it?" Adam asked, getting straight to the point.

"Bad," I said. I told them everything I had learned from the INS.

"As a matter of fact," Brooke said, when I had sketched the outlines of our dilemma, "it's not exactly news, Lynn."

Ronnie and even Adam nodded solemnly, so I knew she wasn't lying.

"It's not?" I asked.

Brooke had just had her nails manicured, I noticed, in a rather unflattering shade of maroon. "Well, no," she said. "I called Harrison, and he—"

"Harrison talked to you?" I asked, trying not to sound as flabbergasted as I felt.

"Why wouldn't he?" she said, smirking a little. "We were close. He'd already asked me to look out for things in his absence—"

"Because he was under advice from counsel not to speak, for one thing," I said, more sharply than I intended. I hadn't told them about Harrison's suicide attempt, and they hadn't asked, although I'm sure they had guessed. I reached across the table and snatched up a chocolate cruller, my favorite. I needed it, bad.

"Maybe he didn't think that applied to Brooke, because she's not a partner," Ronnie said kindly. "Maybe he hoped to get a message to you that way."

"Maybe," I said grimly. "So what did he say?"

"He told me he was sorry if he'd screwed things up for me," Brooke said. "And for the rest of you, of course."

Of course. "I don't suppose he gave you any idea of how many bogus cases we're dealing with?" I asked.

"Well, he could hardly do that without admitting outright that he faked them," she said, with some justice.

"True," I said, "but it would be much easier if we knew how far back we have to go in checking documents."

"If we don't find any problems or discrepancies, should we assume the documents are okay?" Ronnie asked.

"I think we have to," I said. "We don't want the INS reevaluating every approved visa application unless it's clear that there was something fake about the approvals. It's bad enough as it is."

"So what happens now?" Adam asked soberly.

I took a bite of the cruller, which turned to dust in my mouth. They all looked at me, waiting while I stalled. I knew what I had to say; I just didn't want to say it.

"I don't want to lie to you," I said finally. "I may not be able to hold the firm together. We have overhead, and we can't charge for all the time we'll have to spend working through this mess. As you know, the H-1B business was already slowing down because of the tech implosion, and—"

"I can't take a pay cut," Brooke said.

"I can," said Adam.

"Me, too," added Ronnie.

"Thanks," I said, to those who deserved it. "Let's

just take this a day at a time. I have to go see Kojima
Bank later this week, and then we'll have to see how
many clients we have left if the shit hits the fan. Probably ninety-five percent of our work is perfectly legit-
imate, but it's the five percent in question that everyone
will be worried about, and I can't really blame them.
Please be discreet about this, for heaven's sake. And if
anyone wants to start looking for another job right
away, believe me, I'll understand."

Brooke extended a crimson nail toward the plate of
doughnuts and raked a finger's width of vanilla icing
off the top of the one on top. She raised her finger to
her lips and licked it theatrically.

"You know you can count on us, Lynn," she said.

"There is one bright spot," Adam said.

"What's that?"

"We might have a new client. That Dr. Strela is coming in this afternoon."

"I checked," Brooke said. "Harrison got him a re-
newal on his H-1 a year ago."

"Maybe he's heard something," Ronnie said in a
stricken voice.

CHAPTER 13

Alexei Strela was twenty minutes late and arrived rumpled in khaki pants, running shoes, a T-shirt, and a black leather jacket.

"I'm sorry," he said in perfect, nearly unaccented English, when he was shown into my office. "I got held up." He sank into the client chair with the ease of someone settling in to watch *The West Wing* in the comfort of his own living room. "I left my bike in the lobby," he said. "I hope that's okay."

I assured him that it was, although in fact the building management frowned on it. *If you let one do it, you have to let everybody. . . .*

Even though all of my clients were foreign, I never knew what to expect, particularly from the Russians. Many of them had had very little practical English in the former Soviet Union and still spoke it very hesitantly. They were a friendly group on the whole, but for whatever reason—the system of government they had grown up under or some cultural conditioning I was unaware of—they were often wary and excessively private. A number of my clients objected to receiving faxes where they worked and even seemed to harbor suspicions of phone calls. A lot of them were apparently nocturnal and asked if they could call me at home late at night. (No, they couldn't.) Alexei Strela, with his easy English and easier manners, was, if not a rarity, at least intriguingly different.

"I'd like to know," he said, suddenly dropping the bonhomie, "if there's something wrong with my visa."

So he had heard something.

I was ready for him. "I reviewed your documents," I said, "and I don't think so." I had this down pat by now—I'd already gone through it with a number of clients. "I'm sure there's nothing to worry about, but—"

"I work at SLAC," he said. "I have to be careful."

SLAC (pronounced "slack") is the Stanford Linear Accelerator Center, a national research laboratory operated by Stanford University for the Department of Energy. SLAC designs, constructs, and operates state-of-the-art electron accelerators and related experimental facilities for use in high-energy physics and synchrotron-radiation research, and though it used to be a bigger deal than it is now, it still has plenty of clout in the scientific community.

"I know that," I told him. "To be doubly sure, it wouldn't be a bad idea for me to examine the documents the INS has sent you directly."

He sat back in his chair and regarded me coolly. "Why is that?" he said. That was another thing different from the stereotype—he had very black hair, flecked with gray, and his eyes were dark brown. A Russian George Clooney, or Sean Connery when he had hair. Just at the moment, he looked like no one to be put off with half-truths.

I met his gaze with an effort. "I'm sorry to say, Dr. Strela, that we've discovered some irregularities in our own files," I told him. "It's really in your own best interests if we look over the documents the INS sent directly to you."

"Define 'irregularities,' " he said, leaning forward in his chair with the air of a professor delivering a particularly nasty pop quiz.

I closed my eyes and sighed. "One of the members of the firm appears to have . . . altered . . . some approval notices, or worse," I said. "It's still under investigation, but in the meantime we'd like to be sure all our clients are perfectly safe."

"Thank you," he said, sitting back. "I was wondering if you would be honest with me."

I raised my eyes. "What do you mean?"

He smiled slightly. "The word is out about Mr. Grady."

"Oh, Jesus," I couldn't help saying, although it was no worse than I'd expected.

He seemed amused at my reaction. "The immigrant community . . . gossips a lot, at least at a certain level. These things get around. Everybody knows about it."

I resisted the urge to hold my head in my hands and moan. I might as well close up shop right now. "I see," was all I could manage.

He appeared not to notice my distress. "Anyway," he said, "you passed the test, Ms. Bartlett. What is it you'd like from me?"

I got hold of myself and told him what I needed to be sure his status was in order.

"Okay," he said. "I've got most of that stuff in my pack on the bike. I'll just go and get it." He'd also come prepared, apparently.

I nodded, though he was not asking permission.

If you were not from Northern California, you might wonder why a forty-eight-year-old Ph.D. in theoretical nuclear physics was riding around on a bicycle like an impoverished graduate student or a resident of Beijing. The truth is, bikes have a cachet on the Peninsula that extends far beyond the university community. Drive down Foothill Expressway along the edge of open land, and hordes of cyclists, helmeted and tricked out in the latest high-tech racing gear, go whizzing by you in the bike lane with the purposeful air of Africanized bees en route to the hive. Secure in the recognition of their environmental superiority, they often feel free to ignore regulations (such as lane markings and stop signs) formulated for less noble conveyances, so you really have to watch out. Since I was even less adept at bicycling than I was at driving, I had never been tempted to join them, but Jack sometimes went riding with friends on weekends. Still, the ultimate status symbol, at least in certain circles, was not having to drive to work.

Alexei came back with the documents, which

matched, thank God, the ones in our files. "I think you're fine, Dr. Strela," I told him after I'd looked them over. "I don't see any problems."

He reached for the folder with his left hand. "Thank you," he said. He didn't get up from his chair, so I wondered if he had understood.

"You're all set," I told him.

He folded his hands and looked at me. "Yes," he said. "I know. I wondered if I could discuss getting a green card."

I was surprised that he would consider the firm for further work and concluded that he was information-gathering at minimal expense. Potential clients did it from time to time—they'd get the answer to their questions and then find somebody cheaper to do the work. It was a version of cornering a doctor at a cocktail party to get a free diagnosis of your symptoms. It came with the territory, I suppose.

"You have time enough on your visa," I told him. "You can probably get a labor certification before it expires." A labor certification, a permanent residency petition approved by the Labor Department after the employer gave evidence that the alien was not taking a job away from an American, took about three years, depending on the INS backlog.

"I don't think the position will last that long," he said. "I would like to be safe . . . and free."

"Are you thinking of changing jobs?" I asked.

He laughed, but I didn't get the joke. "Possibly," he said.

"And you would like to have your immigration status assured before you do?"

He nodded.

I understood; a lot of potential employers don't want the hassle of dealing with immigration difficulties and require a green card before they take you on. In addition, the employee can be a kind of slave (subject to lower wages and fewer options) as long as he's on any sort of a temporary work visa. I looked at the documents Harrison had filed for the H-1 at SLAC. Strela had a Ph.D. from Moscow University, the most prestigious school in the former Soviet Union. Presumably he'd done high-level work in Russia before he came here. "Has anyone talked to you about an extraordinary-ability petition?" I asked.

"I've heard of it," he said levelly. His expression gave nothing away. Perhaps after all he had the Russian sense of caution.

"You might qualify for that," I told him. "It allows people who are at the very top of their fields to get first preference for permanent residence," I said. "The INS created the category so that someone like Albert Einstein could come to this country without having to prove that he isn't robbing an American of a job."

He smiled. "I'm not exactly Einstein, Ms. Bartlett."

I smiled back. "You don't have to be," I told him, although anyone who could get a Ph.D. in physics automatically qualified as a genius in my book. "The INS accepts evidence in a number of categories to prove your extraordinary ability—your original work, your publications, articles about you, awards, your compensation—"

He laughed. "My compensation is . . ." He named an improbably low sum. "I don't get much more than a postdoc at the university."

"In that case I can see why you might want to look for another job," I said lightly. But even I was shocked. I wondered how you could live on a salary only slightly above librarian level in the Bay Area, where even cheap apartments rented for thousands a month. "There are ways around the salary issue, so don't worry too much. If you want to pursue this, I would need to know more about what you're doing now and the work you did before you came to the United States."

The smile dropped from his face. "In Russia, you mean?"

I nodded.

"A lot of it is classified," he said.

"That's not necessarily a problem," I told him. A physicist was unlikely to be a pornographer, or a spy, or something equally undesirable from the INS's point of view. "In fact, it probably shows that your work was prestigious and important. We'd have to say what you did, but we wouldn't have to go into detail."

"You're very optimistic," he said. He sounded skeptical.

I knew it must seem as if I were desperate for business, which was true, and willing to say anything, which wasn't. "I have reason to be," I said. "The firm does a lot of different kinds of immigration work, but this is my specialty."

"Assuming you decide I'm qualified, what would you charge?" he asked.

I told him.

He blanched.

"It's a very labor-intensive process," I said hurriedly. "This sort of case takes a lot of time to prepare, unless you have a major international prize like the Nobel."

"Not even the Order of Lenin," he said with a wry smile.

"Well, if you did, you wouldn't need me, or anyone. You could just send in the clipping of yourself in Sweden with the medal around your neck and approval is pretty much automatic. Otherwise you have to build the case."

"There's no other way?"

"As I've said, there's labor certification, or you could apply for the lottery."

"You're joking," he said, not looking amused.

"I'm not. If your name gets picked, no matter who you are, you get a green card, as long as you haven't committed any crimes."

"That is bizarre," he said.

"I agree." It *was* bizarre to make the Dr. Strelas of the world jump through incredible hoops to get the privilege of staying here and then offer thousands of slots to anyone whatsoever who happened to draw the winning number. "I'm not an apologist for U.S. immigration policy," I told him. I cleared my throat. "Another way to get a green card is to contract a bona fide marriage to an American," I told him.

His whole body stilled. "I'm already married," he said. I couldn't read his expression.

"Not to an American, I assume?"

"No."

"Is your wife here with you?" I asked.

"No," he said, in the same flat tone. A shadow of something—pain or longing or what?—crossed his face.

My position gave me a certain license to pry, but I knew a closed door when I heard it. "Well," I said.

He got to his feet abruptly. "I'll think it over," he said. "I'll get back to you."

I knew I'd never see him again. "That will be fine," I said. "Thank you for coming in." I extended my hand, and he took it, without the uncertainty that sometimes troubles foreigners when a woman offers a handshake.

He slipped his hands into the pockets of his jacket, and his expression changed. He pulled a card out of his pocket and glanced at it. "I almost forgot," he said. "Do you remember David Peh?"

I didn't. "I don't think . . ."

He laid the card on the desk. I looked at it. It was mine. "How did you . . . ?"

"He was my roommate for a while," he explained. "David said you were nice to him when they repossessed his car," he said, watching my face.

Now I remembered: the kid who got bested by Repo Man at Jack's party. "Oh, yes," I said. "I do remember.

But in all honesty I didn't really do anything. He never called."

"You were kind," he said gently. "That counts for a lot." He picked the card up again and put it back in his pocket.

I blushed. "Um, did he get another job?" I asked.

He smiled. "He married an American," he said. "He's starting his own company."

CHAPTER 14

My stepdaughter was less than enthusiastic about my dinner invitation. "I'm not sure we can make it," Meredith said. "I'll have to get back to you. Justin might be tied up. What about some other night?"

"Your grandmother's only going to be here for the weekend," I reminded her.

Silence.

"It means a lot to your dad to have a family dinner," I said.

"I know that, Lynn," she said. "But the health club's really busy right now, after the holidays. Justin's putting in a lot of extra hours."

I forbore mentioning the obvious, that it was not Justin's grandmother who was coming. Moira would scarcely lament his absence in any case; live-in boyfriends were entirely off her radar screen, something like second wives. "Well, whatever you decide," I said. I wasn't going to beg her; I knew she would come in the end anyway. She always did.

"You remember my food issues, right?"

"Right," I said. I was scarcely likely to forget. Jack said Meredith's diagnosis was orthorexia nervosa, which might be defined in layman's terms as "picky eater to the hundredth power." It seemed to be an obsession with health food, an apparent fear that ordinary sustenance would contaminate her body. Egged on by Justin, she also pushed herself to rather astonishing physical feats, including running in the Badwater, an absurd (to my mind, anyway) 135-mile race from the floor of Death Valley (in summer!) to eight thousand feet up the slopes of Mount Whitney. Dehydration and exhaustion had put her into the hospital for three days afterward.

"Because," she added, "I noticed there was nothing I could feel comfortable eating at Dad's birthday party."

"There were several platters of raw vegetables," I pointed out.

"From the *hotel*," she said, her voice rising. "Who knows what they were grown in? They might not even have been organic. They might have been genetically modified."

Genetic modification seemed like an excellent idea at the moment. I sensed I was supposed to apologize, but I refused. "Well," I said, striving for a neutral tone, "if you and Justin do decide to come this weekend, you should probably bring your own entrée, just in case."

More silence.

I thought that would be the end of it, but she said,

"Lynn, you know Mom and Grandma were very close."

I closed my eyes and exhaled.

"And Valerio's in Italy right now. . . ."

I waited, gathering strength. No wonder I always felt drained after these conversations.

"I don't suppose Mom—"

"I'm afraid not," I said firmly. At least I hope it was firmly. "But I'm sure Moira will want to go over and see her. At her house," I added, for emphasis. "So they can talk."

"Well," she said, after a moment, "I might have to miss it anyway."

"That would be a shame," I said.

"IS MEREDITH COMING?" Jack asked over dinner.

Patrick looked up from his shrimp and surimi salad—a take-out staple when it was my turn to cook—and shrugged. "She said Justin might have to work."

I was surprised—and then alarmed—that they'd talked about it. After Jack's party I found myself looking for conspiracies.

Jack sputtered. "Well, Justin—"

I touched his arm. "She's coming," I said. "I'm sure she's looking forward to it."

Patrick studied his plate. "She just likes to jerk your chain, Dad," he said eventually. "You should know that by now."

I was thrilled by this astute observation, but I

doubted that Jack would take it to heart. He was an eternal optimist where his children were concerned.

"I'm sure she doesn't mean to," he said decisively. "Not to change the subject"—there was a lie if I ever heard one—"but did you catch the Stanford game last night? I didn't see who won."

I knew that this sports camaraderie was not directed at me and smiled demurely. Jack knew better than to ask me for information on any topic having to do with balls, pucks, goat carcasses, or anything else people liked to play games with. I remained happy in my ignorance.

"Pat?"

Patrick shrugged.

I'd heard him listening to it in his room. I wanted to swat him.

"We've still got this morning's sports section," I offered.

"Thanks," Jack said.

NAOKO WATANABE, the head of human resources for Kojima Bank's West Coast operations, was one tough cookie. She dressed like a model and had Japanese manners, but, like most Asian businesswomen, she knew how to hold her own. Today she was all sober business.

"I see," she said when I told her that the vice president, information technology, in the Menlo Park office, who owned a house in Atherton and had three children in Peninsula private schools, was technically in the United States illegally. If she was surprised by this distressing news, as the VP and his family doubtless would be, she didn't show it.

"I know it's something of a shock," I said. "It was to me, too."

"It must be," she said noncommittally. "You're saying that the labor certification that was approved by the INS was never actually filed."

"Apparently not," I said.

She folded her hands on the desk and looked at me. "So . . ."

"So there are several things we can do. Fortunately, the INS has agreed to waive the penalties. Since he's run out of time on his H-1B, we can apply for another kind of visa—an O-1—while we work on getting a green card. It's some work for the client and the company to put together, but that's what I'd suggest."

She nodded.

"I would charge you for disbursements," I said, "but there would be no legal fee. Naturally."

"Naturally." She looked at me. "You must realize there are other . . . firms interested in handling Kojima's work."

Elson Larimer, our big-time rival, for one. I didn't doubt it. "I understand," I told her. "But I hope I can salvage my firm's relationship with the bank. I think you know that I had nothing to do with the problematical documents, or we wouldn't be having this conversation."

"It doesn't really matter, though, does it?" she asked.

I knew what she meant, but I couldn't leave it there. "It does to me," I said.

As a female executive in a Japanese bank, Naoko knew all about trying to break through the "rice-paper ceiling," and I thought she would be reasonably sympathetic to another woman struggling to clean up a mess some man had made. If she saw it that way, however, she didn't say so.

She nodded. "I'll have to get back to you," she said.

"HOW DID IT GO?" Adam asked when I got back to the firm.

I sat down on the edge of his desk and sighed. "It was a less-than-supportive environment, to say the least."

"What happened?" Ronnie asked, coming out of her office.

Now that we were in crisis mode, distinctions of rank, such as they had been, were notably absent.

"They'll get back to us," I said. "It was so humiliating to stand there and beg to do all this work for free in order to keep them as a client. Naoko Watanabe—the head of HR—sat there and didn't turn a hair. It was almost eerie."

"Maybe it wasn't new news," Adam suggested.

Ronnie, standing behind him, poked him on the arm.

"What?" I said.

"Nothing," he said.

"Give," I told him.

He shook his head. "I don't know anything. I just answer the phones."

This time I was the one who punched him on the arm. "Skip the self-deprecating crap," I said. "You notice everything. *I've* noticed that."

He grinned. "Sorry. I really don't know anything. It's just speculation. It's just possible, isn't it, that somebody got to Kojima with the news before you did? And . . . well . . . undermined you?"

I looked at Ronnie. She nodded.

"It's possible," I said grimly.

CHAPTER 15

"Y ou've changed a lot of things around the house," Moira Hughes remarked, in a tone not entirely suggestive of approbation.

"Well, naturally," Jack said, much too quickly. "Once we got married, we wanted to redecorate."

Jack's mother looked at him assessingly. "Is my room still in the same place?" she asked.

"Well, actually, Mother, Patrick's using the guest room just now. We thought we'd make you comfortable in L— in the office. There's a fold-out couch in there."

"How . . . convenient," she said.

Jack stood hesitating with his mother's suitcase in his hand. He looked at me helplessly. Well, we are all reduced to fifteen-year-olds in our mother's presence, but I was starting to get a clearer picture of their relationship.

"If you don't think that will be comfortable," I said, "we'd be happy to give you our room and take the office ourselves."

"Perhaps that would be best," Moira said, "if it wouldn't be too much trouble."

"No trouble," I said. "I'll just go and change the sheets."

Moira Hughes was a widow in excellent health, as she liked to say. If her husband—the late, apparently unlamented Foster Hughes—had left her in better financial circumstances, she could have spent every day playing shuffleboard and comparing symptoms with other survivors of long-term marital dysfunction on the deck of some Nordic cruise ship tricked out in a middle-class fantasy of opulence. Instead she was forced to limit these excursions to annual aquatic pilgrimages up and down the coast of Mexico, or to Alaska, but it was a sufficiently satisfying schedule, enabling her to garner an entire framed series of pictures of herself (posed for the most part in the same sequined dress) with The Captain. The Captains seemed interchangeable, too, in their mature Scandinavian competence and serenity. Not a single one of them looked Excitable.

Foster (who had expired long before I came onto the scene) had liberated his widow from a lifetime of passive-aggressive reaction to the tyranny of his ill humor and infantile tantrums, a legacy that had also left Jack with a deep-seated aversion to confrontation and emotional displays. Unfortunately, the dynamics of family interaction do not switch off, even when the Prime Mover is . . . well, removed. You're left to deal with the aftermath, like the eddies and swirls of a passing ocean liner. The Hugheses were still caught in the wake.

I was in for a little buffeting of my own.

"I've changed my will," Moira announced, settling herself on the sofa in the living room.

Jack's coffee cup rattled on its saucer. "Oh?"

She nodded grandly.

"Do you want to talk about it?" Jack asked.

"I'll just see to something in the kitchen," I said.

Jack shot me a look of chagrin. *Sorry,* he mouthed.

Moira ignored my departure. Since she wasn't wearing her hearing aid, her voice was loud enough for me to hear anyway, unless I was going to be really noble and turn on the faucet or something like that.

I wasn't.

"I've made a living trust," Moira told him. "This nice man contacted me by phone and said his firm was holding a seminar, so I signed up. I never realized I should be putting my assets in trust like that," she added, with a hint of accusation.

I could almost hear Jack's sigh.

"Anyway, it's all taken care of now," she said. "I knew you'd be pleased."

"Do you want me to look over the papers?" Jack asked, with, I thought, remarkable restraint.

"Oh, I don't imagine that will be necessary, dear," she told him. "But of course I'll send you a copy if you'd like."

"Is there anything I should know about?" my husband asked.

"What do you mean?"

"I mean, is there anything you want me to do?"

"As a matter of fact, I'd like you to keep whatever you get from the trust in a separate account. I know there won't be that much, but—"

"Mother—" Jack protested.

"I mean it. It's what the lawyer said. *Advised.* If you keep it in a separate account, it stays your own property. That way it will go to Patrick and Meredith after you're gone, and *she* won't get any of it."

"Mother, that's ridiculous," Jack said. "It's insulting, too."

"You never know about marriages these days," Moira said. "How do you know you can really trust her?"

She, the untrustworthy daughter-in-law, shredded her fingertip peeling a carrot and had to turn on the faucet anyway, so she never got to hear how her husband replied to that.

COSTCO WAS INVENTED for occasions like The Family Dinner. In fact, Costco, which was probably invented or at least inspired by a woman with too much to do, was about the only form of market I really enjoyed, even though the portion sizes were usually too big for two people. Most of the other stores on the Peninsula, including all the formerly humble little corner grocers, had gone so upscale in the dot-com boom that they resembled miniature versions of Harrods Food Hall. I mean, I am as much an admirer of 171 types of exotic cheeses as anyone, but sometimes the cheese you're really going to buy is cottage, and nonfat at that. The rest was like a museum visit—informative but essentially a spectator sport. Besides, I got tired of being sharp-elbowed by twenty-somethings weighed down by Dallas-size diamonds and demanding, *alto voce,* "that really special caviar you set aside for my husband last time." Of course there were fewer of those these days, but the temples of gastronomy remained, like high-water marks of the Valley's affluence.

Costco, on the other hand, was a microcosm of Bay Area life. The Sunnyvale store, where I shopped, was teeming with Sikhs, other Indians, and Chinese, along with the usual mix of retirees creeping out of parking places in their luxury sedans and teenage boys pulling into the handicap spots (*There was no place else to park!*), cell phones in hand and caps in reverse. The SUVs were lined up in rows in the parking lot like Sherman tanks waiting for D-Day.

I entered the store with a fixed menu in mind, but the cart kept filling all by itself, like some bountiful fairy-tale chest of gold. I bought salmon, but then I couldn't remember if Moira liked it, so I thought I should add some baby lamb chops, too. And what about the following night? The chicken Kiev looked promising. And then there were luncheon fixings and an assortment of breads (breakfast and lunch), vegetables, appetizers, and dessert. It occurred to me, as I wheeled the over-flowing cart from place to place, that I was losing my composure pretty early in the visit, not to mention my perspective. I'd told Jack I was going to keep it simple. I kept finding all my best intentions overturned.

By the time I'd stopped at Whole Foods for organic

vegetables for Meredith and Justin, I was far later getting back than I'd planned. Jack and Moira would be sitting in the living room wearing, respectively, looks of unease and disapproval, or so I imagined. The freeway was crowded (the freeway is always crowded, as people in the Valley will tell you) by the time I headed back, and nobody would let me on. Jack kept telling me to speed up to get into the line of traffic, but my natural inclination had always been to slow down. Sometimes I just hoped for the best and went anyway, and so far nothing terrible had happened. In L.A. that behavior got you a horn blast and the finger, but in the Bay Area usually the worst that befell you was a head-shaking gesture of reproof. Northern Californians were too civilized to honk, if a withering look sufficed. I maneuvered into the line of enemy cars the best I could and staked out a spot in the right lane, my default driving position despite Jack's insistence that it was the most dangerous place on the road. I knew that, but I just didn't feel comfortable driving *fast*.

Moira was not glowering with impatience when I returned. Instead she was holding a salon in our living room, entertaining Patrick, Meredith, and Justin, who had arrived well in advance of the invited hour. That was okay—I'd already learned that the hour of invitation didn't apply to family, at least in the family's estimation. "Hi," I said, walking into the room and trying not to notice that the conversation came to a dead halt when I did. "I got stuck in traffic, but I can have dinner ready in a few minutes."

"What are we having?" Meredith asked suspiciously.

"For you and Justin I've brought some vegetables from Whole Foods, in addition to your entrée," I told her.

She looked at me blankly for a second and then with resentment for putting her in the wrong. "I didn't bring one," she said.

I shrugged. "Well, vegetables, then. You can see what I have and pick what you like."

"Whatever," she said.

WHAT DO PEOPLE FIND to talk about if they don't have a shared history in common? If they like you, they'll offer you their pasts/histories/stories (*My mother always liked my sister better than me. My father bragged, and that's what made me shy*) so that you can dip into the wellspring, too. If they don't . . .

"I rarely eat fish," Moira said, bending over her plate to expose the pink scalp at the base of her curls. Like many of her generation, she favored a fixed and sculpted 'do at odds with the diminishing quantity of her hair. She moved the salmon around on her plate before lifting a bite to her lips. She'd selected it herself as the entrée when I'd given her the choice.

The others nodded agreement, even Jack. It made me feel oddly disconnected and in the wrong, as if I should have known. If we had had a past in common, even some shared embarrassments or trivial annoyances, we could have rescued the situation. *Do you remember the time that . . . ?* is a potent social anodyne.

But the only person I really had a history with was Jack, and Jack's mother certainly didn't want to hear about *that*.

I resisted the impulse to apologize and said nothing.

Meredith sampled her vegetables with misgiving, as if she might detect their inorganic origins with the tip of her tongue. Justin, with no family loyalties to worry about, was less inhibited. I watched them, wondering why it mattered to me if they liked what I served. Maybe it was a Norman Rockwell thing (not that *his* family life was anything to write home about), some ingrained symbol of maternal nurturing I was unable to escape.

Jack, at least, looked happy, his fantasy of fully functional family—*all together around the dinner table!*—momentarily fulfilled. He'd told me that, growing up, he'd always had a stomachache whenever his father presided at a family meal. In suffering he was clearly my superior; my stomachaches had resulted only from eating second helpings of my mother's gravy with the Sunday roast. Like all unhappy childhoods, his had fueled a determination to make things different for his own family, a desire that manifested itself in increasingly futile efforts to smooth things over when they got the least bit tense. Unfortunately, there appeared to be an inverse relationship between blood kinship and susceptibility to his charm. It was as if his children had been vaccinated against enjoying themselves, at least around us.

"What are you doing now, Patrick?" Moira's voice cut across my thoughts like a bullet through mist.

Patrick studied his plate. I could even find it in my heart to feel sorry for him. "Not much, Grandma," he said.

"Have you found a job yet?" she asked.

He shook his head. "Not yet," he mumbled.

"What? I didn't hear you."

"He said, 'Not yet,' " Jack interjected. I could see his good mood starting to melt away. "Don't put him on the spot, Mother."

"Why not? Isn't he looking?" she asked.

"Yes, he's looking," Jack said, "But—"

"What are you looking for?" Moira insisted, redirecting.

"Oh, anything, I guess," Patrick said, raising his eyes but focusing just past her. He had the hunched posture of somebody receiving blows on his shoulders.

"I've heard the Layoff Lounge has a pretty good program," Meredith said, attempting a rescue of sorts. "Also, some people I know go to a support group in Cupertino. You bring your lunch on Fridays."

"That's a thought. Good for you, Merry," Jack said, a shade too brightly.

"Yeah, thanks," Patrick said grimly.

"*Seriously,*" she said. "It might do you some good."

"Maybe his father could find him something," Moira said pointedly.

"More asparagus?" I asked.

"I'm keeping my eyes open, Mother," Jack, the Good Son, the Good Father, said. "You know this is a really tough job market. There's no need to panic. We enjoy having Patrick here with us."

Four pairs of eyes shifted to my face. Jack's were pleading, so I nodded. "That's right," I said.

Meredith made an indistinct noise behind her napkin.

Patrick, who was not one of those who had needed to check my reaction, said sullenly, "It's not as if I'm not trying. I've got my résumé out there."

"Right. Of course you do," Jack said, a little desperately. "Was there more asparagus?"

"I've been thinking about day trading," Patrick said. Silence.

"What's that?" Moira said.

"You're kidding, right?" Jack sounded hoarse.

Patrick shrugged.

"What? What is it?" Moira demanded.

"It's a kind of gambling on the Internet," Jack said tightly.

"Dad—"

"Gambling?" exclaimed Moira in horrified accents. "Is that wise?"

"It isn't gambling, Grandma," Patrick said. "It's trading stocks on your computer." He looked at Jack. "Anyway, all I said was, I was thinking about it."

"Also," said Meredith, continuing the thread of her earlier contribution, "you could try Recession Camp. I mean, it's supposed to be for laid-off dot-commers, but I'm sure they'd take you. They have outings and stuff. It might help you . . . you know, find something."

"I don't see how hanging out with a bunch of losers is going to help me," Patrick said. "Now could we please stop talking about this?"

"I've gotten laid off lots of times," Justin said, deciding to enter the conversation just as it was ending. He had the sweet disposition and—unfortunately—the brains of an Irish setter. "And I always find something. It'll work out, Pat, you'll see."

"Of course it will," Jack said heartily.

"Excuse me, Grandma," Patrick said, pushing his chair away from the table.

"Poor boy," Moira said, in what she appeared to think was a low voice, after Patrick had left the table. "You can see how he feels it."

Even I could see how he felt it, though probably not in the sense Moira meant. I considered how it would be to have made your own family afraid to ask you anything directly. It must be terrible to have people worrying about you and waiting in patient silence for some reassurance that you might be all right after all. It must be even worse to be convinced that you were a loser, a conviction not obviously contradicted by the facts. It certainly made a gap between you and others. Even though I shared the rather pessimistic assessment of Patrick's chances of Turning Out Well, at least in the short run, I had to admit a grudging sort of sympathy for his plight. In the midst of this family, I felt as if I were shrinking, too.

Of the two of them—Patrick and Meredith—I guess I preferred Patrick, on the whole. That was a little like preferring Genghis Khan to Attila the Hun, and I certainly had no admiration for his sullen stasis or his passive-aggressive behavior around the house. I'd scarcely forgiven him for using my own cat against me. But at least his bad behavior seemed to be rooted in a general kind of unhappiness that encompassed everyone around him. Meredith was the one who had it in for *me*.

Plus, she was sneaky (I knew who facilitated Janet's incursions into our lives), manipulative, and, despite her resentment of me, not especially nice to her father. She'd somehow acquired an air of superiority—possibly from ingesting so many organic vegetables—and appeared to disdain any opinions not her own. Jack seemed totally unable to handle her or keep himself from getting hurt. Of course, everybody who's ever taken Psych 1 knows that a girl's relationship with her father is complicated, but I mean, come *on*. Meredith seemed to delight in snubbing him, or maybe she was so self-absorbed she didn't even notice. I'm sure Jack thought she was punishing him for the divorce or for not being there enough when she was little or for any of the other textbook resentments kids have against their parents. I don't know. My own relationship to my parents seemed unexamined and bland by comparison, but at least we never kept lists of things we disliked about each other, the way Meredith had done to Jack when she was sixteen. She might have put away the paper, but mentally she was still keeping score.

The worst thing was, Jack appeared to harbor the conviction that he could deflect such treatment by ignoring it. I thought there was very little evidence that giving dictators what they demand begets anything but more demands (what was Chamberlain's visit to Munich all about, if not that?), but his common sense seemed to have deserted him. The more Meredith resisted his friendly overtures, the more polite he acted, as if she were a very exclusive club he was trying to get into. I thought he should stop rewarding her rudeness and quit acting like a paparazzo trying to coax a picture out of Princess Anne. I also thought he should stop making it easier for Patrick to evade responsibility, especially under My Roof. That was the trouble: I'd started assessing and judging, even though I'd promised myself I wouldn't. So far I'd resisted the fatal next step—making suggestions—but my tongue was getting callused from biting back the words.

As long as I'm being completely honest, I might as well admit that I began to look at Jack differently after I started having trouble with his children (mothers-in-law are a given; everybody expects to have trouble with *them*). The judgments and the assessing had gotten to be a habit, and I couldn't seem to turn it off. I couldn't help it: I blamed him—maybe not entirely, but certainly in part—for their flaws. How could someone so kind and talented and smart have produced offspring who were such backsliders on the evolutionary ladder? You were supposed to replace yourself with something better, wiser, more successful—wasn't that the aim of parenthood? And if—by genetic anomaly or misguided actions or whatever—you did happen to produce a neurotic, egocentric troublemaker on the one hand and a lumpen loser boomeranger on the other, shouldn't you try to do something about it? And shouldn't you try to protect, if not yourself then your innocent spouse at the very least, from their bad behavior?

Okay, so I have to admit that that last part is really about me. Maybe I'd lost perspective; I'd undoubtedly lost my sense of charity. Maybe I just didn't like them because they didn't like me. But I couldn't help resenting it that Jack let them make life difficult for both of us without making the smallest push to get them to behave themselves. My mistake was in convincing myself that if you really want things to work out, if your intentions are good, then things will turn out all right. Not that I could necessarily document this philosophy with objective evidence, but by and large I'd believed it anyway. Now I was having my doubts.

So there it was, the family dinner as metaphor for the family dynamic. It wasn't quite *The Corrections,* but it wasn't *The Sound of Music* either. Well, maybe it was, at least while Maria's future stepchildren were still putting toads in her bed. I looked down at my half-eaten salmon congealing on the plate and considered excusing myself, like Patrick. I thought longingly of a good book and a quiet evening, all by myself.

The only trouble was, there was no place to go.

CHAPTER 16

On Sunday, Moira and Patrick trooped off to Janet and Valerio's, there to meet, if I understood correctly, Meredith and Justin. Instant replay, minus Jack and me. Jack looked tight-lipped and harassed; I guessed he'd been invited—make that urged—to go and had refused. At least I hope he'd refused. He seemed tense.

"Will your mother be back for dinner?" I asked.

"Who knows?" he said. He looked at me. "What?"

"I only ask," I said carefully, "because I was wondering if I should marinate the lamb chops."

Not carefully enough, apparently. "Just do whatever you want to," he said curtly.

I said nothing.

He sighed. "Look, I'm sorry, Lynn. I know it's inconvenient. I can't control my mother. I can't control Patrick. Or Meredith."

Or Janet, I thought.

"We'll just have to roll with it and see what happens, okay?"

I nodded. I wondered if he was talking about more than dinner. "Okay," I said. I took a breath. "We probably have a couple of hours at least. Would you like to get out of here and take a walk? We could drive up to Skyline or just walk around the neighborhood. The tulip trees are out," I said.

He looked at me oddly, since I had not hitherto displayed a notable interest in horticulture. But it was spring, which comes to California in fits and starts beginning sometime in December, and besides, the house was feeling a bit claustrophobic. "Not just now, thanks," he said.

"Okay," I said again, putting my arms around his neck, "we could just stay here."

He smiled, but he stayed motionless. I kissed his ear.

"Don't," he whispered.

"Headache?" I asked, sounding more bitter than I intended.

He stiffened. "That's not fair," he said. "They might be back any minute. How would it look?"

As if you put your wife first, I thought. "They aren't two-year-olds peeking into Daddy's bedroom," I said. "They're adults. I bet even Meredith and Patrick have had sex. They'd understand." I exempted Moira out of a sense of delicacy. No one likes to think of his mother having sex, even if the act last took place in 1969.

"I wouldn't feel comfortable," he said. "Also . . ." He trailed off.

"Also?"

"I don't want to be used to make some kind of statement to my family," he said.

"Used?"

"I'm sorry, Lynn; that's the way I feel."

The only thing that kept me calm at that moment was the recognition of a modicum of justice in the accusation. "Fine. But, Jack, I have to say . . ."

He looked at me. "Yes?"

"Things are not going well."

"Of course they're not going well." He sounded exasperated. Your business is in chaos, and I have the tax problems. We—"

"That's not what I mean."

He looked trapped, as if I'd suggested airing our personal differences on *Judge Judy*. But at least he didn't pretend not to know what I was talking about.

"It's only temporary," he said.

"I hope so," I told him. "I—"

"We're *back*," Moira called, her voice floating gaily from the front door. "Anybody home?"

Jack flashed me a look that said, *See, I told you so*, but he had the decency not to say it aloud.

MOIRA'S ARRIVAL DREW ME BACK, relieved, from whatever I'd been about to say. I wasn't even sure myself. Probably I'd been unwise to bring it up in the midst of a family visit. The presence of a blood relative under the same roof as oneself can play tricks on the psyche and subvert the best of intentions. Once Moira went home, Jack could snap out of it, as my mother used to say about behavior of which she disapproved—"it" in this case being his role as an anguished fifteen-year-old desperately trying to keep the peace. We would sit down calmly and tackle the issues, one by one. We would make decisions. We would abide by them.

We would have sex in every room in the house if we wanted to.

Actually, having sex in any room in the house would have been exceptionally gratifying, not to mention rare. Jack and I had each passed the age—about twenty, if I remember correctly—when sex had the kind of desperate urgency generally found between the covers of airport fiction or on Lifetime TV. When you build a life together, other pleasures—good food, a back rub, even a hot shower—get thrown into the physical equation. But still, now that I'd been with Jack for a year, I didn't want to go back to the intermittent asceticism of my intramarriage days. "Appetite comes with eating," Rabelais said, and as the tension built from all the problems in the household, the table wasn't set very often.

It's not as if I were wandering around in some supercharged state of frustrated desire, but I felt cranky and possessed of a kind of restless troublemaking quality I didn't quite like. I was lonely, too, if "lonely" is the right word for what I was feeling, surrounded as I was by all things Hughes.

When Moira left and Patrick was out of the house we could straighten things out. Meanwhile, though, there was the rest of the weekend to get through. I had plenty of time to think things over.

ON MONDAY, clientless, on the verge of debt—or worse—and facing God-knows-what professional calamities, I nonetheless embraced the office with the enthusiasm with which you might greet, say, the sight of dry land in *Jaws*. The scuff marks on the desk, the half-eaten bagel in the wastebasket (the janitor had forgotten to come again), my framed diploma on the wall (a law-school graduation present from my parents) were at least tangible reminders that I had a life, even one that was reeling out of control. I could almost tolerate Brooke's smirks, if not with cheerfulness at least with equanimity. At least in the office, my personal life would take a welcome backseat to other issues, or so I believed. And by the time I left to go home for the day, Moira would be gone.

"Any calls?" I asked Adam hopefully. If things got any quieter, I would have to take to the airwaves or bus-stop benches, like the ambulance chasers on late-night TV (*Had an accident? Whiplash? Bad back? Call . . .*) or the ads that trumpeted help with DUIs.

Adam studied his message pad. "A couple," he said. "That Dr. Strela called. The one who was here before?"

I nodded.

"He wants to come in this afternoon," Adam said. "I said I'd check with you."

"My calendar is clear, as far as I know," I said, trying not to sound too grim. At least Alexei Strela might turn into a paying client.

"Yes, but I thought I should check. I'll call him back, if that's okay with you." He cleared his throat. "Also," he said, lifting the second message pad, "a Mrs. Vivendi called. She would like you to call her back at your earliest convenience."

He said it in such a bland tone of voice I realized he knew perfectly well that "Mrs. Vivendi" was Jack's first wife.

My heart sank. Janet had never, ever called me for anything, much less contacted me at the office. "I don't suppose she said why," I asked.

"No, she didn't," he said, still in the same tone of voice. "She left her number." He reached toward me with the slip of paper.

I took it gingerly, with a caution befitting the weapon of invasion that it was. This would teach me to congratulate myself on my escape to the haven of my office. No place was safe from incursion anymore. "Thanks," I said, insincerely.

"Don't mention it." He gave me a small, pitying smile.

"THANK YOU FOR CALLING ME BACK," Janet said formally. Her tone suggested that she was surprised I had capitulated so easily.

"Your message sounded as if it might be urgent," I said, already on the defensive. "I hope everything is all right."

"Well, I suppose so," she said.

I waited.

"Actually, there are some things we need to discuss," she said.

"I'm listening," I told her, my stomach doing a nasty little flip. Tension always goes straight to my digestive tract.

"Not on the phone," she said ominously. "I was hoping we could have lunch."

"Just the two of us?" I squeaked. I did *not* want to have lunch (or breakfast or dinner) with Janet. I had a fear—possibly irrational, possibly not—of one-on-one encounters with her. I had the feeling she would use the knowledge gained—of my choice of food, my table manners, the way I spoke to the waiter, I don't know—against me somehow. Needless to say, I had never expressed any such reticence to Jack. I mean, I could see how it would sound. Nevertheless, that is what I felt. Now that Gavin de Becker has confirmed that "Trust your instincts" is good advice in potentially threatening situations, I feel vindicated and far less paranoid.

"Yes, of course," she said, as if we were weekly luncheon companions.

"Um, this is an extremely busy week for me," I told her. "Maybe you should just tell me what—"

"Lynn, I am trying to make a friendly gesture here," she interrupted. "If you don't wish to reciprocate, that's fine, but I'm asking for—I *need*—an hour or two of your time regarding a matter of some importance to *my family*. It's important. I wouldn't ask otherwise. Shall I make an appointment to see you at the office?"

Recognizing defeat, I conceded. "That won't be necessary," I told her. "I'll rearrange my schedule," I added, attempting to save face. "What about Thursday?"

"I was thinking tomorrow," she said.

I flipped through some papers on my desk for a long moment. "I guess I can do that," I agreed.

"Good," she said. "I made reservations at Il Fornaio at eleven-thirty."

I noticed that "made" in the past tense (I hadn't overlooked the "my family" reference either). "That's too early for me," I said, in a last-ditch attempt at rebellion. No wonder Meredith and Patrick were so screwed up.

She sighed audibly. "The restaurant's much less crowded then. I thought it would be quieter. What time *can* you make it?"

I looked at the ceiling for inspiration. "How about one-thirty?"

"Just as you like," she said, sounding amused. "I'm looking forward to it."

CHAPTER 17

I'm back," Alexei Strela said, settling into a chair in my office. He looked more European today, in a collarless shirt and a sports coat. Despite his colloquial, almost faultless English, there was something indefinably not American about him. Maybe it was something I sensed in his dark eyes, a hint of melancholy that didn't quite square with New World optimism. Immigrants are all, to some extent, people with secret lives whose pasts are buried deep. Somebody said (or probably said) that the happy and the powerful do not go into exile. At least not of their own volition.

He seemed tense, but not ill at ease. I smiled. "How can I help you, Dr. Strela?"

He leaned forward. "I hope you don't . . . I'm sorry to tell you this." He folded his arms.

I waited, hoping that he had not committed visa fraud or something that would make it impossible for me to help him. "Go on," I said.

"I've been to see another law firm."

I laughed. "That's it?"

He shrugged.

"That's perfectly okay," I assured him. "This is America. We expect competition. Everyone wants the client to be satisfied. What's the problem?"

He studied my face as he spoke. "They told me I couldn't get the classification you told me about."

"Extraordinary ability?"

"Yes." He shrugged. "Not on the basis of my current position. I know we joked about it last time, but they really did seem to think I'd have to get a Nobel Prize or something like that." The words were diffident, but his manner suggested that if circumstances were different, it would not have been out of the realm of possibility.

I sighed. It was not easy to explain to clients what the INS was like. It was inscrutable, maddening, and unpredictable, and there were almost as many viewpoints as to how to fulfill the organization's rules and regulations as there were immigration lawyers. There were lawyers out there who really did believe that the EB-1 requirement for the Nobel or the Pulitzer or whatever meant exactly that, and that nothing less would suffice, while others took a far more generous view of the necessary qualifications. The second group didn't usually trumpet their views to the first, for obvious reasons.

"You'll tell me if I really can't get a green card, won't you?" he asked.

"Yes, I would tell you, but I don't think you need to worry too much." I took a breath to explain. "Look, Dr.

Strela, the other lawyer isn't really wrong. The INS does define evidence of 'extraordinary ability' as winning the Nobel Prize or its equivalent. But the truth is, if they're not here already, Nobel Laureates don't want to leave where they are, so lawyers rarely get a client like that. There are other categories of acceptable evidence, and I've gotten this type of green card for at least two hundred people, not one of whom has ever been to Sweden in a tux to collect an award."

"So it's not hopeless," he said. He had big hands, and a white scar that ran along the top of his wrist under his cuff.

"There are no guarantees," I told him. "But there's SLAC, and, unless I miss my guess, you've done important work before you came to this country. Did you mention any of your prior work to the other lawyer?"

He shook his head.

"Then possibly he—she?—wasn't fully aware of your background."

He smiled grimly, as if at some private joke. "Possibly," he said. "What would I have to do?" he asked, still watching my face.

"You need to give me as much information as you can about your work, now and before this. I'd like a list of your publications, awards, and any articles about your work or conferences where you've spoken." I passed him my standard handout explaining the necessary documentation. "Also," I said, "you will need supporting letters from experts in your field who can confirm your work and ability."

"From Russia?" He sounded slightly alarmed.

"One or two," I said. "The rest should be from non-Russians who are independent of Stanford. Maybe physics professors or other scientists you've met through your work."

"That could be a problem," he said quietly. "I really don't want anyone in Russia to know about this. Also . . ." He cleared his throat. "There may be a difficulty in discussing some of my work."

"Because it was top secret?"

"In a way," was all he said.

I wondered what he was hiding. I couldn't believe it was a criminal past, but stranger things had happened, and these days the Department of Justice was in no mood to take chances. "Don't misrepresent anything," I told him frankly. "Even if you get permanent-resident status, it can be revoked if there's anything false about the application. Remember all those Nazis who lied on their immigration documents? Forty years after the war, the INS still came after them. And today they're far more skittish, for reasons I'm sure I don't have to explain."

"I understand," he said. He looked almost amused and not at all intimidated. "I have nothing to lie about, but there is a difference between lying and telling everything, isn't there?"

He'd probably captured in a nutshell the essence of practicing law, but still. I gave him my best I'm-in-charge-here look and said, "I have to tell you, that kind of statement makes me very nervous, Dr. Strela."

"Fair enough," he said. I waited, but he didn't say anything further.

"This is the point at which you're supposed to offer some kind of reassurance," I prompted him.

He smiled, a slow, confident sort of grin. "How about 'I haven't done anything that would compromise you, Ms. Bartlett'?" he said.

"That's a start," I said. "Full disclosure will have to come eventually. I mean it. We want to make the best case we can, and I have to feel comfortable with the facts as we present them."

"Okay."

His self-possession was intriguing, and more than a little attractive. I wondered if it came from always being the smartest person in the room. I was in the habit of sizing up potential clients rather quickly, and I didn't get what people used to call "bad vibes" from him. On the contrary. He was certainly keeping something hidden, but I very much doubted if it was an affiliation with the Russian Mafia or a history with drugs. Countries like the Soviet Union had produced all kinds of people with reasons to hide things.

"If I get my green card, I can work anywhere in the U.S., is that right?" he asked.

"As long as you stay within your field. If you open an ice-cream store instead, they could revoke it."

He raised an eyebrow. "Really? I like ice cream. It's one of my favorite things about America."

Momentarily distracted, I asked, "Didn't you have ice cream in Russia?"

He looked at the ceiling and rolled his eyes. "Why did the Siberian peasant buy a refrigerator?" He looked at me expectantly.

"Is this a joke?" I asked, caught off guard.

"It's supposed to be," he said.

"Okay," I said. "Why?"

"To have someplace warm to spend the winter," he said.

"Oh. I see. But you take my point."

"Of course," he said.

"I don't know any Russian jokes," I told him. "I never thought about it, but humor probably tells you a lot about the place."

He smiled. "Yes, it does."

I would have liked to ask him more about Russian humor, but business was business. "Anyway," I said, "you can work anywhere, with that limitation. Also," I added, "if your wife should join you here, she can work, too." He'd already told me his wife wasn't with him, but I thought I should mention it. Was I curious? Maybe just a little.

"She will not be joining me," he said flatly.

"I'm sorry," I said. I wasn't sure what I should say.

"I suppose you would say we are separated. Legally separated." He shrugged. "She went home."

I knew how that was, since I'd seen it happen. The wife was unhappy because she didn't know anyone and didn't speak English. Without a job, she was marooned, away from the support of friends or family. It was easy to imagine the loneliness, the isolation. "I'm sorry," I said again.

"I don't blame her," he said.

"Well," I said briskly, "when you decide whether you want to proceed, I'll need a deposit of half the fee. The money goes into a trust account until the work is completed. The other half is due at the time of filing."

"I've already decided," he said. "Will you help me, Ms. Bartlett?"

"My clients call me Lynn, Dr. Strela."

He smiled his celebrity smile. "Alexei."

CHAPTER 18

Il Fornaio is the new Silicon Valley—all glitz and mirrors and upscale menu—in the middle of Palo Alto's funky old main street. University Avenue used to be a fifties-style collection of fairly pedestrian retail businesses, like drugstores and ice-cream parlors, with a couple of aging theaters and a handful of bookshops and cheap eateries, mostly catering to Stanford students, but without the psychedelic tackiness of Berkeley. If you overlooked the brief historical cachet enjoyed because it was the site of the original Mrs. Fields Cookies (where Debbie Fields herself used to hand out samples on the street, to promote sales), there was nothing much to distinguish it from a small-town Main Street in the Midwest.

The dot-com explosion had changed all that, like a fairy godmother sweeping in to tart up a reluctant, dowdy Cinderella. Vestiges remained, but now the merchandise was trendy, the run-down, gilded movie theater was an elegant Borders bookstore, and the burgeoning numbers of cafés and restaurants were neither modest nor cheap.

I circled the block a couple of times, looking for a diagonal parking place. Since I couldn't parallel-park, I was relieved when somebody pulled out of something I could actually get into. Parking on crowded streets makes me start to sweat, and I was already annoyed at the prospect of meeting Janet. Sweaty and irritable— just the way you'd love to be perceived by your husband's ex-wife.

Janet was waiting at the table, in serene, air-conditioned composure. She was very slender, especially for her age, with close-cropped blond hair and a deep voice that sounded as if she smoked. I would have liked to believe that she did, but in the Bay Area hardly anyone committed such an egregious faux pas in public, so you could never tell. Lighting up exposed you to the same social opprobrium for moral laxity as did showing too much avoirdupois on the beach in L.A. or eating a Big Mac on the street in Paris.

She stood when I entered and offered me both cheeks to kiss, like a European. I attributed this action to any number of unflattering motives, not the least of which was to discomfit me, so I went along with it, trying not to bump her with my nose. "Thank you for joining me," she said when we had each smiled insincerely at the other and taken our seats.

I waited for her to tell me the purpose of this luncheon, but she seemed in no hurry. She studied the menu as if it might reveal some secret bit of information indispensable to making the right choice. I glanced at my watch. I'd been there only five minutes, but they were long ones. I mean, what did we have to say to each other? I wanted to get this over with and get back to work. At length I skimmed the menu and told the waiter, "I'll have the ahi salad and iced tea."

Janet didn't look up from her perusal.

"Would you like me to give you a few more minutes?" the waiter asked.

Janet glanced at me, saw my look of consternation, and smiled. She hesitated. "I'll have the abbacchio al forno," she said. "The lamb," she repeated, for my benefit.

"So," she said, when the waiter had gone, "how are you getting along with Patrick?"

I let out my breath. I had to stop myself from shrugging. "Fine," I said, as cheerfully as I could manage. "I don't see him all that much, actually."

"Really?" she asked.

I heard the implied criticism but tried not to react to it. "I'm not home that much these days," I said.

Her lips twitched. "Well. Meredith says he's depressed."

"I imagine he is," I said, more sharply than I intended. "Who wouldn't be, living at home at his age and having no job?"

"Then, if you understand that, perhaps you could persuade Jack to find him something," she said. "Also, maybe you could find it in your heart to be just a little more patient with him. He thinks you don't like him."

I had to bite my tongue on that one. "He told you that?" I asked.

"Not in so many words. Something Meredith let slip."

Meredith appeared to have been very busy letting things slip. "Quite honestly, Jack's the one you should be talking to, not me," I told her. "He's in the better position to help him. I'm happy to have Patrick living with us for the time being, but I think his mood has very little to do with me."

"Then you aren't the one who imposed the time limit?" she asked pointedly.

I flushed. I couldn't believe Jack would have told her that, so Patrick must have assumed it. "It was a mutual decision," I said, in what I hoped was a tone indicating that the subject was closed. "Thank you for your thoughts. I'll bear them in mind. And, of course, if he feels too uncomfortable, you can always invite him to live with you."

She parried my thrust with a shrug. "I'm just trying to be honest. I thought you'd appreciate that."

I've noticed that people who say unpleasant things often defend them on the grounds of honesty, as if that were some kind of ultimate justification, like an appeal to the Ten Commandments. It's useless to argue with those who are determined to feel themselves your moral superior, however speciously. More to the point, she didn't respond to the suggestion that she might take her son in herself, but in her case I would have pretended not to hear it either. I looked desperately for the waiter, who was, of course, nowhere to be found. I wondered how we were going to get through the rest of this lunch. "I understand that some of your ceramics are on display at the crafts gallery in Los Altos," I said at length. Moira had gleaned that on her visit to her former daughter-in-law.

Janet nodded. "Yes, they are. Have you seen them?"

I said I had not had that pleasure. I did not add "yet," but that is what she assumed.

"I'll be interested in your opinion," she said. "It's always interesting to see what someone who is not artistic perceives in a piece."

Thus consigned to the Philistine hordes, I occupied myself with buttering my roll in silence, until I remembered I didn't eat butter anymore. I was determined not to let her provoke me. It was better to hold the high ground and get out early.

"Anyway," she said, "Patrick isn't what I wanted to talk to you about."

"No?" I said, my heart sinking.

"No," she said firmly. "It's Meredith."

Uh-oh. "I hope nothing's wrong," I murmured.

"Not at all," Janet said, sitting back in her chair. "She's getting married."

"To Justin?" I asked, sounding, I'm afraid, a bit dim. Who else would it be? But what a surprise!

"Well, yes," Janet said.

"How nice," I said. I wondered what Jack would say about his daughter's marrying a fitness instructor at a health club. I mean, Justin was nice enough, but he was hardly the sharpest knife in the drawer. Plus, he was not a good foil for Meredith's own somatic absorption and fear of unhealthy food. Come to think of it, I had to wonder why I hadn't heard this news from Jack first.

"Does Jack know this?" I asked her.

"Probably not, unless Meredith has told him. I thought it might be a good idea to discuss the news with you first, before he finds out."

"Why?" I asked.

"Several reasons," she said as the waiter at last set our lunches in front of us.

I took a bite of the tuna while I waited for her to continue. Delicious.

"Meredith has lived in the community for a long time," she said. "She has her heart set on a—how shall I put this?—showpiece wedding. I've tried to talk her into something smaller-scale, but she's exceptionally romantic. She always has been."

I hadn't noticed. I understood that she meant that the wedding Meredith wanted would be—how shall I put this?—expensive. "I'm sure you must be very excited to help her plan it," I observed.

She hesitated. "Yes, of course, but the truth is that I can't afford to pay for it, and neither can she."

I remembered that this was the woman who had declared bankruptcy rather than contribute to her children's college education, so I knew what she was angling for. It put me in a ticklish position, though. It was clear she couldn't know about Jack's financial difficulties, and I didn't know how much to say. I put down my fork. My appetite was rapidly evaporating.

"I'm sure Jack will be happy to contribute," I told her. "I don't know on what scale. It wouldn't necessarily . . . Well, look. You really need to talk to him."

She looked as if I had just handed her a Christmas present, and a big one at that. "I will," she said.

Too late, I realized my error. I should have said *Meredith* really needed to talk to Jack.

"It's just that our friends have expectations . . . ,"
Janet said.

"Yours and Valerio's?"

"Jack's and mine," she said matter-of-factly. "Well, they *are* still our friends, even though we're not together. I hope you understand. I wanted to have this talk so that you would know that you don't have anything to worry about—"

"Worry about?" My voice rose involuntarily.

"—even though Jack and I are going to be involved in this wedding," she said.

"Of course I'm not worried," I lied, "although I can't imagine that Jack will want to be involved in the details. Does Valerio go in for that sort of thing?"

She took a bite of lamb and swallowed it with apparent satisfaction. "You might as well know," she said, "that Valerio has gone back to Italy." She wiped her lips delicately with the napkin and looked at me. "I'm not sure he's coming back," she said.

CHAPTER 19

I called Meredith at work (she taught at a local Montessori school), because I wanted to ask her right away whether she wanted me to break the news of her wedding to Jack. I knew if I remained silent I would be seen as uncaring and manipulative, whereas if I was first with the tidings I would be seen as uncaring and manipulative. It seemed prudent to find out what Meredith wanted and dodge the ball, if I could, but the school secretary said she had called in sick. Thus thwarted, I put in a call to Naoko at Kojima Bank and got her voice mail. I knew she was ducking my calls, and I certainly knew what that meant. But I couldn't see losing the client without a fight.

I put my half-filled coffee cup (my sixth of the day) down on the desk, listened to the acid rumbling of my stomach, and suddenly felt very tired. I decided to pack it in.

"I'm out of here till tomorrow," I told Adam. "Call me if anything important happens."

"You mean like if Hewlett-Packard decides to change immigration counsel?" Adam asked with a smile.

I laughed. "On second thought, why don't you close up shop, too? We could all use a break."

"Not from too much work," Brooke said from the doorway.

Much as I would have liked to, I couldn't disagree with her.

My parents always told me I could be anything I wanted, and then they left me to decide for myself what that was. Since I had stumbled into someone else's ready-made family life, I'd come to realize the extent to which they'd left me alone. Not physically alone, certainly, but just more or less to my own devices, as long as I was content and reasonably successful. I did not in any way resemble today's micromanaged child, scheduled from dawn to dusk and schlepped from music lessons to soccer games to play dates to tutoring sessions by hypervigilant parental attendants eager to provide every advantage. My parents apparently felt that every advantage was being provided by two benevolent if somewhat preoccupied adults, adequate food (if you don't count the overcooked vegetables), and a house full of books. Since I was a quiet, independent child who loved to read, their method of child rearing probably succeeded as well as anyone else's.

Of course, that business about being anything I wanted was a crock. Ballerina was clearly out, despite my youthful fantasies and dancing lessons, as were cellist, race-car driver, baseball player, or anything remotely having to do with sports. Nor did I conceive an early inclination for the law by watching *Perry Mason* reruns. I drifted into law school because I was curious, because there isn't much you can do with an English major that will earn a living, and because my grades were good enough to get in. Until Harrison's bizarre peccadilloes had landed me in a royal mess, I'd been content enough with my choice, though I have already explained about my aversion to a big-time corporate practice. I liked the clients, I liked the way you had to be looking down the road, legally speaking, all the time, and I even liked, in a peculiar sort of way, the jousting with the INS. It suited my nature, which was, I suppose, critical and objective. What I didn't like, just at the moment, was being responsible for the futures of all the people I'd inherited with Grady & Bartlett.

Before I left, I put in a call to Kay. "Could you be looking around for some cheaper office space for me?" I asked her.

"What about your lease?" she asked.

"It's a month-to-month. The landlord wanted to be able to raise the rates when space was at a premium."

"They're a bunch of greedy bastards," she said. "They squeezed people on the way up, and now they squeeze them when the companies fail. I could see it if you bought the building at the top of the market and have to make your payments, but a lot of them owned the properties long before the dot-com bubble. Anyway, I'll keep my eyes open. How many people will you want space for?"

"I'm not sure yet," I said.

"Oh, Lynn," she sighed. "How are things going? Are you okay?"

"I'm not really sure," I said again.

She was silent a moment. "Now, don't bite my head off . . . ," she began.

"Am I that cranky?" I asked.

"Of course not," she said loyally. "It's just that you maintain a dignified reticence on certain subjects."

I laughed. "What is it?" I asked.

"The society is meeting again next week," she said. "And I thought—"

"When?" I interrupted her.

She told me.

"I'll be there," I said.

"Really?" She sounded surprised.

"Really," I said. I mean, look where reticence had gotten me so far.

MEREDITH'S VOLVO, a college-graduation present from her father, was parked in front of the house when I got there. I felt the way you might feel if you were expecting chateaubriand at a restaurant and the waiter lifted the dome to reveal fried tofu instead. Not objectionable, but not what you were hoping for either. My expectations of a tolerably pleasant evening were dashed.

"Hi," I said, smiling insincerely, a talent I seemed to be exercising quite a bit of late.

Jack and Meredith were sitting on the couch. Meredith was sipping out of a teacup filled with ocher-colored liquid. Nothing from our pantry, I was sure. Jack had a drink.

"Meredith has some news," Jack said.

I did a quick calculation and decided that honesty was the best policy, or at least the one with the fewest risks. "So I've heard," I said, still beaming. "Congratulations."

"Mom told you," Meredith acknowledged.

"Yes, this afternoon. That's wonderful news. We're very happy for you."

Jack said nothing.

"Thanks," Meredith said.

"Is Patrick here? Should we bring out the champagne?" I asked. I wasn't sure what I'd walked in on. The mood seemed a trifle glum for a wedding announcement, but that might just have been Meredith.

"You know I don't put that kind of poison in my body, Lynn," Meredith said. "It destroys your brain cells."

I couldn't think how to respond to that. Jack was still silent. "Um, when's the wedding?" I asked.

"We're working that out." She looked at Jack. "Aren't we, Dad?"

He smiled thinly.

I attempted a rescue with the usual bride-y questions—"What are your plans?" "When did you decide?" "Have you told Justin's family?"— but at best I got monosyllabic answers and a demeanor that boded ill for nuptial bliss. At length I sank back into the pillows, exhausted. Let them sit in silence if they wanted to. I couldn't do any more.

"Well, I have to be going," Meredith said as soon as I had ceased chattering. It was probably a rebuke, but I didn't care.

"WHAT WAS THAT ALL ABOUT?" Jack asked me as soon as she had left. I'd been about to ask him the same question, but he jumped in first. "What did she mean about Janet?"

I thought longingly of a glass of sauvignon blanc but decided to save it as a reward for getting through the conversation. "She called me," I said. "We had lunch."

He looked at me as if I'd lost my senses. Maybe I had. "You have to do what you think best, but I really don't feel comfortable about your socializing with Janet," he said. "It sort of gives me the creeps."

It sort of gave me the creeps, too. "I didn't feel all that comfortable about it either," I said. "But she said it was important."

"I wonder why," he said.

"Actually," I said carefully, "I think she wanted to give notice that she expects us to pay for the wedding."

He nodded. "I gathered from Merry that they're envisioning something . . ."

"Baroque?" I suggested.

He smiled. "Vegetarian Baroque anyway. But very expensive nonetheless."

"Well," I said, "you'll have to level with them sooner or later."

Jack stopped smiling. "About what?"

"About our financial situation," I said, my voice rising a little. "Until you conclude an agreement with the IRS, we still don't know how much the tax liability will be. How can you afford to fund a lavish wedding?"

"She's my daughter, Lynn."

We were back in dangerous waters. "Of course you want to contribute to her wedding," I told him, "but we can't bankrupt ourselves to put on something we can't afford. If you're candid with Meredith, I'm sure she'll understand."

"I doubt that, based on this evening's conversation," he said dryly. "But in any case, this is one of the reasons we didn't commingle our money. This is my problem, not yours."

I was getting a little tired of hearing that. "I don't agree with you," I said. "And beside, what is this marriage about? We only share the good things and we deal with the bad ones on our own?"

"Don't pick fights, Lynn." he said grimly. "I'm trying to spare you. The money's not the worst of it, anyway. The really sad thing is that she's agreed to marry that muscle-bound half-wit. I thought she'd grow tired of him before now."

I finally understood the source of the tension in the atmosphere when I'd walked in. "He's probably not genius material," I agreed, "but he seems devoted to Meredith. Plus he's easygoing, and you know she's a little . . . high-strung. He might be good for her."

"He doesn't read," Jack said. "Probably not even the newspaper."

"Probably not," I said, suppressing a smile at the thought of Justin toiling over the *San Jose Mercury,* much less a dog-eared copy of *War and Peace.* "Although he might read the comics."

"It's not funny, Lynn," Jack said.

"You have to admit they both have a certain"—I almost said *obsession* but thought better of it—"interest in health issues and the body. They'll have lots to talk about. And they'll probably live forever, and Meredith won't be left a widow."

Jack smiled. "You're making fun of me. And them."

"Neither," I said, which wasn't exactly true. "But you know it's futile to make a fuss about it. Would you have listened to your father if he didn't like the person you wanted to marry?"

"My father always approved of Janet," he said.

Just what I wanted to hear. I said nothing.

"But I see your point," he conceded. "I only hope he can support her."

She'll have to support herself, I thought, *like all the rest of us.* But I didn't say it. "I'm pouring a glass of wine," I told him. "Can I get you anything?"

"No thanks," he said. "Oh, Lynn?" he said when I'd gone a few steps toward the kitchen.

"Yes?"

"Did Janet say what Valerio thinks of this marriage?"

Ha. "Um—I'm not sure he has an opinion," I said.

Jack nodded thoughtfully. "That's probably best," he said.

CHAPTER 20

To: Lynn Bartlett, Esq.
From: Alexei Strela, Ph.D.

Russian Joke: During his visit to the USSR, President Nixon was intrigued by a new telephone capable of connecting with hell. He spoke briefly with the devil, and the call cost him 27 cents. When he returned home, he found out that this same service was now available in the U.S. He tried it again and received a bill for $12,000.

Nixon, notoriously frugal, was distressed. "What happened? The same call only cost me 27 cents in the USSR!"

"Well," said the operator, "over there it's a local call."

To: Alexei Strela, Ph.D.
From: Lynn Bartlett

A Nixon joke! I can't believe it! I'm adding it to the collection.

Thank you for the expanded résumé and materials for your case. I'm impressed with that, too. I didn't realize you'd gone to high school in the United States.

To: Lynn Bartlett
From: Alexei Strela

What collection?

My father was a diplomat under the Soviet government. I
know lots of Nixon jokes. Ford, Carter, and Reagan jokes,
too.

To: Alexei Strela
From: Lynn

You've sent me five Russian jokes so far. That constitutes a
collection, at least a small one.

That explains your perfect command of English anyway.

It must have been hard growing up in Washington during
the Cold War.

To: Lynn
From: Alexei

Yeah.

I was starting to get the sense of Russian humor. It
was self-deprecating with a twist, like the Nixon joke.
I didn't usually have such a personal correspondence
with my clients, but it wasn't outside the bounds of experience either. My capacity as biographer and chron-
icler of extraordinary achievements gave me a certain
license to ask for details generally considered socially
off-limits—salary, for example, or bonuses, or grades

in grad school. Straying into emotional territory was something else, but some people you just clicked with in the weeks it took to develop a case.

To: Lynn
From: Alexei

Russian joke: A New Russian comes in to buy a car. He tells the salesman he wants a black Mercedes. The salesman finds exactly the car he wants, and the man pays for it in cash. As he is about to leave, the salesman asks him, "Didn't you buy a car just like this from us last week?"

"Oh, yes, I did," replies the New Russian, "but the ashtray got full."

Lynn, there is something I need to talk to you about in person. Can I come to your office?

"What's a New Russian?" I asked.

Alexei grimaced. "Just what I didn't want to be," he said. "I guess you'd say 'nouveau riche' here."

I smiled. Since I knew how much Alexei was making at SLAC, I didn't think there was the remotest possibility of that. "What did you want to see me about?" I asked him.

"Have you read about the International Linear Collider SLAC wants to build?"

I shook my head. "Uh, no." To my shame, I passed right over articles about physics projects en route to topics more suitable for early-morning scrutiny. Virtually any topic fit that category.

He smiled, as if he'd read my mind. "Since they shut down the linear collider here in 1998, there's been a lot of interest in building a huge new atom-smashing center that would take the work to the next level. There are lots of things we still don't know in physics."

"I'm with you," I said. "Do they want you to work on it?"

"Yes," he said. He looked unhappy.

"Is there a problem?"

"It's a dream project," he said. "And there could be unparalleled trickle-down benefits. Did you know the World Wide Web was born at a particle accelerator near Geneva, and the first Web site in the United States was at SLAC?" His eyes, so brown they were almost black, burned with intensity.

"Then why not go for it?" I asked. There had to be a catch, or he wouldn't be talking it over with me.

He sat back in his chair. "It might be in Germany," he said.

"Ah."

"I mean, at this point it's still a dream. The design and site haven't been chosen. But Germany is the front-runner."

"Well, you're right to be concerned," I told him. "If your primary residence isn't the United States, you could lose your green card."

"Which I don't have yet," he pointed out.

"Which you don't have yet," I agreed. "But you will."

He smiled his unsettling languid smile. I had to fight

the urge to smooth my hair and moisten my lips. *Down, girl.* "I like your confidence," he said.

He should talk. "You have a good case," I said, as blandly as I could manage. "Anyway," I added, recovering, "you can just wait and see, can't you, as long as it's all still up in the air? Maybe they'll build it in Stockton or someplace like that."

His expression told me he had been to Stockton.

"Or not," I said hurriedly. "My advice would be to proceed as planned and see where you are when some decision is made. But you're right to be concerned."

"Okay," he said.

I expected him to take his leave now that he'd learned what he came for, but he stayed in his chair, looking around. "Nice office," he observed, although this was already his third visit.

"Thank you," I said. I didn't add that it probably wouldn't be mine much longer. That sort of information does not inspire confidence in clients.

He seemed to be searching for something—in his pockets, on the surface of my desk. I waited.

"Sorry," he said. "I used to smoke, and when I get nervous, the urge comes back."

"I don't have any cigarettes," I told him. I wondered what he was nervous about.

He laughed. "Neither do I. I shouldn't smoke them now anyway. But when I first came here, people used to stop me on the street and urge me to quit. They seemed angry. I couldn't believe it. In Russia everybody smokes."

"That's the Bay Area," I said. "There's a sort of tendency to reprove people for activities that aren't supposed to be healthy. Sometimes people will even scold you in restaurants for eating red meat. They probably mean well, but it's annoying."

"I'm familiar with a paternalistic society," he said levelly. He shifted in the chair in a way that made me aware of his physical presence. He sighed. "I have an offer from Cooper Livingston in New York. They want me to create and trade derivatives once I have clear permanent resident status. I could start at about three hundred thousand dollars a year."

"That's wonderful," I told him. "You'll make more, if the economy comes back," I observed. I knew what people could make in the field. Derivatives no longer enjoyed the innocent reputation they once had, but as a means of risk management, they were probably here to stay. People with the intense mathematical background necessary to understand them, much less formulate them, were in big demand. "An embarrassment of riches," I added. "And no problem with your green card."

"It's selling out," he said flatly.

"You mean as opposed to discovering the true nature of dark matter or something like that?"

He looked amused. "I thought you didn't read about that kind of stuff," he said.

"You're forgetting the Discovery Channel and PBS," I reminded him. "Anyway, it seems to me it's only a sellout if you really don't want to do it."

"It's more complicated than that," he said.

"You don't want to be a New Russian in America," I said, recalling his joke. I was trying to keep it light. It wasn't part of my job description to pry into his life, intriguing as it was.

"My father was in the war," he said suddenly.

I nodded. I knew what "the war" meant, though someone twenty-five might not.

"He hated Stalin, and he was nearsighted and not very strong, but he put his life on the line anyway. After he retired, after the breakup of the country made his pension worthless, I wanted to bring him and my mother here. He refused. He said he didn't want to give up seven centuries of culture and his homeland for an SUV and a condo in Florida. I didn't make that choice, but I admire him." He ran his hands through his hair. "You said 'an embarrassment of riches.' You probably can't see it, but all this . . . affluence"—he waved an arm around my office, but I was pretty sure he wasn't referring to *that*—"takes getting used to, when you've been conditioned not to . . . approve, I guess you'd say. There's too much of everything." He shrugged. "Things are going that way in Russia, too, so maybe it's just human nature. But I feel guilty about accepting the rewards when I haven't made the sacrifices."

"I think some ambivalence is natural," I said. "A lot of ambivalence, actually. I mean, I saw an ad for Las Vegas that said, 'Seven Deadly Sins—One Convenient Location.' Do I want to lay my life on the line for *any*-

body attracted by a slogan like that? I don't even think they should be allowed to vote."

He laughed. "That's not a very democratic sentiment."

"I know," I admitted.

"There is one thing, though," he said.

"What?"

"My father said that one of the happiest days of his life was the day he met up with the Americans at the Elbe."

Germany again. "That should count for something, shouldn't it?" I asked him.

He looked at me. "I'd like to think so," he said.

CHAPTER 21

Naoko Watanabe summoned me to her office to give me, finally, the news I'd been dreading. Because she was Japanese, friendly, and uncomfortable with disagreeable topics, it took longer than it might have to get to the point.

"I'm so sorry," she said at last, offering me tea in her tiny, spare office. "The decision came from much higher up. From Tokyo." She sighed. "It's regrettable. I know none of this was your fault."

I nodded, and we sipped our tea in silence.

"We might still be able to use you for extraordinary-ability petitions," she said. "Quite frankly, no one else seems to know what to do with them. But the head office felt that the bulk of our business should go to a larger, more established firm."

That probably meant Elson Larimer. "I understand," I told her.

"I hope you do," she said. "I feel terrible about it. I know what a bad time this must be for you."

All this sympathy made me wonder if things weren't worse than even I realized. "Well, thank you," I said.

She looked into her lap. "Your partner told me there were some problems in your personal life," she said. "But even with assurances that we would be well served—"

"*What?*" I said, my jaw dropping. "What do you mean?"

Her expression told me I had interjected the very note of discord she'd been hoping to avoid.

"Harrison told you something?" I pressed her, incredulous.

She shook her head. "Not Harrison. Your other partner. Brooke."

"I don't have another partner," I said, trying to keep my voice under control.

Naoko was no dummy. "I must have misunderstood, then," she said.

"That's probably it," I agreed, suppressing the urge I felt to rush back to the office and throttle Brooke right on the carpet of her paid-for-by-me office.

"She was very helpful," Naoko said, trying to cover. "She's so impressed with your abilities as a lawyer, and she offered to do anything for us herself if you were unavailable."

" 'I come to bury Caesar, not to praise him,' " I murmured.

"*Julius Caesar.*" Naoko smiled. "Well, you know best," she said. She stood and offered me her hand. "Good luck."

*   *   *

"I WAS JUST TRYING TO HELP," Brooke said. "I thought that if she realized there were a number of people available to do the bank's work—not just you and Harrison—that it might be . . . well, more reassuring."

"You can see how reassuring it was," I told her.

"She'd already made up her mind," she said. "It's not my fault."

"Then why did you tell her I had personal problems that might prevent me from doing her work?" I concentrated on keeping my voice low and steady, not without some effort.

She shook her head. "I didn't say that."

"Did you imply it?"

She looked away. "She probably misunderstood. English isn't her first language, is it? Maybe she misinterpreted something I said."

"I see," I said. "Do you remember what I said about not being ready to deal with the clients directly? About running things past me first?"

"You don't trust me with anything important," she said. "Every time I take the initiative, I get in trouble with you. How am I ever going to learn anything this way?"

"By watching and listening and not opening your mouth till you're sure of what you're saying," I said. "You've way overstepped the boundary here."

"Well, it wasn't really a conversation with a *client*," she argued. "Naoko's really more of a friend, in a way. Harrison used to take me to meetings with the bank, and we sort of hit it off."

I remembered my suspicion that Kojima had some-how gotten wind of the false documents even before I'd informed them. "You didn't by chance give your friend Naoko some kind of early warning about their possible immigration problems, did you?"

She looked wounded. "Of course not. I wasn't even informed myself, if you remember," she said accus-ingly. "Harrison gave me a lot more responsibility," she added.

"I don't think we should forget that Harrison was creating a smoke screen to hide the fact that he was fudging on a lot of the work," I told her.

"That's cruel," she said.

"Tell that to all the clients who trusted—not to men-tion *paid*—us to help them," I said.

"I'm not defending what he did, but, I mean, maybe he couldn't help himself."

I looked at her.

"Well, we don't really know why he did it, do we? Maybe he was being blackballed or something like that."

"Blackballed?"

She closed her eyes. "I mean *blackmailed*. I'm upset, so I'm getting confused." She gave me a look that suggested her confusion was all my fault.

"Brooke, I sincerely doubt that anyone would black-mail Harrison into forging documents when he could have gotten the approvals at all events in the ordinary way. I have to believe he did it to cover his tracks. I think he had a much more serious drinking problem than anyone realized."

She put a hand to her ample chest and said dramatically, "I feel so guilty. All this time together, and I never had a hint of it."

I thought of reminding her that associates rarely have a hint of anything that goes on with the partners, at least if the partners have anything to say about it, but of course I didn't.

"I mean," she continued, "he did miss a few meetings, and sometimes he seemed a little *blank,* if you know what I'm saying. But I didn't think it was anything serious. Besides, he was old. He was supposed to have trouble remembering things."

I sighed. "Not that old. Anyway, it's a big problem," I told her. "A surprisingly large percentage of attorneys have alcohol issues. That's why the bar makes us take all those continuing-ed courses on substance abuse. There's no need for you to feel guilty. It was Harrison's responsibility to deal with it."

"That seems a little hard," she said.

I was feeling the temptation of some alcohol abuse myself at just that moment. "Well, put it this way, how sympathetic would you be if he'd been driving drunk and killed somebody?"

Her mouth dropped open. "He didn't kill anybody," she said at last, in a whisper.

"No, just the firm." I couldn't help letting the bitterness show. I folded my arms and looked at her. "Listen, Brooke, I'm not firing you, but I think you should be looking for another job."

She reached over my desk and patted a pile of papers into a neat stack. She said, over her shoulder, "Do you think I'm not?"

"WELL, THAT'S THAT," I told Jack. We were sitting at the table after dinner. It was his turn to cook, so we'd had what he almost always fixed, pasta with some kind of vegetables and a little meat. He made it a point of pride not to get takeout, but frankly the repertoire was getting a bit stale. We ate dutifully, like post-op patients with their hospital trays.

I set aside my napkin. I wasn't hungry anyway. "I don't see how I can keep the office open any longer," I said. "Without Kojima and the other clients who've left because of Harrison, there's scarcely enough business for one person, let alone three."

"You'll get new clients, Lynn," he said. "You still have a good reputation."

I shook my head. "Thanks, but Felix Frankfurter might have trouble getting clients after this. In this economy I can't afford to wait till they see the error of their ways and come flocking back."

"I'm sorry," he said. "What will you do?"

"I've asked Kay to find me some cheap office space," I told him. "I'll go it alone, answer my own phone, and do the work for the clients I still have. I'll have to try to find jobs for the others, though. They deserve better than this." At least most of them did.

"That's tough. But there are people out of work all over the Valley. They'll land on their feet."

"Maybe," I said.

"Have you considered working out of the house?"

I looked at him. "The extra room isn't available right now." I had to fight the surge of panic that arose from merely contemplating the idea of working out of the house. It surprised me. I hadn't realized how much of a refuge my office had become.

He frowned. "Patrick won't be here forever," he said.

I didn't respond to that one. "There are probably too many distractions," I told him. "Anyway, you don't want clients coming here. They keep odd hours, and some of them get paranoid when they don't hear anything and start dropping in to see if just by chance you might be keeping the news from them. Trust me, you don't want that."

"Not when you put it that way," he said. "It was just a thought."

"Also," I said, "there's going to be a certain amount of activity here because of the wedding, and—"

"I get the point, Lynn. You don't want to work here. It's fine." He sounded hurt, but since he was, in effect, correct, I didn't see how I could make it better without agreeing to something I would find surprisingly intolerable. The person you are at the office and the person you are at home may not be all that compatible, and increasingly I found I liked the office person a lot better.

Jack pushed his plate away. "It's probably not the best time to bring this up, but I might as well tell you now. I've reached a settlement with the IRS."

I swallowed the last bit of wine in my glass and tried to smile. "And?" I prompted him.

"Two hundred thousand." He said it briskly, which was his way of signaling that he didn't want to argue about it.

I closed my eyes. "How soon?" I asked.

"Payable over two years," he said.

"Can we do that?" I asked.

"Not without borrowing," he said.

"What about selling the house?" I asked impetuously.

"And do what? Anything decent would be just as expensive."

"Well, actually I was thinking we could move away. Almost anywhere would be cheaper than this, and we could . . ."

He looked at me as if I'd suggested a hiking tour of the Afghan countryside. "Leave the Bay Area? What about my business and . . . your practice?" He added the second part out of politeness, as we both knew.

"I could start over somewhere else. It would be better to do it now than wait to build things up again. I don't know about your business, Jack, but you aren't one of the principals, and so far it's caused us a lot of grief."

"I still believe in it," he said. "And anyway, what about Merry and Patrick?"

"You think they would resent it if you moved away? Even though Meredith is getting married and Patrick has his own life?" *I hope.*

"I guess it does seem foolish," he said, "but they've always depended on having their parents close by."

"Well, Janet would still be here," I pointed out. I couldn't seem to drop the topic, even though I have to admit that I knew I should give it a rest. It was as if someone with no self-control and little judgment had taken over altogether while I was distracted by something else.

He frowned. "Is that what this is about? Janet?"

"No, of course not," I said, hoping I was telling the truth. Or at least not an outright lie.

"You don't have to feel threatened by her," he said.

That statement, like "You can trust me," generally inspires the opposite of what it professes to invoke.

"If that's what this is all about," he concluded, in the face of my silence.

"Give me some credit," I said finally. "Don't you ever think it might be fun to live somewhere else? Somewhere less materialistic?"

"Materialistic?" he said.

"Well, focused on material things, I mean. Half the people here live in million-dollar homes, and the other half can't afford any place to live. And all those slick dot-commers riding around in their expensive sports cars pulling fast ones on the shareholders and the grocery stores that seem to be Fauchon's knockoffs specializing in carrot fetuses or some other vegetables so precious you could wear them as jewelry. I mean, whatever happened to *produce?*" I stopped to catch my breath.

"Where did all this come from?" he said, sounding incredulous. "A month ago you wanted us to get a bigger house. Now you sound postively puritanical, like Jonathan Edwards." He tried to smile. "What gives?"

"I'm not sure," I said truthfully. "I know it's not consistent. But sometimes it all seems . . . excessive somehow."

"You're just tired," he said. "I can't blame you; it's this thing with the firm. Things will work out eventually, you'll see." He stood and started clearing the plates. "We'll sort out the tax situation somehow. We don't have to sell up. And besides, I like the Bay Area," he said. "We have a good life. All our friends are here. The kids. Why would we want to move away?"

I looked at him. I opened my mouth, and the Jonathan Edwards voice came out again. "All of *your* friends are here, you mean." I didn't add, *And that's exactly what I want to move away from.*

Silence.

"I'm sorry, but that's the way I feel sometimes," I told him. "Like a guest in your life. And anyway, don't you think it might be good for us to start over somewhere else?"

He paused, dishes in hand, and gave me a bleak look. "I didn't know you felt that way," he said. "I really thought you were happy here."

CHAPTER 22

O f course, I'd assumed I *would* be happy. Jack had gone to great pains to arrange my first meeting with his children, which I thought was a very good omen for our future life together. He'd chosen a lovely restaurant (neutral territory, as I realize now) and prepared them with a description of my wit, charm, and accomplishment that would have done credit to a combination of Madeleine Albright/Condoleezza Rice (pick your administration) and Princess Diana. It was a stage set, and I was cast in a leading role. Sort of like Lady Macbeth.

Meredith and Patrick had arrived early and were already sitting alertly on tapestry-covered chairs, watching us enter the restaurant. They looked formal and a bit stiff, something like the chair backs, but not unfriendly. I put the stiffness down to nervousness and uncertainty, emotions I was only too aware of in myself.

Jack bent and kissed Meredith on the cheek and patted Patrick on the shoulder before shaking hands.

"This is Lynn," he told them, putting his arm around me. "Lynn, my children, Meredith and Patrick."

I shook hands with each of them. We sat down and busied ourselves with the settling-in rituals—napkins in lap, menus, water glasses—while we studied each other covertly. Jack picked up the wine list.

"Would anyone like a drink before dinner?" the waiter asked.

Meredith shook her head firmly, Jack and Patrick had scotch, and I had a glass of white wine. I wanted to keep my wits (overhyped as they were) about me, so I resisted the urge to gulp it down.

Meredith was studying the menu as if it were a Mafia hit list and her name was on it. She was a slender and rather pretty blonde, with aquiline features. Jack leaned over. "Is there anything you can eat, Merry? I didn't think to call ahead and ask."

I remember wondering if she had some health problem, like diabetes. "No, I'm okay," she said. "I can have some steamed fish, I guess."

Jack settled back with an air of relief. At the time I thought such solicitude was touching.

"I'll have the bifstek fiorentino," Patrick said, jumping the line. "Rare."

Meredith closed her eyes.

"And for you, ma'am?" the waiter prompted.

I wish there were some age-appropriate form of address falling between "miss" and "ma'am." I was too on edge to be hungry, so I ordered the first thing I saw on the menu. "I'll have the swordfish," I said.

Meredith coughed spasmodically and gripped the arms of her chair. Patrick laughed. I looked from one to the other of them, but I didn't get the joke, if that's what it was. Afterward I realized they rarely addressed a single word to each other—they spoke mainly to their father or, occasionally, to me. I had no direct experience of siblings, but I'd expected familial ribbing or in-jokes or some manifestation of a bond beyond genetic inheritance.

Meredith was definitely not smiling. She leaned toward me and said seriously, "Are you sure that's what you want?"

"Merry—" Jack said.

"Is there something wrong?" the waiter asked.

She ignored both him and her father. "Aren't you worried about mercury poisoning?" she asked.

"Should I be?" I inquired.

She nodded emphatically. "Swordfish is one of the *worst* offenders. Children and pregnant women should *never* eat it."

I stole a glance at Jack and smiled. "Well, I'm definitely not pregnant," I said.

Big mistake. The introduction of just that much sexual innuendo lowered the room temperature perceptibly. You could almost see their postures hardening along with their misgivings. Hitherto I might have been some visiting nun in civilian dress their father had somehow invited to dinner, but no longer.

The waiter stood holding his order pad, his face an impassive mask. "Would you care to choose something else?" he asked. He deserved a big tip just for keeping his tone so neutral.

"I guess I'll have the halibut," I said spinelessly. I didn't really care what I ate, and I didn't mind deferring to Meredith if it would help things go smoothly between us. I think even then I had the suspicion she would not be mollified.

"Did I tell you that Lynn's an attorney?" Jack said eventually, in an overenthusiastic tone of voice not inappropriate for Back-to-School Night.

"How nice," Meredith murmured.

Patrick laughed again. "What kind of work do you do?" he asked.

"Immigration, mostly," I told him, prepared to elaborate.

No further questions were forthcoming, however, so I asked him, "What do *you* do?" to reciprocate. Jack sat back, apparently pleased with the conversational ebb and flow. I was starting to sweat in my silk blouse.

"I'm in advertising," he said.

"That must be interesting," I said.

"It isn't, actually," he said. "I'm just a very low-level copywriter."

"Yes, but so many interesting things have been going on in advertising since the eighties," I said, hoping to coax at least some topic out of this exchange. "Ads are so much better than they used to be, don't you think? That Super Bowl ad for Apple just blew me away."

He shrugged. "That was Jay Chiat," he said. "Not

me." He set down his roll and butter knife. "Also, it was a long time ago. And he's dead."

Mercifully, the waiter brought our dinners at that point, so I didn't have to reply. The waiter poured everyone except Meredith a glass of wine. She was having some kind of mineral water from Napa-Sonoma, but I didn't catch the name. In the Bay Area, the Napa Valley has the kind of cachet Burgundy does in France, and everything from toilet water to tofu tries to cash in on the association.

"Let's have a toast," Jack said. "A toast to welcome Lynn."

Jack beamed at me while the others raised their glasses with expressions of mild puzzlement.

"Thank you," I said.

"Are you here on business?" Meredith asked me after a moment.

"No, just visiting," I told her.

"Where are you staying?" she asked.

Was this an innocent question? I doubted it, but I couldn't be sure. Before I could answer, Jack said, "With me, Merry. Of course."

Neither of them reacted to what was, essentially, a declaration. At the time I remember feeling a bit relieved that nothing more was said. Ha.

Meredith was pushing rice grains around her plate with the tip of her fork. "I think there's coconut in this rice," she announced. "Could you get the waiter?" she asked Jack.

Jack signaled the waiter with a look of resignation.

"Is there coconut in this rice?" Meredith asked him when he approached the table.

Did his lips twitch just a little? I hope so. "I believe the dish is made with coconut milk," he said. "Also a bit of onion and some garlic." He straightened. "All the ingredients were on the menu," he said. "Should I bring you the recipe? The chef is very happy to share them with our customers."

"I won't be *making* it," she said sternly. "Not with *coconut milk*. I won't be eating it either."

"I'm very sorry," said the waiter. "Would you like me to bring you some plain rice instead?"

"Not white," Meredith said. "Brown, if you have it."

"I'll check with the chef," he said. "Will there be anything else?"

"Not just now," Jack said quickly. "Thank you for your help."

"I was telling Mom," Meredith said when we had resumed our meal, "that the school is *finally* getting around to wiring my classroom for the Internet. Every other grade level has already had access for ages. The parents have been complaining right and left."

"What grade do you teach?" I asked.

"Third," she said. "Anyway, the electricians and the phone company came in first thing this morning while I was teaching class. Right in the middle! And they . . ."

She proceeded to tell a lengthy but largely innocuous (if you don't count the invocations of her mother's opinions, which occurred with suspicious frequency) story about the installation, directed for the most part toward her father. Patrick yawned conspicuously while I sat attentively, the model guest. I might have spared myself the trouble; she rarely glanced my way.

The brown rice came at length, followed rather closely by the check. (No dessert. No coffee. A family tradition, apparently, since no one even asked.) "It's on me, of course," Jack said, although, as far as I could see, there was no discernible reaching for wallets. "My treat."

"Thank you, Jack," I said. "This was lovely."

"Well, I've got to be going," Meredith said. "I've got an early day tomorrow."

Jack smiled. "Tomorrow's Saturday, Merry."

"I *know* that, Dad," she said. "Justin and I are going for an early run."

"I'm taking off, too," Patrick said.

We stood and shook hands and pronounced "nice to meet you"s all round.

Afterward Jack said, "That went well, I thought."

"It was a lovely dinner," I repeated.

"They liked you a lot," he said. "I can tell."

I smiled at the hyperbole. "You're prejudiced," I said.

He took my hand. "This is the point at which you're supposed to say, 'I liked them a lot, too.' "

I felt a rush of affection for him, for his concern that all of us should be happy together. "It went fine, Jack," I said. "I think we'll all be friends."

"Patrick was a little quiet," he said, "but when you get to know him, you'll see that he has a wonderful sense of humor. And Merry . . ." His voice took on an indulgent tone. "She's very . . . oh, I guess you'd say *rigorous*. Her standards are very exacting."

"Yes, they must be," I murmured.

He grinned suddenly. "Actually, she scares the hell out of me. I mean, how can anybody ever measure up?"

Good, I thought. *At least he can laugh about it.* "She's certainly very pretty," I said.

He smiled fondly. "She takes after her mother, not me," he said. Then he looked at me quickly, to see if I'd taken offense.

"Janet must be very attractive, then," I said.

"Yes," he said. "I suppose she is."

LYING IN THE DARK in Jack's house in what would, in time, become our bedroom, I had leisure to examine the evening more objectively. I didn't share Jack's certainty that his children liked me, but I hardly expected that. They hadn't attacked me (verbally or physically) or implied I was after their father's money or any of the other hallmarks of second-wife horror stories. (In fairness, they didn't exactly know I was going to be the second wife, but I doubted the news would come as a shock.) They had seemed, for the most part, indifferent to my presence, as if I were a stranger they'd encountered in an airport. That was perfectly okay with me. As long as the relationship remained cordial, I didn't need to be the center of attention. In fact, it mirrored, in some respects, the relationship I'd had with my own parents.

Quite frankly, I thought Jack's children were a little weird, particularly Meredith, but if she wanted to regard the entire spectrum of edible creation with suspicion, I supposed there were worse neuroses. I foresaw some difficulties with family dinners, but I figured I could always prevail on Jack to cook. On the whole, their initial bland indifference was comforting, even hopeful. In time we might even be friends. I permitted myself a brief, warm fantasy of a loving family around the dinner table, trading jokes and catching up on one another's news.

And then there was Jack, lying beside me in a gentle, contented sleep. His body—I loved his body and the way my body felt when I was with him—was both familiar and mysterious. I felt a deep kind of peace, the kind that comes from a long-term emotional investment after a lot of relationships where my bags were always packed, literally and figuratively. So what if his family was a bit eccentric? It felt like home.

I decided that Jack's assessment, that the evening had been a success, was right after all. We would be happy; things would work out.

That's what I hoped anyway.

I never claimed to be clairvoyant.

CHAPTER 23

To: Lynn
From: Alexei

Russian physics joke:

—Ivan, did you know that Albert Einstein is coming to Odessa?

—Who's he?

—A famous physicist. He is the author of the Theory of Relativity.

—What's that?

—Well, how can I explain this. . . ? Let's see, you have two hairs on your head. Is that a lot or a little?

—A little.

—And now let's imagine you found the same number of hairs in your soup. . . .

—Can this be true? Somebody's really coming to Odessa with this stupid joke?

To: Alexei
From: Lynn

Thank you so much for referring Drs. Sidykh and
Pushkin for their H-1s. I look forward to working with
them and appreciate your confidence in my work.

I suppose I ought to try to explain how things got
started with Alexei. I mean, obviously it wasn't just the
Russian jokes, some of which were little better than
"Knock, knock . . ." I hope it wasn't just that I felt myself shrinking in my life with Jack and needed a life-
line to keep my ego afloat either. I can't even say
Alexei flirted with me, although I think he did. He just
noticed, and, paying attention, he somehow slipped
under my guard. I found him touching—brave and
playful and serious all at once. He was also so *alone.*
Under the circumstances, that was undeniably part of
the attraction.

That is, once I realized it *was* an attraction. At first I
didn't think it was any different from the admiration I
felt for a lot of my clients, who were, by definition, extraordinary. But then I started to anticipate the e-mails
and the corny jokes and the little snippets of biograph-
ical data with the same sensation I used to feel when
Mikey Stewart would leave notes taped to my locker in
junior high. In the featherweight, anything-goes banter
of e-mails, the crush got going almost before I realized
it had begun.

Okay, I told myself the times I found myself thinking, surprisingly often, about a moment in my office

when I had leaned toward Alexei, at the end of the conversation, and had had to stop myself from putting my hand out to touch him. As long as I didn't act on it, the feeling would probably go away on its own. Whatever, I had to cure myself of the little involuntary twist inside my stomach when I saw him, but since it was involuntary, the best antidote was obviously not to see him in person.

Send me your backup documents and the letters as soon as you have them, I e-mailed him. *You can just drop off the materials when you're ready. I'll get in touch if I have any questions.*

Nevertheless, when I finally got the box of documents, I called him up.

"The awards are great," I said, determined to sound businesslike. There were at least five gold medals for mathematics olympiads—the Russian academic competitions in scientific fields. "And the publications." (Sixty of them, in major journals, on suitably arcane-sounding physics-related topics no officer in the INS in his or her right mind would ever consider reading.) "But all the letters are about what you're doing now, at SLAC. We really need something about what you did in the Soviet Union."

"I'm sorry, Lynn, but I don't know anyone to write such a letter," he insisted. "Not anymore."

I had prepared for this contingency. "I might know someone who could help us," I said. "A former client, a Ukrainian here in the U.S. He's not in your field, exactly, but he could at least write a generic description of your reputation and achievements, if you give him just a little something to work from. Shall I contact him?"

"He's not a nuclear physicist?" he asked.

"No. Computer science."

"That might be okay," he said. "But I would have to approve the letter before it goes in." He was silent a moment. "I know I'm being difficult," he said.

"Yes, you are," I agreed.

"But I have my reasons."

"I just want to help you," I said.

He laughed. "What is that American expression? 'I'm puddy in your hands.' What do I have to do?"

"Putty."

"What?"

"You're putty in my hands."

"Yes, I am."

I swallowed a giggle. "No, I mean the word is 'putty.' It's a kind of cement."

"That doesn't make sense," he said.

ILYA KOPYLOV WAS A STAR in the former Soviet Union in the development and implementation of computerized-automation technologies critical to optimizing nuclear-power and thermal-energy electrical-generating facilities. I'd gotten him his green card several years before when I had my own practice, and he and his wife still kept in touch. Now he was a consultant in automated large-scale information-management and -control systems for American technology clients and, I hoped, making a bundle. I always liked to see my former clients doing well.

Because he'd been through the process himself, I didn't mind asking him for a favor.

"Yes, I would be glad to help," he said, as I knew he would, after I'd explained what I needed.

"That would be great, Ilya," I said. "I'll send you a model letter so you don't have to write it from scratch."

"From . . . ?"

"Make it up out of your head," I amended. Ilya's English was not yet up to colloquialisms. "I'll ask him to call you, if that's all right, and give you some background about his work. Maybe it will be easier for him to tell you. I haven't been able to get much out of him."

"What kind of work?" Ilya asked.

"He has a Ph.D. in physics," I said. "He hasn't said much beyond that. He works at the Stanford Linear Accelerator now. I just want some idea of what he did in the Soviet Union. It doesn't have to be really specific."

"I'll see what I can find out, Lynn," he said. "What is the man's name?"

"Strela," I told him.

There was a silence on the other end of the line.

"Ilya?"

"Dr. Strela?" he said at last. "*Alexei* Strela?"

"Yes," I said, surprised. "Do you know him?"

"I know of him, certainly." He paused. "So this is where he went!"

"Ilya, you're making this sound very mysterious. Is he famous or something like that?"

"Dr. Strela was one of the most brilliant young nuclear physicists in the former Soviet Union," he said soberly. "He was one of the first people they called right after Chernobyl. Since my work involved nuclear power facilities, naturally I heard about it."

"You're kidding!" I said. "If he was that well known, can you think of any reason he doesn't want the INS to know about it?"

Silence.

"Ilya, if you know something, you should tell me."

"I don't know anything," he said firmly. "But he disappeared sometime after Chernobyl. When prominent people disappear from conferences and things like that, you assume they're dead or they've left the country. There was no notice of death, so . . ."

"So you assumed he'd gone," I prompted.

"Yes," he said. "It was certainly not uncommon. Things may be changing now, but there was little future in science in Russia or Ukraine. But . . ."

His sentences kept trailing off, I noticed. I waited.

"Well, somebody like Strela is not easily replaced, do you see what I mean? He was a big loss to the country, and the government would not have been happy about it. Also . . ."

He paused so long I wasn't sure if he was still on the line. "Ilya?"

"I don't like to repeat gossip," he said.

"I'll keep it to myself," I assured him.

"It's not like computer science or pure mathematics," he said modestly. "To the right sort of people—or maybe the wrong sort—Strela's knowledge could be extremely valuable. Extremely."

He said something in such a low tone of voice I had to ask him to repeat it.

"I said, there were rumors that he might have gone to Saudi Arabia," he said. "Or even Pakistan."

"Yikes," I said.

"That is an expression I haven't heard," Ilia said, "but I can guess the meaning. Yes, you are right, yikes. But let me tell you one thing, Lynn: It was not unheard of for the government to make up such stories itself to cover the embarrassment of losing so many scientists. I personally do not know anything . . . bad about him, so I would not believe it so easily. If you still want me to, I will write the letter."

"Thanks, Ilya. I appreciate it. I'll get back to you. Give my best to the family."

"CAN WE TALK?" I asked Alexei when I had tracked him down at SLAC.

"Business or pleasure?"

"Business," I said, as sternly as I could manage. "I apologize for disturbing you at work, but I wasn't sure if you got my e-mails."

"I'm sorry. Is it urgent?" he said. "I haven't been checking. I've been here pretty much around the clock on a project for the last few days."

"I wouldn't say it's urgent," I said, "but it could be important. In any case, I didn't mean on the phone. We need to discuss this in person."

"I'm free at lunch tomorrow," he said. "But if you could possibly come over here, we could spend more time together. Otherwise it would have to be a very brief meeting."

He sounded brisk and rather businesslike himself, which made me feel both relieved and a bit disappointed at the same time. Though moments before I'd vowed to keep things professional, now I wanted the rapport, the sense of connection. The chemistry. *Get a grip,* I told myself.

"Do you have an office?" I asked him.

"I'd much rather get something to eat, if you don't mind. Could we meet at the café on Sand Hill Road?"

I hesitated. "This is a discussion about your green card," I said.

"Of course it is. But I still need to eat, and so do you. Okay?"

"Okay," I said.

ALEXEI WAS ALREADY SITTING at a table in the spring sunshine when I arrived. He was the only person sitting by himself; everyone else was engaged in intense conversation with at least one other person. It made him stand out, like the eye of the hurricane. Oddly enough, no one was jabbering into a mobile; Sand Hill Road, the bomb center of Silicon Valley technology, is, ironically (and largely inexplicably), a dead zone for cell-phone reception.

"Hi," he said, half rising from his chair. He had on a

dark blue golf shirt and khaki pants. His ID badge brushed the table as he bent over.

"Hi," I said. "Am I late?"

He shook his head, smiling. "I'm early," he lied. "A bad habit."

"I'm always behind," I confessed. "That's worse."

He pushed the menu in my direction. "Not to rush you, but . . ."

I nodded. "You don't have much time. I understand." This was not going quite the way I'd planned. I felt as if I'd lost the upper hand somehow, and I needed Authority if I was going to extract the truth from him. At least, that's what I had assured myself was the purpose of this meeting.

I studied the menu, salads first. Then it caught my eye, a meat-loaf sandwich. Suddenly I really, really wanted a meat-loaf sandwich, something I hadn't had in years. I wondered if it came with bacon. Probably not. "I'll have . . . um, number fourteen," I told the waitress, lacking the courage of my convictions.

"Meat-loaf sandwich?" she asked, in stentorian tones.

I could have sworn that heads turned and conversation stopped, like one of those old EF Hutton commercials (*When EF Hutton speaks, people listen. . . .*). I half expected someone to get up from his chair and talk me out of it. Even the waitress seemed to disapprove.

I nodded faintly. "Chicken salad," Alexei said, "and I'd like pickles, please."

We both ordered iced tea. "I learned to like it in Washington," Alexei explained.

After the ordering, he looked at me expectantly.

"Here's the thing," I said, lowering my voice. "I've talked to the computer expert I told you about, the guy who could possibly write a letter?"

He nodded.

"He says you were a very prominent nuclear scientist in the former Soviet Union," I said, watching his reaction.

He didn't look in the least discomposed. "Go on," he said.

"Go on?" I asked. "Is it true?"

"That's probably not an unfair statement," he said mildly.

"Why didn't you tell me?" I demanded. "This is no time for modesty. This sort of information alone will probably get you an approval from the INS."

He smiled. "If your expert told you that much, he might have hinted at the reason I didn't tell you. Am I right?"

I was surprised at his directness. I decided to respond in kind. Not that I had any choice. "He said you sort of disappeared after Chernobyl. He suggested . . . well, he said your skills were so valuable you might . . ." I couldn't think how to finish the sentence.

He did it for me. "Have sold out to the highest bidder, you mean?"

"Something like that," I said.

"Well, it's possible. I certainly had offers," he said.

"And?"

"And I didn't. I could have, but I didn't." He searched in his pockets. "Now I really do need a smoke. Do you mind?"

"You can't smoke here," I said, hating it that I sounded like someone's prissy aunt. "It's a restaurant."

"Even outside?" He looked surprised.

"Yes," I told him. "Anyway, I thought you quit."

"It's a rare indulgence, but sometimes necessary," he said.

"Like a meat-loaf sandwich," I observed, as the waitress put a mammoth sandwich and a mound of fries down in front of me. The chicken salad looked anorexic by comparison.

"Is it good?" he asked with a grin. "I've never had one."

I pushed the plate toward him. "If I give you half, will you tell me the truth?"

He eyed the sandwich. "You drive a hard bargain," he said. He picked it up gingerly, as if it might contain explosives. He opened his mouth wide and took a bite. After an eternity of chewing, he smiled. "Not bad," he said. "Actually, I was going to tell you anyway."

"In that case you owe me a pickle slice," I said.

He offered me his plate, and I speared the pickle with my fork. "Okay, now we're even," I said, "so tell me."

AFTER CHERNOBYL, Alexei told me, many of the Soviet Union's nuclear physicists were drafted into the cleanup. The world's scrutiny notwithstanding, the results, for various reasons, were not an unmitigated success. "People are probably too frightened of radiation," Alexei said. "There's a lot of fearmongering."

As someone who had read *On the Beach* in high school, I found this view surprising, not to mention a little disconcerting, and said so.

"Well," he said, "a lot of people agree with you. The area around Chernobyl has been turned into a giant parking lot without cars. Some people still live there, but, let's face it, that's probably not the best option."

"Plus, I've read that Chernobyl is leaking again," I told him.

"Yes, I've read that, too," he said.

In response to the accident, an elite team of scientists was formed to develop strategies to prevent similar disasters. Not just at nuclear power plants, but also measures to safeguard the many thousands of nuclear warheads warehoused around the country.

"Because of the defense concerns," Alexei said, "the identity of the team was top secret. Your computer guy is right—we did 'disappear' from public view—from conferences and panels and university faculties. I told myself it was worth it, that the potential safety of millions of people was at stake, and not just in the Soviet Union."

He reached absently for one of my french fries, then realized it was mine and stopped. I inched the plate toward him. "Be my guest," I said. "So what happened?" I asked him.

"You have to understand that I can't tell you anything more about what I did for those years," he said. "I'm sure I don't have to explain why." After the Soviet breakup, he said, the potential for nuclear nightmares increased a thousandfold. With an economy in ruins, the state could no longer afford to maintain the reactors. Disgruntled, underpaid soldiers tried to sell weapons to rogue states like North Korea or to individual terrorists. "You've heard the story about the officer who prevented nuclear war when obsolete equipment identified a flock of birds as incoming missiles from the United States?" he asked. "He was given the order to retaliate, *and he didn't push the button.* There were near misses like that all the time."

"So what happened to you?" I asked him.

His hands stilled, and he let out a long breath. "My father told me that sometimes in combat, soldiers in desperate situations have an irresistible urge to give themselves up," he said. "Not to capture, but to death. Just to get it over with." He rubbed his eyes. "Maybe I'm not explaining this well. Maybe it's like having some terrible disease. For a while you fight it, and then you're just . . . resigned."

He looked at me. The Russian jokes, the banter, the cosmopolitan ease with which he moved between two cultures were a cover for this naked anguish, and for just a moment he let me see it. "It was something like that," he said. "Russia is a country with more than its share of corruption, not enough money for appropriate safeguards, homegrown terrorists, and a military that is unstable, underpaid, and unhappy. There is a thriving black market." He shook his head. "What does anyone think will happen? It is not possible," he said slowly, "to prevent some kind of nuclear disaster from happening. Not possible." His eyes held a look that chilled me to the bone. "Once I realized that, I could not go on," he said.

"You had a breakdown?" I whispered.

He smiled grimly. "Not quite that dramatic. But I couldn't face it anymore. Not another day, not another sleepless night. So I quit, or I tried to." He drummed his fingers on the table. "I really need a cigarette," he said.

"Have another french fry instead," I said, pushing the plate at him. "It's almost as bad for you."

"I know," he said, picking up two. "I should give them up, too."

"So you left your job," I prompted him.

He shook his head. "It's not that simple," he said. "It's not exactly a job, is it? What I had to do was . . . arrange my disappearance, I guess you'd say. I ran away. There wasn't any other choice."

"Why?" I asked.

His look told me I was naive. "For the same reason a lot of less-than-upright people have tried to buy my services," he said. "I know things. Nuclear-warhead disposition, power-plant sites, construction vulnerability." He lowered his voice. "I could even make a bomb, if I had to. It's not that hard."

I shuddered involuntarily, which did not escape his notice.

"Precisely," he said. "So now do you understand why I'm tempted to get into a different field altogether? I took a postdoc fellowship at a university and then got the job at SLAC, but even that is—what's the expression?—too close to home. And if I did start work on the big international project in Germany, the rumors would start up again. It might be nice to do something restful and lucrative for a change. At least till the end of the world comes."

He sounded as if he were only half joking.

The last bite of sandwich turned to sawdust in my mouth. I swallowed with difficulty. "This is the scariest conversation I've had since . . ." There was no need to finish the sentence.

This time he was the one who touched me. He put his hand over my arm, and the warmth was surprisingly comforting. "I know," he said. "I'm sorry. I shouldn't have told you. It's not something you should share, even with a friend."

"Yes, of course you should. I asked you. I wanted to know."

He shook his head. "You can't stare down this fear, Lynn. All you can do is inventory the possibilities. It can poison you. It ruined my marriage, my hopes, my career. That is why it has to stop." He had not removed his hand, and I put my other hand on top of his.

"I'll help you any way I can," I said, in a far-from-businesslike manner.

"I know you will," he said. He smiled.

I had a thought. "Alexei?"

"Yes?"

I lowered my voice conspiratorially. "Do they know where you are?"

"Who?"

"Whoever employed you before," I said.

"The Russian Ministry of Defense? Probably."

"And?"

"And if I get a green card," he said, "I'll be safe."

"Safe?"

He smiled grimly. "I'm a dangerous man, Lynn. They want me back."

"Well, they can't have you," I told him. "Not if I have anything to say about it."

CHAPTER 24

To: Lynn
From: Alexei

Lunch at your office next week? I promise—no more
gloomy topics! Let's talk about you next time.

To: Alexei
From: Lynn

What makes you think that isn't a gloomy topic?

To: Lynn
From: Alexei

I have eyes, Ms. Bartlett.

Ever since Alexei's revelations, I'd been feeling like
some Calvinist sure that the Dreadful Day of Judgment
was close at hand. The happiness of everyday life—the
daily routine, the security, the freedom—was a chance
event that could disappear at any time. It altered your
priorities, that's for sure. I mean, would you want to be

spending your time doing the dirty laundry during Armageddon?

So what did I want to spend my remaining days doing? I was smart, I was (or at least I had been) successful, and a certified genius from the Soviet Union not only entrusted his future to my competence but found me attractive to boot. Whatever I decided to do with my life, what I did *not* plan to do, to use my father's expression, was take any more guff.

THE HUGHESES WERE THE FIRST to feel the effects.

"Um," Jack said to me one morning, "I've been finding a bunch of garbage in the family room. Apple cores and banana peels, stuff like that. Um, is Patrick leaving his trash in there?"

I took a leisurely sip of my coffee. "Afraid so," I said.

He looked puzzled. "Why would he suddenly turn into a slob? Do you think he's upset about something?"

"I imagine he's upset about a lot of things," I told him. "But there's nothing sudden about it."

"What do you mean?"

"I mean I stopped picking up after him. That's why his garbage is still in there."

"Why didn't you say something? I didn't know you were doing that."

He didn't *want* to know either. Family life is easier with blinders on. I shrugged. "I've been sort of busy cleaning up other people's messes at the office. I just got tired of doing it at home, too."

"I'll take care of it," he said. "I'm sorry."

"That's not the big issue, Jack," I said.

"No, I suppose not," he said. "But the job market's really tough now, you know that."

"I've noticed," I said dryly. "But we're still coming up on six months."

"I know, but . . ." His voice trailed off.

I didn't help him.

"You seem a little distant," he said eventually. "Is everything all right?"

Of course it wasn't. "I'm sure it will be," I said.

"I WONDER IF YOU FORGOT to give Jack my message about the invitations," Janet said on the telephone.

She'd called with the information that the printers were expecting a check in advance. Far in advance, apparently, since the wedding was still eight months away, and even the locale wasn't definite yet.

"I didn't forget," I told her.

"Well, did you tell him?" she demanded.

"Of course I did. If there's nothing else, I have a lot—"

"He didn't call back," she said in an accusing tone.

I'm shocked. "I gave him the message," I repeated. "I'd leave a message with his secretary, if I were you. Sometimes when he gets really busy, he forgets things."

"*I* know that," she said. Her tone suggested that leaving a message with Jack's secretary was precisely what she thought she was doing. "You know," she said, just when I was ready to hang up, "Jack doesn't seem very enthusiastic about this wedding."

"Mmm," I said, in what I hoped was a noncommittal tone.

"You wouldn't happen to know anything about that, would you?" she asked sweetly.

I sighed. "What do you mean?"

"I just wondered if the explanation might be that the wedding is interfering with some plans the two of you might have. I know you were looking for another house. I thought that might be putting pressure on Jack not to—"

"Stop right there," I said.

"I hope I'm not offending you," she said.

Of course, when people say that, that's precisely what they do hope, and moreover they hope to get away with it by pretending politeness. "The only pressure I'm putting on Jack," I told her, "is to level with you and Meredith about how much he can afford to contribute to this wedding. Otherwise I'm staying out of it."

"Jack's rolling in money," she said.

"Open your eyes, Janet," I said wearily. "Haven't you noticed what's happened in Silicon Valley? Why don't you two just sit down and discuss it frankly and stop playing games?"

"It's your *business,* isn't it?" she asked. "Jack's rescuing your law firm, isn't he? That's why—"

I hung up on her.

"I DON'T KNOW WHAT'S GOTTEN INTO ME," I said, taking a serious gulp of some wine that had doubtless

emerged from a container with square corners. Someone less oenophilic had brought the refreshments this
time. The other Anne Boleyn–ites nodded sagely, waiting for me to go on. "I mean, I thought I was sure this
marriage is what I wanted, and now I'm not." Not only
that, but here I was babbling away about my personal
life to, with the exception of Kay, a group of relative
strangers. I felt as guilty as if I'd spilled my guts to the
National Enquirer or *60 Minutes*.

"We've all been there," Claire Billings, the doctor,
said. "You just have to decide if it's worth all the has-
sles." She sighed. "Sometimes it's not."

"See, last time you were here, you were far more
concerned with behaving decorously," Melanie, the
Suburban Bombshell, suggested, surprisingly. "That
made it easy for all of them to take advantage of you.
Even your husband."

"So now I'm turning into a bitch instead," I said. "I
still believe in behaving decorously, on the whole, but
I don't seem to be able to do it."

"Being assertive about what you want doesn't make
you a bitch," Kay said.

"And if it does, so what?" said Claire. "It's better
than being a doormat."

"Repeat after me: 'I am not a doormat,' " Melanie said.
The others laughed. "That's our mantra," Kay said.

"I don't think I'm a doormat," I said. "But I don't
think I'm getting much respect either. I mean, I've got
a lot of important things going on in my professional
life, and my husband is focusing on why his son is sud-

denly leaving garbage in the family room. I'm really tired of running interference for my husband with his ex-wife, of fending off her innuendos about the reasons for my actions, and of dealing with what is essentially an appalling lack of manners on the part of my stepchildren. It's such a . . . dispiriting way to spend your life. I have other things to focus on, and I just don't want to do that anymore."

"Amen," said Claire.

"So how do you feel about your husband now?" Melanie asked me.

Amazingly, I was not offended by the frankness of these questions. In fact, it was a kind of relief to get things out in the open.

"I don't know," I said. "Of course I still love him, but the context has changed. I admire his loyalty to his family, but I didn't expect that they would so often come first. This is sort of over the top, but . . ." I hesitated.

"Just say it," Kay urged. "You'll feel better."

The others nodded. It was an organizational mantra that the less you held back, the better.

"Sometimes I think my life is so arid," I said finally. "I mean, where's the passion? Maybe I settled. Or maybe I'm just evolving a set of elaborate rationalizations."

"For what?" Melanie asked.

"For leaving him," I said, shocked at the words after they came out of my mouth, but not taking them back either. At least I didn't say, *For having an affair.*

"Robert died," Lorraine, the elderly woman whose stepson had abducted her husband from the nursing home following a stroke, said suddenly.

"Oh, Lorraine, that's so terrible," Kay said. "We're so sorry." The others murmured their sympathy.

"I never got to see him again. I wasn't even treated as his widow when he died," she said. "I wasn't invited to the funeral." She shook her head sadly. "I should have fought for him when I had the chance. I shouldn't have just let him go."

"I'm sure there wasn't anything you could have done," Kay said soothingly.

Lorraine raised her head and looked directly at me. "There's always something you could have done," she said.

"ARE YOU REALLY THINKING OF LEAVING JACK?" Kay asked afterward, over coffee.

"I was almost as surprised as you were to hear myself say it," I told her. "I really don't know." I took a big gulp of coffee, then another. "Maybe I'm just tired," I said.

"I gathered that," Kay said. She gestured at the coffee cup. "Go ahead, fuel up."

"I'm going to pay for it later," I said. "I can feel all that cheap wine fighting the caffeine for dominance."

"So what's really wrong?" she said after a moment.

"Do you ever stop to think about how short life really is?" I asked.

"Sure. So many houses, so little time," she said.

"I'm serious," I said.

"So am I. So life is short. Make the most of it—is that what you were going to say? Find something that gives you joy? Don't waste your time on the trivial?"

"Something like that," I said.

"So get a T-shirt," she said.

"I realize it sounds trite," I said.

"Good." She poured half a pitcher of cream into her coffee and swirled it around. "I've thought of leaving Mike, too," she said, still looking down at her cup.

"Why?"

She shrugged. "The usual reasons. He's never home. He lives for his work. My stepdaughter hates me." She studied her magnificent diamond wedding ring. "Also, he has absolutely no sense of humor. None. And he tells orthopedic-surgery stories at the dinner table."

I laughed, assuming she was only half serious.

"I'm not kidding," she said.

"Then why do you stick around?" I asked her.

She spread her hands, palms out. "I can't afford the very big house in Woodside on my own," she said.

"I don't for one minute believe that's the only reason you stay with him," I told her.

"Thanks for the vote of confidence, but don't be too sure. I'd lose a lot financially if I left Mike. Socially, too. I don't fancy being just another divorcée real-estate agent showing condos in San Jose. I don't kid myself—I get a lot of business because of who my husband is." She sighed. "Also . . ."

"Also?"

"I don't want to look like a loser," she said. "And I *really* don't want to give *her* the satisfaction of saying 'I told you so.' "

"Who?" I asked.

"Suzanne. The ex–Mrs. Burks," she reminded me. "*She* left him because he was never home. He lived for his work. He probably even told her about the latest hip-replacement technique over a plate of prime rib." She dabbed at her mouth with her napkin. "Trust me, that's enough to put you off rare meat for at least a month."

I laughed. "Well, presumably at least, her own daughter didn't hate her."

"I wouldn't be too sure," Kay said thoughtfully. "She seems to hate just about everyone."

We sipped our coffee in silence. *Jack isn't like Mike,* I thought. *He's funny and tender and generous.* At least he was. We hadn't laughed together about anything much in a long time.

"So anyway," Kay said, "it all comes down to the bargain you made, doesn't it? We each get some things, and we have to give some things up, too. You have to decide for yourself when it stops being a good deal."

"Do you believe what Lorraine said? That there's always something you can do?"

"Probably," she said. "But you have to want to make the effort. Otherwise what's the point?"

"What about love?" I asked, sounding, I'm sure, like some dewy, censorious adolescent. But I couldn't believe she really took such a calculating point of view.

She shrugged. "What about it? Mike loves me, or at least I think he does. I love him. Jack loves you. You love him. But if love were enough, we wouldn't be having this conversation, would we?"

"I guess not," I said.

CHAPTER 25

I wrote Alexei's petition myself, focusing on his activities at Stanford and downplaying his career in the Soviet Union. I made references to top-secret work so awesomely classified and significant that it could not be discussed on the pages of a mere INS document, and hoped that would do the trick. Ilya Kopylov backed up the assertions. It was still an impressive case, but not as exceptional as it might have been if I'd been allowed to document what Alexei had told me. There was only one small hitch.

"The company has agreed to help with the legal fees," Alexei told me over sandwiches.

We were alone in the remnant of my offices; I'd already found Ronnie another job as an office administrator/paralegal at a medium-size white-shoe law firm. It was a step up from Grady & Bartlett (even in the firm's palmiest days), and I was happy for her. Adam had decided to seek his fortune in Los Angeles, where he was going to write screenplays by night

and work as a lifeguard by day. "A lifeguard?" I'd .
asked.

"Just for the summer," he said. "It's research."

"What do your parents think about it?" I couldn't
help asking.

He shrugged. "I promised to come home if I don't
make it in a year," he said.

"Define 'make it,' " I said.

He grinned. "Precisely."

Brooke was still officially employed, but since there
wasn't much to do, I rarely saw her. Boxes were
stacked everywhere; I was moving out into a tinier,
much cheaper space at the end of the month. Meanwhile I couldn't find anything and kept unpacking the
things I'd already packed. It made me crazy and frustrated, which must have been why I welcomed Alexei's
appearance with such enthusiasm.

"I've brought lunch," he said, bearing a Draeger's
sack that wafted wonderful odors. "Sandwiches." He
smiled. "Not meat loaf, though. Nobody has it for
takeout."

"That's fine," I said. "I'd rather have it as a special
treat. Familiarity breeds contempt."

He smiled. "No it doesn't," he said. "That's such an
American way of thinking. There is comfort—probably even more—in the familiar."

The way he said it made me wonder if he was home-
sick. "Are we talking about meat loaf?" I asked.

"And then there is that admirable American directness," he said, reaching into the sack and placing two

wrapped sandwiches in front of me. "I've brought shrimp with . . . sprouts, I think, and turkey with almonds or maybe pecans. I can't remember. You choose."

"What about half and half?" I asked. "We can share."

"Okay," he said, but he didn't make a move toward the food. He managed to look almost insolently relaxed.

"What were you going to say? About the fee?" I asked, to cover the slightly exhilarating nervousness I was feeling.

He sat back in the chair. "The company will reimburse me for half the cost of the petition," he said. "But they have their own immigration counsel, and they want to run it by them first."

"That's okay," I said, although of course it wasn't. Competitors had every incentive to find fault with your work and none whatsoever to approve it; plus, they could hold up the process for weeks. "Who is it, do you know?"

"Elson Larimer, I think."

It would be. "Well, fine," I said insincerely. "But remind them we need to file quickly, won't you? Sometimes these things can languish on someone's desk for months."

"Languish," he said. "English is such an incredible language."

One of the manifestations of Alexei's intelligence was his curiosity about virtually everything. "Yes," I said. "You're not eating," I pointed out after a moment.

He smiled and reached for a sandwich half. "So tell me about you," he said. "I said it was your turn, remember?"

"What do you want to know?" I asked.

"Whatever you want to tell me," he said. "You have my complete biography from the petition, and I don't know a thing about you."

"I don't know where to start," I said, blushing. I was carrying on like a seventh-grader at an eighth-grade dance. "I'm bad at math," I said finally. "Seriously bad."

He laughed. "Thanks for warning me. I'll remember to double-check the bill." He looked at me. "Are you married?"

I nodded.

"Children?"

"Stepchildren," I said. "Adults."

"Do you like them?"

"Not excessively," I said. "We get along."

"And your husband?"

"We get along, too," I told him.

He shook his head, smiling. "I meant, what does he do?"

"He was a lawyer, too. Right now he's a consultant and part owner in an Internet company." I felt acutely uncomfortable talking about Jack with Alexei, as if I were betraying one or the other.

Alexei was watching me. "You don't like to talk about him," he said.

I shook my head. "Not really," I said. I couldn't exactly say why. Well, possibly I could have, but I didn't want to. One way or the other, I had the feeling I was going to get my heart broken.

"Do you think," he said slowly, "we could have lunch sometime? A real lunch, I mean. Not this."

"I'd like that very much," I said.

I DON'T THINK other people thought of me as particularly vulnerable or susceptible to getting hurt. Not because of some inherent chirpy optimism or general obtuseness (at least I hope not), but because of that straightforward self-possession Jack thought he had spotted in me the first time we met. But now I realized that, far from demonstrating some admirable character trait, this inability to be touched was a manifestation of the poverty of my emotional life. I hadn't had that much to lose. Now I felt the fear of loss, the foreboding that nothing could be guaranteed. The conviction arose with increasing regularity, at least in my own thinking. That I would get hurt. That I might hurt someone else. That it might not matter.

"HOW ARE THE WEDDING PLANS COMING?" I asked Jack when we were alone in the bedroom. Patrick had gone out to dinner with friends, and they'd come back "just for a few minutes" to take over the living room. I felt parental and superfluous at the same time and retreated to the only part of the house that was completely off-limits to stepchildren. Even the cat seemed to hang out there more frequently.

Jack was wearing pajamas, a concession he'd made

to his son's presence in the house. He shrugged. "I don't know. They don't ask me anything. They just send the bills."

"That's the dad's role, I guess," I said lightly.

He pushed Brewer gently aside with his knee and slid under the covers. "Does he *have* to be on the bed with us? I get leg cramps from not being able to turn over."

"He gets scared when strangers are in the house," I said. "I'll put him out after Patrick's friends leave."

"Whenever that is," he muttered. "They looked like they were settling in for the night."

"Well, it must be hard on Patrick not having a place to entertain his friends," I said, sounding, I thought, appropriately sympathetic.

Jack looked at me suspiciously. "There are restaurants," he said, "and clubs. Listen to them. It sounds like a fraternity party out there."

As someone who had once lived in the same metropolitan area as San Diego State, I could have told him he was dead wrong. "He can't afford restaurants and clubs," I said instead. "And anyway," I added, using his line, "it's only temporary."

He looked as if he would have liked to respond, but by now the topic was dangerous. Silence trailed the mention of Patrick's name in any conversation. What he did say was, "There's something I've been meaning to bring up, Lynn. I don't want to make too much of this, but I don't think you should have discussed my finances with Janet."

I closed the book I'd been planning to start before bed, the latest Lisa Scottoline, with regret. "I didn't *discuss* anything," I told him. "She hinted that the reason you seemed to be less than enthusiastic about Meredith's wedding was that what you've referred to as *your* finances are going to support my law firm."

He looked startled, as if he'd never considered the possibility. "We agreed that . . ."

"That we'd keep that separate. I know. But Janet apparently doesn't, not that it's any of her business. Moreover, she told me you were, and I quote, 'rolling in money.' "

He looked away. "Good God," he muttered.

"Jack, why don't you just level with her? That's all I suggested, really. That you two sit down and have a frank discussion about finances."

He looked away. "It's embarrassing," he said indistinctly.

"So is bankruptcy," I said. "That's where we're headed if you try to float the cost of this wedding on your own."

"It won't come to that," he said. "Look, I don't expect you to understand why I don't want to disappoint Meredith—"

"This isn't about Meredith," I said, "although I really think you should be honest with her, too. It's about Janet. You don't want to expose your own financial situation, but you're perfectly willing to expose me—falsely, I might add—as someone who can't manage her own business without your intervention. Try to see it from my perspective, Jack. I'm the one who had to sit there and listen to her."

"You wouldn't have if you hadn't accepted her lunch invitation," he pointed out.

"A mistake I don't plan to make again," I said. "But—"

The sound of music—some ghastly Generation X, Y, or Z anthem—suddenly assaulted my ears. "They'll blow out the speakers," I said worriedly. *My* speaker*s*, in fact. "The Magnepans may not be able to handle that much bass."

Jack sighed and threw back the covers, displacing the cat. "Sorry, big guy," he said. "I'll deal with the acoustical terrorists," he told me, "if you'll promise to drop the topic of paying for the wedding."

"I'll drop it willingly if you tell Janet the truth," I said. "Otherwise she'll keep on with the insinuations, not to mention the importunings." This might have been going too far, but the boom boom boom was starting to resound in my head.

Jack ran his fingers through his hair in exasperation. "Where does that leave us, Lynn?"

He folded his arms over his chest. We stayed stiff and motionless while the volume jolted us like an artillery shelling.

Boom boom boom.

"At a stalemate, I guess," I told him, covering my ears.

CHAPTER 26

Much to my surprise, the detritus from the previous night's festivities was nowhere in sight when I went out to the kitchen to get my breakfast. Jack had left the house early, before I was even awake, so I was planning a quiet cup of coffee and some toast along with the *San Jose Mercury*. The *San Francisco Chronicle* was more frivolous and more fun (where else could you find a lengthy exposé of Danielle Steel's twenty-odd parking permits?), but the techies and serious Valley entrepreneurs all read the *Mercury,* and Jack's business life depended on keeping up.

I started another pot of coffee and sat down at the kitchen table, bleary from lack of sleep. I am not at my best in the mornings, and lately I'd been plagued with bouts of insomnia, the multiple sources of which probably do not need to be analyzed. I'd finally drifted off when the stereo shut down just before midnight, but 4 A.M. found me, as my mother used to say in a throwback to her rural girlhood, bright-eyed and bushy-tailed. Now I was anything but.

"Hi," Patrick said, striding into the kitchen and startling me into almost spilling my coffee. I hadn't seen him before ten in the morning since he'd moved in. Moreover, he was wearing a good shirt and decent pants. Like everyone young, he was noticeably more able to shake off the effects of a late night (and whatever else) than were those of us with a few more years under our belts. At that moment, propping up my eyelids, I sort of hated him.

"Good morning," I said, swallowing the impulse to say, *You're up early*. "I've made a new pot."

"Thanks. And, um, thanks for last night, too. I mean, I know it was loud and all. We just . . ."

I nodded, unsure what I was agreeing with.

"I might be getting a job," he announced.

"That's great," I said, in a tepid tone. I knew better than to shout, *Hallelujah!* even if that's what I was feeling. "What is it?"

"I don't exactly have it yet," he said. "I've got an interview today."

I was glad I had not been too effusive in my congratulations. "That's a start, though," I said.

"Yeah, I guess."

"So what's the interview?" I prompted him.

He looked away and mumbled something so indistinct I wondered if it was "Jack in the Box."

"Sorry?" I said.

He sighed. "It's in Dad's old firm," he said. "Paralegal."

"Oh, well. That's great," I said.

"I know what you're thinking," he said. "I don't have any training, and Dad's just getting me the job. But if they hire me, I'd start as a kind of assistant, and if that works out, they'll pay for paralegal training."

"Great," I said for the third time.

"The thing is," Patrick said, with unexpected candor, "I really wanted to find something on my own."

Even though I thought part of his problem was that Jack kept rescuing him from his failures, I was not entirely unsympathetic. "It's a tough economy," I said. "And anyway, lots of people get help from their parents," I added truthfully. "Business is all about connections of one sort or another, and so are a lot of other things. The movies, for example." I smiled. "Or politics."

"That's not necessarily the most flattering comparison," he pointed out. At least he smiled in return.

I laughed. "Well, but you take my point."

"Yes, and you take mine. It's kind of humiliating."

I couldn't believe we were having this conversation. "Cheer up," I said, deciding to venture a joke. "You can always blow the interview."

He looked startled for a moment. "Yes," he said, looking rather buoyed at the prospect. "I could, couldn't I?"

BROOKE GREETED ME at my tiny new office as if we were still colleagues. I suppose in a way we were, since I'd agreed she could work out of the new space till she found another job. I'd stopped paying her at the end of the month, which effectively ended most of whatever power I'd exerted. Now that she was on her way out, I felt less irritated by her presence and succumbed, in my weaker moments, to a nostalgic affection for her as the last remnant of Grady & Bartlett. It was, like the retrophilia for bell-bottoms and lava lamps, entirely without a rational basis.

"Hi! Guess what?" Brooke's perkiness was apparently immune to both unemployment and lack of space. She waved at me from her cramped corner, her work area a small table the last tenant had left. My own desk was pretty modest, too; I'd tried to sell the one I bought when Harrison offered me the partnership, because it was too big for my diminished circumstances. Unfortunately, there was such a glut of expensive office furniture on the market that even Goodwill was overstocked. I had to put it into storage and make do with something tiny, cheap, and serviceable from Cost Plus.

"What?" I asked.

"Strela got a denial," she said breathlessly.

"Shit," I said. My heart sank. I'd been hoping for a seamless approval. It was unwise to count on anything from the INS; each agent is, by the organization's own admission, something of a loose cannon, and the visa-classification process was anything but scientific. Nobody could really stop you if you wanted to reject an applicant because your baby sister once got stood up by someone with a Russian-sounding last name. Still,

Alexei had a good case, and now I was going to have to respond to a bunch of issues before he got approved. "You mean a kickback," I corrected her automatically. "They have to give you a chance to respond before you get a denial."

"I *know* that, Lynn," she said. "But nevertheless it is a denial. See for yourself."

I took the paper she was holding. "Jesus, you're right," I said. "It must be some officer who doesn't know what he's doing. They don't even give any reasons." I turned the documents around to see if by chance I was missing something. "I can't believe this," I said.

"What will you do?" Brooke asked.

"I'm not sure," I said. "Try to check it out, I guess. If I can't pin it down, I suppose we can always refile, but the backlog is already huge, and Alexei could run out of time."

"I thought he was extending his H-1," she said.

"Well, it's complicated," I told her.

"Okay," she said. "Let me know if I can do anything to help."

I looked at her with surprise. "That's very kind, but it would hardly be fair. I'm not even paying you," I said.

"I know, but I'm not exactly busy," she said.

"Well, thanks," I told her. "How's the job search going?" No one had called me for references, so I had an idea, but I thought it would be polite to ask anyway.

She made a face. "They seem to like my résumé, but when I go to an interview . . ." She looked at me.

"Lynn, I know you'll tell me the truth. Is there something about me that turns people off?"

I had to bite my tongue, literally, to keep from answering that one. After all, we were still crammed together into a small space, and absolute truth in a situation like this was probably dangerous. "Um . . ." I began.

"I mean, I know I come across as really smart, but I don't *intend* to show up the interviewers. It's just that some of them are so geeky. Do you think that could be it?"

"Very likely," I said solemnly.

She sighed. "You can't imagine what a burden it's been all my life to be labeled gifted," she said.

"I guess not," I agreed.

"THEY KNOW," Alexei said, when I told him. "Someone's throwing up roadblocks."

We were sitting on a blanket having a picnic lunch in a beautiful little park in the foothills of the coastal mountains, an informality that was entirely suggestive and entirely my fault. Since the park was open only to Palo Alto residents, there was almost no one there in the middle of the week. (You can't afford to live in Palo Alto unless you work.) As I was now a resident of Los Altos, I hadn't been there in years, but today there was no one at the entrance checking IDs. The park brought back all kinds of memories. Plus, I was pretty sure I wouldn't run into anyone I knew. Despite being the instigator of this *déjeuner sur l'herbe,* I felt guilty over possibilities that were becoming increasingly less distant.

"You can't know that," I told him. "The INS isn't a scientific organization. They screw up all the time."

"What makes you think scientific organizations don't screw up?" he asked with a smile.

"All the more reason not to jump to conclusions. It's probably just a mistake."

He shook his head. "I wish I could believe that."

"Then try to, at least till I investigate," I told him. "We can always refile if we have to. Aren't Russians supposed to be notoriously pessimistic?"

"*Fatalistic,*" he corrected me. "Just like lawyers are supposed to be sharks. There's some truth behind every stereotype, don't you think?"

"Not that one. Lawyers are always getting a bad rap," I said.

He brushed my cheek with his finger, which caused a surge of sensation—neither unexpected nor unwelcome—all the way to the soles of my feet. "Not this one," he said.

"Alexei . . ." I drifted off, enmeshed in some dazed state of desire. I was unable to think. Scratch that. I didn't *want* to think.

"I don't want to go back, Lynn," he said. "The last time I was there, a woman tried to sell herself to me for three dollars. When I refused, she offered to throw in her younger sister, who looked about ten." He shook his head. "Some Mafia guy lives in my old house. I saw the BMW out in front. Everyone is depressed. I don't want to go back there," he repeated.

I touched his hand. "I've told you before I'll help you any way I can," I said.

"I know that," he said. He put his hand behind my head and drew me to him. He kissed me and then pulled back, seeking permission. I imagine I gave it to him, because the next one, the definitive kiss, left no questions unanswered. He put his arms around me as if he were encircling me in a cloak. "I didn't misread you, then?" he asked.

"No," I told him. "I'm afraid you didn't." I'd probably been sending up semaphores of lust. My self-discipline had deserted me entirely, and I was waving good-bye to it with unbridled enthusiasm.

"It's okay," he said. "We don't have to do anything. We don't have to decide anything right now. There's time."

I could feel the dry grass poking up through the blanket, tickling my arm. I'd almost forgotten we were outside. I'd almost forgotten just about everything. "The thing is . . . ," I said, looking into his eyes, which were very dark. You could lose yourself in those eyes, if you weren't careful. "The thing is, I don't want to wait."

I felt him relax against me. The possibilities were now clear. He stroked my hair. "Shall we . . . ?"

"I don't know where to go," I said. It seemed such a ridiculous thing to be hung up on, now that I was going to go charging into unknown, possibly life-changing territory, consequences be damned. But even in my love-bead days I would have drawn the line at having sex in a public park.

"I do," he told me. He looked at the untouched picnic lunch. "Do you want to eat first?" he asked.

"No," I said.

CHAPTER 27

A lexei lived in the poolside guesthouse of a Stanford professor and his wife, the ex-CFO of a dot-com business that had suffered the stereotypical rise and fall. They'd bought the house on her options exercised and sold in boom times, so they were safe. The professor paid his debt to the underclass by renting out his guesthouse at a nominal charge to visiting faculty or postdocs.

It was very nice, although I was in no mood to evaluate the furnishings. All the life in my body had collected in one place, and I had to bite my lip to keep from crying out when he touched me.

Don't analyze this, I told myself. There were forces welling up that waylaid my conscience. I wanted just to be wanted, even if only this once, without anything else getting in the way. I wanted to surrender.

So I did.

Afterward we lay dozing on the bed, the afternoon sun coming in through the blinds. I tried to lie perfectly still; as soon as he woke up, I'd have to start thinking about leaving. The first departure, and probably not the last. I could see into a future of big lies and little ones, the probable unhappy denouement.

Russian joke:
A popular French magazine held a contest for the best short essay describing a typical morning.
The winning entry: "I wake up, eat breakfast, put on my clothes, and go home."

Eventually he woke up and stretched—I'd been lying on his arm. He looked at me and smiled. "What are you thinking?" he said.

"I was thinking how nice it would be to be French."

He propped himself up on one elbow, laughing. "Why would you think that?"

"Because then I could be puritanical about food and philosophical about sex, instead of the other way around," I told him.

"Lynn—" he said.

I put a finger over his lips. "Don't talk about it. Not just now."

He nodded.

Now that I had more leisure for inspection, I noticed that the room was very plainly furnished, like a motel on an interstate. There was nothing personal about it except the shelves of books with titles in several languages. It had the air of being inhabited by someone ready to move on at a moment's notice. At least it was neat, a quality I now realized I had undervalued at the outset of two marriages.

I looked at my watch. "I have to go," I told him.

"I know," he said, pressing his hand to my face.

"Alexei," I asked, "have you ever read *Anna Karenina*?"

"No, I haven't," he said.

"Neither have I," I lied.

"I HOPE YOU DON'T MIND," Janet said when I opened my front door and discovered her enthroned in my living room, "but we had some things to discuss, and Jack preferred to meet here."

"Not at all," I said shortly. There was so much going on in my head that all I wanted was to be alone.

Jack looked irritated, but not at me. "Come and join us," he said. "Please."

Janet looked around with an air of mild approbation. "I've been meaning to tell you, Lynn, you've done such nice things with the house. I *know* none of that was Jack's doing." She cast him the fond, tolerant look an overindulgent owner might bestow upon a mischievous dog, which irritated *me*.

"Actually, it was mostly the decorator's doing," I said. "But thank you."

"I tried to reach you all afternoon," Jack said, "but your cell phone was off."

"Sorry," I said. "I turned it off at lunch, and then I must have forgotten to turn it back on."

"I called your office," he said.

"I've been trying to track down some information about a client, and I had a meeting," I told him. How easily the lie came to mind, and how hard it was to say it. I suppose that if things went on, lying would become second nature. The realization made me intensely uncomfortable.

"Well," Jack said, "Janet said you suggested we go over the finances for the wedding, and I thought you'd want to be in on the discussion."

"Thank you," I said, "but whatever you two decide is all right with me. As long as everyone is in full possession of the facts."

Janet looked as if she'd bitten into a lemon. "I hadn't realized, of course, about the tax problem."

Jack and I said nothing.

She picked up her glass and stared into it, then took a big swig. "Vodka tonic," she said to me, by way of explanation. "No one makes them like Jack."

I bet.

"The thing is," she continued, "a lot of the arrangements are already made. I'm afraid we planned things on a rather grander scale than if we'd known . . ."

I refused to help her. I didn't look at Jack but kept my gaze focused on her face. I hope she squirmed, at least inwardly.

"The problem is, you see, that it's much too late to cancel now, so I'm afraid . . ."

Jack leaned forward. *I* was afraid he was going to fall for that line without protest, so I intervened, although I had promised myself that I wouldn't. "The wedding is still months away, Janet. There would be cancellation fees for the caterers and the room, but we're certainly not locked in to the arrangements."

Janet played her trump card. "I suppose it might be possible," she sighed, "although of course we'd never find decent alternatives at this late date. Poor Meredith really has her heart set on this wedding, and it meant *so* much to her that her dad wanted to give it to her. She'll be very disappointed."

A look from Jack silenced me before I could respond. Now I understood why it was a bad idea for people to carry weapons. If I'd had something, I probably would have used it on her.

"How much have you committed for so far?" Jack asked.

Janet raised a fluttery hand. "About forty thousand dollars, I guess."

A mere drop in the bucket. Jack paled ever so slightly. "And how much of that can you and Valerio put up?" he asked.

She had the grace to look embarrassed. "Well, Valerio and I aren't exactly on the best of terms right now, so it's just me, I'm afraid." She consulted the ceiling. "I guess I might be able to come up with, oh, two thousand. Maybe twenty-five hundred."

That left a mere thirty-eight thousand—thiry-seven five, if she sold a few more pots. "What about Meredith?" I asked.

Janet looked at me with, I thought, feigned horror. "What about her?"

"Can she contribute? If an extravagant occasion means that much to her, perhaps she—"

Jack laid a hand on my arm. "Lynn, we won't ask my daughter to pay for her own wedding," he said.

I had definitely said "contribute to," not "pay for," but I reluctantly held my tongue.

"She's a *teacher,* Lynn," Janet reminded me. "She doesn't make very much money."

Which was precisely why Jack had been helping support her since she started work. You had to ask yourself whether saddling him with a mountain of debt for a wedding more befitting a society princess than a member of a profession supposedly marked by altruism was really an appropriate act of gratitude. Nevertheless, I had made a mistake. I had nudged Jack into an alliance with Janet, and if I weren't very careful, I'd find myself looking like the bad guy. I just didn't think I had the stamina for that kind of battle, at least not at the moment.

I stood. "Well, I'll just leave you two to sort things out," I said. I couldn't help adding, "I imagine there can be some room for compromise."

Jack stood, too, so Janet had no choice but to get up. "I've got to be going anyway," she said. "I promised Merry we'd go shopping for some curtains for her apartment." She looked around the living room. "Such a shame she and Justin can't afford a house. It wouldn't have to be anything grand, just something modest." Her look said, *Like this one.* Since the median price for a house in Santa Clara County was well over five hundred thousand dollars, even "modest" was far beyond reach. But I knew what she was getting at: *Wouldn't it be nice if you bought her a house?*

"We'll get back to you about the wedding," Jack said.

Janet looked from one to the other of us. "Yes," she said. "Talk it over."

I WENT INTO THE KITCHEN and started taking out the ingredients for a salad. I set them on the counter precisely, like surgical instruments. Jack came into the kitchen with the drink glasses, but I kept on rinsing and chopping.

"It's my night to cook," he said.

"That's okay," I said, without looking up. "I'm really not hungry. I'll fix us both a salad, and then you can have whatever else you want."

"I'm not very hungry either," he said.

"Just a salad, then?"

"Fine," he said.

Chop chop.

"Lynn," he said after a moment. "I know you're angry."

"I'm not angry," I said.

"What, then?"

"Do you really want to go into this now?" I asked him.

"Janet said we should talk things over," he pointed out.

I put the knife down, extremely carefully. "Otherwise we wouldn't be talking?"

"I didn't mean it that way," he said. He sighed. "Why don't you just say what you're thinking?"

Not a good idea. I dried my hands on a paper towel and turned to face him. "Okay," I said. "For the record, I'm not angry, I'm . . . dismayed."

"Dismayed," he repeated.

"Yes," I said. I tried to choose my words with care. "At the way we're being manipulated into paying for a wedding we can't afford."

His jaw tightened. "I'm perfectly well aware of what Janet is doing. This isn't about her; it's about Merry. And anyway, I've told you this is my responsibility, not yours."

"So you keep saying. Is that supposed to be comforting? We're supposed to be partners. A team. A *couple*."

"We are, in most things. But I had a life before you. I have obligations to my children. You must understand that."

"Of course I do. It seems to have escaped your attention that I had a life before you, too. Obligation is a two-way street, Jack. And what I see is your ex-wife egging Meredith on in ways that show very little consideration for either *your* opinion or *our* finances. You can't expect me to like it."

He ran his hands through his hair. "I know you had—have—a life of your own," he said, "but you didn't have children. It's not the same. I'm sorry if you're hurt or angry, but I can't ignore my children's needs, not even for you."

"There isn't any question of ignoring their *needs*," I said, knowing his visceral dislike of confrontation and trying to control my own anger. "But really, Jack, even though you want to please your daughter, even though you want to make it up to her for whatever it is you think you might have done to make her life less than perfect, I think you really have to tell her that you can't afford to finance this wedding on such a grand scale."

"I don't think I can do that," he said. "I'm not even sure it's the right thing to do."

I turned back toward the counter and dumped the contents of the chopping board into the salad bowl. "Then there's nothing more to be said, is there?"

CHAPTER 28

American optimism, in the end, proved no match for Russian fatalism.

When I got through to an officer at the INS (no mean feat), I was told that Alexei's petition had been "held up" at the special request of the State Department.

"He got a denial," I pointed out. "Not even a Notice of Action."

"I couldn't really comment on that," he said.

"Do you know the reason given for the holdup?" I asked.

"I couldn't really comment on that."

Translation: *no.*

"Well, do you know if they ran a security check?"

"I couldn't—well, actually, at this point, our computer system isn't yet compatible with the Interagency Border Inspection System."

Translation: *no.*

"But we expect to remedy that soon," he added brightly.

"Well, could it be that the denial is a mistake, and what's really intended is a hold until they cross-check him with the computer system?"

"That's possible, but I really can't say," he said. "Do you have any reason to believe your client is a security risk?" he asked.

"Of course not," I said.

"WHAT ARE YOU GOING TO DO NOW?" Brooke asked me.

I put the heels of my hands to my forehead and massaged my temples. It didn't help. "Christ, I'm not sure," I said. "The INS is so frustrating." It was a measure of how much things had changed that I would make a confession of uncertainty to Brooke. I didn't think she'd hesitate to use it against me, but I just didn't care anymore.

"Are you going to appeal?"

"Probably," I said. "But it's hard to build a case for appeal when I don't know what the grounds for denial were. If they even meant to deny him. You certainly couldn't tell from talking to the INS officer."

"Um . . . you probably wouldn't want to do this, but . . ."

"What?" I said. "I'm open to suggestions."

"I think you should . . ." She frowned. "I mean, it's just an idea, but . . ."

I resisted the impulse to grab her by the shoulders and shake her. Clearly if she didn't find another job soon, I was going to have to find her one. It was so ironic that of all the people in Grady & Bartlett, she was the one who was still around. She was my curse, my albatross, my punishment, my . . . I gritted my teeth. "I'm listening, Brooke."

She made a little fluttery motion with her hands. "I was just thinking that you might want to consult Harrison."

Whatever I'd imagined she might suggest, it wasn't that. "I don't think so," I said.

"I knew you wouldn't like the idea," she said, "but you really should think about it. Harrison knows a lot."

I made a gesture encompassing our cramped, diminished office. "Harrison is the reason we're in this cubbyhole. Harry Potter had better accommodations than this with the Dursleys."

Her eyes widened. "You read Harry Potter?"

"Sure," I said. "Does that surprise you?"

"Well, yes," she said seriously. "You seem so . . ."

"Never mind," I said quickly. "More to the point, Harrison is the reason I'm here and you're no longer on salary. I don't think we should trust him to mess up anyone else's life, do you?"

She mumbled something I didn't understand.

"What?"

"He's dying," she whispered.

I had my doubts about that. "How do you know that?" I asked.

"He told me." She shook her head. "He didn't exactly say it in so many words, but I could tell that's what he meant. And the thing is, if he knows he's dying, he's not going to deliberately mislead you or anything like that, is he? Besides, what motive would he have for hiding things now?"

For a lawyer she was incredibly naive. "I've never heard that being on the point of death confers any special virtue," I told her. "If he *is* on the point of death, which I doubt. And anyway, his case hasn't gone to trial yet. He's still under house arrest."

"I know that," she said. "I went to see him."

I didn't know whether to find her loyalty touching or exasperating. "Why?" I asked.

She said, very quietly and patiently, as if she were explaining something to a non-English-speaking psychotic, "I told you. Because he's dying. I'm almost positive."

"Because of something you thought he implied," I said.

"Well, don't forget he was in the hospital. In intensive care, remember? It had to be *something* serious."

I closed my eyes. "Oh, right." A serious attack of guilty conscience, most likely. I was surprised Harrison had been able to keep the truth about his suicide attempt from getting out.

"I can't believe you'd forget something like that," she said.

"I haven't forgotten," I told her.

"Then you'll go see him?"

"Well . . ."

"I don't mean to lecture," she said, in the pious tone people assume when they mean to do precisely that, "but Harrison did say he asked you to come see him and you promised you would. You *promised*. I know you well enough to know that a promise means something to you."

This was not a topic I wanted to explore at the moment, especially not with Brooke. "I'll think about it," I said.

"But—"

"Let's drop it for now."

HARRISON WAS SO BORED BY HOUSE ARREST that he would have opened the door to Jeffrey Dahmer peddling homemade sausages, but he was undeniably surprised to see me. "I didn't think you'd really show up," he said.

"I called first," I pointed out. "I left a message."

He shrugged. "Come in," he said.

Harrison's house, like Harrison himself, had a defeated look. The upholstery was worn. The coffee table had beverage rings. There were stacks of newspapers—at least a week's worth, by the look of them—piled in the corner. The air smelled sour, like unlaundered clothes.

Harrison gestured toward a geriatric La-Z-Boy facing an oversize TV. "Have a seat," he said.

I obeyed him. My feet swung upward toward the ceiling as my head sank back. I scrabbled madly for the control lever.

"It's on your right," Harrison said. "I should have warned you. The mechanism's a little loose."

I sat up gingerly, using my arm and leg muscles to keep from tipping back again. "Well," I said, "how are you doing?"

"Fine. Okay. Thanks for asking, Lynnie." He had a day or two's growth of beard and an indoor pallor, but otherwise he didn't look moribund.

"Enjoying good health, are you?" I asked.

"Sure." He smiled. "My liver's not what it used to be, but you can't have everything." He gave me a shrewd look. "Why? Have you heard differently?"

It was my turn to shrug, which caused my legs to soar again.

Harrison laughed. "Sorry about that," he said. "So what have you heard? Out with it. I'm immune to gossip by now."

"Brooke thinks you're dying," I said bluntly.

He looked amused. "Brooke is very impressionable," he said. "Also, I might have helped her impression along a little."

"Why?" I asked.

"It's probably pointless, but I didn't want her to know the real reason I was in the hospital," he said. "Anyway, it's true in the essentials. My life is over. There's nothing left, whether I go on physically or not." He said it so matter-of-factly I saw he believed that it was true.

"Are you at least in AA?" I asked.

He raised his shoulders. "It's a condition of my house arrest," he said, which was not a totally straightforward answer.

"Brooke's very concerned about you," I said, unwilling to say that I was concerned about him, too, though I was, at least a little. There was an air of, if not death, *disintegration* about him. Because of Alexei, because of dealing with the crises Harrison had left me, because of the Anne Boleyn Society, I'd begun to believe that no matter what calamity occurred in my professional life or my home life, I would somehow handle it. I had shaken off failure like a sickness. I could find it in my heart to pity Harrison, who wrapped himself in it like a cloak.

"Brooke's very loyal," he said.

"Yes, she is," I agreed. "Surprisingly."

"You've always misjudged her," he said.

"And you've always given her too much credit," I said. "Have you ever seen anyone with more confidence in herself? *Unwarranted* confidence, a lot of the time. It leads her into foolish mistakes. She shoots from the hip."

"She's young. She's overeager." He gave me a shrewd look I remembered from the old days. "Not everyone has your self-control, Lynn."

If only he knew that self-control didn't seem to be my strong suit these days. Lately it seemed that everyone's conversations were laced with double entendres.

"Also," Harrison said, "Brooke thinks you think she tried to steal Kojima Bank's business away from you."

I did think so, but I didn't have any proof, and anyway, what did it matter now? But I couldn't believe he had the nerve to bring it up. We'd have Kojima, the firm, and a passel of other clients if he hadn't screwed up.

"You probably think I'm out of line to bring this up,"

he added, reading my mind. Harrison's downfall had not affected his acumen, apparently.

I said nothing.

"Okay, so there's no 'probably' about it," he said. "But I wanted you to know she didn't do it. In case *you* want to do anything."

"Like what?" I asked him.

"Like ask her to stay on," he said.

"She is staying on. I'm just not paying her. I can't afford to," I added pointedly.

"No, of course not," he said, and I was suddenly ashamed of shaming him. He was heading for prison, his life was in ruins—what more did I want? Blood?

"Actually," I said, changing the subject, "I need your advice."

"Problems at home?" he asked softly.

I was shocked. We'd never discussed personal things, at least not at that level. I wondered if he'd been spending too many afternoons watching *Oprah*.

I drew back, probably with a look of horror, because he added, "I'm sorry. It's none of my business. It's just that you look . . . stressed. You used to look so happy, Lynnie. I know I've done my share to take that away. I'm really sorry."

"No, no," I said quickly. "It's not a personal problem." I told him about Alexei's circumstances and the INS's curious response. Naturally I omitted the part about sleeping with the client and how it would rip my heart right out of my chest if I couldn't help him to stay in this country. Ms. Cool, that's me.

Harrison, however, was not taken in. "Special client, I take it?"

"Something like that," I said.

"Well," he said, considering carefully. Harrison was never precipitous in offering advice, and he never, despite his defense of Brooke, shot from the hip. It was one of the things I had always liked about him when we were in practice together. It made his screwup—his betrayal—all the more shocking. It just proved you never knew people as well as you thought you did.

"I'm really not sure how to proceed," I told him. "I mean, I'm not even sure what the objections are or what information they're acting on."

"Well, that's nothing new with the INS, is it? One time the State Department objected to a client I'd already gotten an approval for, and the INS rescinded the visa status. They said he'd lied about something he'd done in the Philippines. When I asked the client about it, he admitted that he'd lied, so I didn't feel a bit sorry for him. He could have gotten me in big trouble."

I decided to overlook the irony of this statement and said nothing.

Harrison looked at me over the top of his reading glasses. "Are you sure your client isn't lying to you?"

That required either a very long answer or a very short one. I took the short one. "Yes," I said. "I'm sure."

"Well then, I guess I'd start the appeal process with a request for full disclosure. Unless he's going to be arrested for something, it will take some time to resolve, and in the meantime there's something else you could try."

"What?" I asked eagerly.

He told me.

I looked at him. "That's so simple," I said.

He smiled.

"Do you think it will work?" I asked.

"It might."

"Harrison?"

"What?"

"How do you know Brooke wasn't trying to steal Kojima?"

"Ah," he said. "Because I know who tipped them off about the fake documents. It wasn't Brooke."

"Who was it?"

"Me," he said.

I sat back, being extremely careful not to tip back in the chair. "Why on earth would you do a thing like that?"

He looked at me as if the answer were the most obvious thing in the world. "Because," he said slowly, "once the INS started calling me, I knew that the truth was bound to come out. I told Naoko Watanabe at Kojima because—" He hesitated.

"Because?" I prompted him.

"Because, Lynn," he said finally, "I didn't want them to think it was you."

CHAPTER 29

My problem, if you want to call it that, lay in thinking that as long as you didn't exceed any egregious boundaries, you should be able to live your life as you see fit. My life before this hadn't even been such a bad advertisement for that principle: I'd left my first husband because I didn't—couldn't—live the way he wanted to, and I'd chosen my career because I found it compatible with my temperament and style. Now that my smug choices threatened to end up in ashes, I wasn't so sure. The pursuit of happiness had turned into a dead-end pilgrimage, and it was up to me to find my way out.

"I've been contacted," Alexei told me.

I almost remarked that that sounded like something out of a spy novel, till I reflected that Alexei might not find it amusing. "Contacted how?" I asked.

"By e-mail. By phone," he said. "It's the twenty-first century." He laughed mirthlessly. "I'm invited back," he said.

"You'll have to be more specific."

He sighed into the phone. "I am invited to take up a very high position with the Russian Ministry for Atomic Energy. My job would be devising and directing a new program to prevent nuclear disasters."

"Like before," I said.

"Yes, but with an official title and a salary that is decent by Russian standards."

"It's an honor to be invited," I said carefully. My blood sounded in my ears. *He could leave.* The memory of kissing him—and more—liquefied my nucleus, to put it in atomic terms. Still, I had no right to ask anything of him or try to influence any choice he might make. None whatsoever. "After all this time."

"Well, 'invited' may not be the correct word. 'Pressured' probably comes closer to the mark. And no, it is not an honor. The existing program is in shambles. They are desperate. Really desperate."

"Why now, particularly?" I asked him.

"You know about Chernobyl," he said.

"Leaking, you mean?" I asked.

"Yes, and there are other— Lynn, I'm not free to tell you, even now."

"Oh, Alexei," I said. "Do you think someone's been manipulating the State Department to make you go back?"

He didn't answer me. His silence was an answer of sorts, I suppose.

"What will you do?" I asked. "You don't want to accept, do you?" I caught myself up short. "I mean, I—"

.

"No," he said firmly, "I don't." He paused. "I miss you," he said.

I smiled. It had been only six days. And twenty-five e-mails. "I miss you, too," I said.

"Lynn?"

I knew what he was asking. I felt the same kind of push-pull vertigo you feel when you're on the top of a tall building and the height seems to be sucking you down. "Yes," I told him.

I could hear the smile in his voice. "How did you know what I was going to ask?"

"Because it's what I want, too," I told him. Truthfully. "When?"

"Now," he said. "Please."

"YOU'RE NEVER IN YOUR OFFICE ANYMORE," Jack said.

My heart stuttered, but he sounded only mildly pissed.

"And your cell phone is turned off," he added.

"I went to see Harrison," I told him.

He looked at me as if I'd confessed to an afternoon tête-à-tête with Anna Nicole Smith. Utter disbelief. "Why?" he gasped.

"I needed to ask him something about a client," I said. "Also, Brooke thought he might be dying, so I thought I should go."

Jack looked dubious. "Is he?"

"No, but he looks pretty shabby," I said. "It's sort of sad, to tell you the truth."

"I find it hard to feel sorry for him," Jack said.

"So did I, till I went there," I said. "But it's impossible to hold a grudge against someone who's got nothing left. He's going to plead guilty, did you know?"

"Mmm," Jack said.

"So why were you wanting to reach me?" I asked.

"Patrick got the job," he said. "I thought we might go out to celebrate."

"That's great," I said. "The paralegal job with your law firm?"

"Yes," he said stiffly. "But I don't think it had that much to do with me."

"I'm sure it didn't," I said. If that's what he wanted to tell himself, I didn't see how it could hurt to play along. "Of course I'm happy to go," I said, "but do you really think he wants to go out celebrating with *us?*"

"I don't think he has anyone else," Jack said in a worried tone.

"Of course he does," I said, though I was far from sure of it.

PATRICK SAT BETWEEN US AT THE TABLE, wilting under the force of his father's enthusiasm. Even I could see that it was too much, like praising your dinner guest for buttering the bread. The very excess of it emphasized his deficiencies. Besides, what guy in his twenties regards a formal dinner out with his parent and stepparent as a rollicking good time? Since the dot-commers had brought their youth and wealth to the Peninsula, there were far cooler places to celebrate. I thought about Jack's comment that Patrick didn't have anyone else. There must be *someone* one of his friends could fix him up with.

Jack seemed impervious to the effect of his forced jollity. "Too bad Merry and Justin couldn't make it," he said. "I know your sister is really proud of you, too."

Patrick guffawed. "Right, Dad."

"I'm perfectly serious," Jack said. "You know how much she admires you."

Patrick stared in mute disbelief at his father. I couldn't blame him. I was startled into silence myself.

"So what kind of training will you have?" I asked, recovering.

"There's a course I have to take," he said. "The firm will pay for it," he added quickly.

"They must think a lot of you if they'll pay for your training," Jack said. "Don't you agree, Lynn?"

"Sure," I said. "Harrison and I always expected people to get their training on their own."

Patrick's face turned sour. "I'm sure the firm pays for everyone, not just me."

I had apparently said the wrong thing. Jack looked at me. "Maybe Lynn can give you some pointers about working in a law office," he said.

I saw the desperation in his eyes and realized, suddenly, that his mood, his overreaction, had as much to do with me as with his son. What had I thought? That he wouldn't notice that I was preoccupied and distant? "I'd be happy to," I said.

"Thanks," Patrick mumbled dismally.

"Great," Jack said heartily, raising the wine bottle. "Another glass, anyone?"

Patrick shook his head. I lifted my glass to be filled. "Here's to your success," I said. "I hope it's a lot of fun."

"Fun, yeah," Patrick said dubiously.

"I'm serious. You might actually enjoy it. I did— *do*—at least when I'm not preoccupied with how to get business. And you won't have to worry about that."

"No, I won't have that much responsibility," he said.

I wondered how it would be to have this sad sack around the office, his leaden pessimism the complete opposite of Brooke's maddening perkiness. I wondered which was worse. Then I was struck by an idea that sprang from either an extremely generous impulse or an extremely diabolical one, I'm not sure which. "Well, you can always go to law school if you find you like the practice," I said recklessly, considering who was bound to pay for it if he did. "But in the meantime, when do you start?"

"Monday," Patrick intoned, as if he were announcing the imminent commencement of the Apocalypse.

"Then, if you're not busy, could you come over to the office tomorrow afternoon and help me out? I have some files I need to go through with my associate—"

"What associate?" Jack asked.

"My *former* associate," I said quickly, "who's still sharing the office till she finds something else. Anyway, we could use your help for a couple of hours, and it might help you to get the feel of things before you actually start."

"Yeah, I guess I could do that," Patrick said. Despite himself, he looked rather pleased.

"Of course you can," Jack said heartily.

"THAT WAS REALLY NICE OF YOU," Jack said afterward. He sighed. "I don't know what happened to him. He used to be so energetic and curious about everything. Now he doesn't seem very interested in anything."

Patrick had already gone home, and we were lingering at the restaurant. Being alone with Jack made me feel edgy and uncomfortable, the probable signs of a guilty conscience. There was a kind of wary formality between us, like people who meet at a class reunion after having slept together a decade before. I was determined that until I decided what to do, I should go on behaving normally, if that's the right word for it. But it was getting harder.

"I'm glad you asked him to help you," he said. "It was a kind gesture."

It wasn't all that kind, actually. I hoped it didn't boomerang. I wasn't going to tell Jack that I planned to foist Patrick on Brooke and see what happened. It was something like mixing two entirely incompatible elements to find out if they would combust. At least it might prove interesting, and I didn't think that either one of them had that much to lose. Maybe they would sort of cancel each other out, and if they focused on each other, I could get both them out of my hair.

"We'll see," I said.

"What do you mean by that?" he asked sharply.

"Nothing," I said. "I mean, I really hope things work out for him."

Jack smiled tightly. "You seem to be in a very forgiving mood today," he said. "First Harrison and now Patrick."

I said seriously, "I have a lot to forgive Harrison for, but not Patrick. He hasn't done anything to hurt me."

"I wish I believed you really felt that way," Jack said.

"Well, I do," I assured him. "Anyway, forgiveness is good, don't you think?" I asked lightly.

"For most things, I suppose." He looked at me. He put his hand over my wrist in a gesture that should have been comforting but wasn't. "But some things are . . . unforgivable."

The contents of my stomach congealed into a leaden, indigestible ball. My throat was dry. I lifted my water glass and took a big swallow, trying to keep my hand steady.

"The trick, I guess, is knowing which is which," I told him.

CHAPTER 30

I tried to exercise a certain degree of discipline and not think of Alexei—at least not think of him in *that* way—while I was at home, as if even the passing thought would mark my forehead with the scarlet you-know-what. But my self-control was eroding. I mean, bigamists did it—the newspapers were full of stories about men (always men, never women) who maintained separate wives, separate families in different states, with neither one the wiser. Pilots carried it off, too, if you believe Anita Shreve. I wondered whether the key to success in such deception didn't lie in not caring too much, because when you did care, the unbridled fluctuations between . . . well, what? *joy? rapture?* and the anguished conviction that you could be causing pain to someone else were almost too much to bear.

I'd had a modern Protestant upbringing, so my notion of hell was sanitized and shrouded in myth and no more threatening than, say, a ride on an un-air-conditioned subway car on a particularly warm day. Warm, not hot. Still, the pit beckoned. There weren't any words to describe my afternoons with Alexei, even though I knew that my feelings were fueled in part by the overhanging sense of jeopardy, the probable brevity of this impulsive affair. Alexei's emotions, I thought, were driven as much by loneliness and the need to connect as by passion. None of that mattered. For the first time, I understood why poor Hester Prynne, who probably did believe in Hell with a capital *H,* had risked perdition to be with Dimmesdale. Sin, which I had previously equated with stealing from department stores or cheating on your income tax, suddenly acquired both gravitas and allure.

COOPER LIVINGSTON, which had offered Alexei a job once his green card status was assured, changed its mind under pressure and promised to sponsor his petition, provided they didn't have to pay. There is a reason the comic strip *Dilbert* makes the evil Catbert the head of human resources at its mythical company. Normally I had to suck it in and take whatever HR dished out or risk losing the institutional client, but Alexei was, to put it mildly, special. I went around HR, who insisted that not only could company policy never be changed but that even the mere suggestion made Dr. Strela's future with Cooper Livingston doubtful. I contacted the head of the department where Alexei would be working and pointed out the obvious advantages of helping my client with his immigration status, evoking the specter of SLAC's international project if they didn't. Besides, as I pointed out, it would cost them nothing. Since I'd already written the petition once, it was relatively easy to reformat the work and resubmit it.

Now we were both out on a limb if it didn't come through.

"I don't know what will happen," I told Alexei, "but it's a different INS service center and a company petition, so it might not trip whatever alarm went off the first time. If we get an approval, we could still have trouble down the line, but at the very least it buys you some time."

"Time," he said, as if it were an alien quality. He sighed. "This means I have to take the offer with Cooper Livingston, doesn't it?"

"No, you don't have to," I said, "although they'll be rightfully pissed if you don't." Also, I would never get another piece of business from them as long as I lived, but I didn't mention that.

"Pissed," he said, drawing out the *s* sound. Certain words in English amused him, although he spoke it so well I sometimes forgot it wasn't his first language.

"Anyway," I said, "I thought you wanted to accept."

He sat up and pulled the blanket up over his knees. "I've been alone a long time," he said. "Most of my life, in one form or another." He turned toward me. "I don't particularly want to leave right now. . . ."

I feel a sharp stab of doubt. I didn't want to say anything that would make him stay, or go. It wasn't fair when so much was still undecided. He'd made my life more supportable, but the possible complications threatened to upend it altogether.

"You could come with me," he said after a moment.

My fingernails dug into my palms. "I could," I acknowledged.

"I don't want to pressure you, Lynn," Alexei said, no doubt encouraged that I hadn't refused outright. "But we could live in New York. You could start a whole new practice. Whatever you wanted."

We'd always understood, I'd thought, that this was temporary. The sudden surge of possibilities made me mute.

"I *am* pressuring you," Alexei said. "I'm sorry." He grinned suddenly. "I'm just waiting for a little guidance. Something to put a man out of his misery."

I smiled back. "It's my misery, too," I said lightly. "I don't like leaving you either," I conceded, wanting to give him something. "It's like a phantom limb. I feel you even when you're not there."

Alexei, the scientist, corrected me. "The severed nerves keep sending signals to the brain," he said.

"The way you can still see light from stars that are already burned out?" I asked.

His hand closed over mine. "Yes, like that," he said. "But that's an image of loss."

"I suppose so," I said, trying hard for a breeziness I didn't feel. "How about 'We'll always have Paris'?"

Alexei said, "I've seen *Casablanca,* too, Lynn. Do you call that a happy ending?"

I shrugged.

"Have you heard of quantum entanglement?" he asked. He lifted our entwined hands as if they were Exhibit A.

"Is that something in physics?" I asked.

He laughed. "I guess you haven't."

"It isn't my strong suit," I said. "I did warn you. Anyway, what about it?"

"It's very romantic," he said.

"If you say so," I said dubiously.

"Oh, very," he said, releasing my hand and tracing a line down my hip with his fingertip. "Just listen: A pair of subatomic particles that have interacted at some point, like this"—he demonstrated a particularly pleasant sort of interaction, which made my concentration slip—"retain a connection forever. If you know the spin state of one entangled particle—up or down—you'll know that the spin of its mate is in the opposite direction. What's really amazing . . ."

"Yes?" I breathed, in something of a spin state myself.

"Yes," he agreed. "What's amazing is that the spin state of the particle being measured is decided at the time of measurement and then somehow communicated to the other particle, which then simultaneously assumes the opposite spin direction."

"I don't get it," I said, bewildered.

"Neither did Einstein. He called it 'spooky action.' But here's the romantic part," he said. "No matter how far apart they are, even millions of light-years, they'll remain entangled as long as they're separated."

"Why?" I asked, my head pressed against his chest.

"Nobody knows for sure. But it's been demonstrated repeatedly through experimentation."

"Like this?" I asked, a minute later.

"Yes," he said. "Like this."

"I think I could learn to like physics," I murmured in his ear.

BROOKE, who, despite the annoying qualities enumerated ad nauseam here, was not lacking in the brains department, saw right through my little scheme.

"Why are you throwing your stepson at me?" she asked. Since I wasn't paying her anymore, she had abandoned all pretense of sucking up, which was okay with me. "I don't need any help getting dates."

I tried to look as if I were shocked—no, horrified—at the very idea. "It probably did seem that way," I said apologetically. "I'm sorry. I didn't think. As a matter of fact, I don't think you'll like him particularly." I sighed a rueful, affectionate-stepmother sigh. *Please don't throw me into the briar patch.*

"Why not?" she asked suspiciously.

I shrugged. "Forget it," I said. "I can go through the files with him on my own. I'd just like him to get a feel for what goes on in a real office, such as it is, and since you've worked with Harrison, too, I thought . . . Anyway, just forget it."

"What's wrong with him? Is he one of those e-holes?"

"Oh, no, nothing like that." I turned back to the papers on my desk, shuffling through the pile.

"What, then?" she insisted.

I shook my head sadly. "Patrick's smart, charming, and good-looking. I'm not sure why, but he seems to lack self-confidence. That's why I thought, before he started his new job, a sort of dress rehearsal might make him feel more comfortable."

She let out a breath. "He got a job?"

"As a paralegal," I said. "And he had help."

"Maybe your husband could put in a word for me, too," she suggested.

I winced inwardly. "I could certainly ask him," I conceded.

"Does your stepson say 'dude'?" she asked.

"Definitely not," I assured her.

She twirled the ends of her hair around one finger. "I guess I wouldn't really mind taking him through some of the paperwork," she said. She looked at me. "I know how busy you are with the Strela case."

Despite my best intentions, I blushed. "That's very kind of you, Brooke, but I don't want to impose unfairly."

"It's okay," she said. "You can owe me one."

WITH A MAN IN THE OFFICE, Brooke suddenly started tossing her head and speaking in brittle phrases, like someone being interviewed for a part in a movie.

"We used to represent a lot of *very* important clients," she said, posing next to the filing cabinet, her hand draped possessively over the top. "Of course, the list is highly confidential, but I can assure you that you'd be impressed."

Patrick stood transfixed, his glance darting back and forth between Brooke and me in confusion. I knew what he was wondering: *Who's in charge here?* At such moments Brooke reminded me rather forcibly of Janet, which, in my heart of hearts, I knew was the real reason I'd arranged this introduction.

"If you like, I can show you the process we go through to file a visa application for a client," she said. "Will you be doing any immigration work, do you think?"

"I don't know," Patrick said. He looked at me.

"Probably not," I said. "It's a corporate practice."

"Um, then what did you want him to do, Lynn?" Brooke asked me.

"I thought maybe you could sort the files into 'viable' and 'not viable,' " I said. "That way I'll have some place to start building the new practice."

"Can do," she said, in her chirpiest tone.

I looked at Patrick to see how he was taking it. He looked puzzled, as well he might have. Since he didn't look actively hostile or sullen, I wasn't positively discouraged with my efforts.

"Great," I said. "Brooke will walk you through what you need to know. In the meantime I haven't had lunch yet, so I thought I'd go bring back a sandwich. I'd love to get you two something as well. Brooke? Patrick?"

"I've eaten," Brooke said. "But I wouldn't say no to a croissant. Provided it's a good one," she added.

Patrick laughed and looked at me to check my reaction.

"My sentiments exactly," I said. "Patrick?"

"I guess that would be okay," he said. "Thanks."

I TOOK MY TIME, detouring by Draeger's to find fresh croissants, which, owing to their fat-laden qualities, were not as ubiquitous as they had once been. Almost everyone I knew claimed to be on a low-fat diet, but nobody was getting any thinner. Someday people would probably discover that what you really ought to be eating for optimum weight loss was food cooked in lard. I personally am waiting for the Chocolate Éclair Diet. But I digress.

When I got back to the office, the door was open, and I could hear Patrick—*Patrick!*—recounting a story about Meredith in animated detail. His voice carried into the corridor, and I hesitated before going in, because I knew that my presence would douse whatever warmth might have been kindled in the room. A sad admission, that.

"Anyway," he was saying, "my sister heard about this sect called the Breatharians who were supposed to live in some monastery like Shangri-la in Bolivia or someplace like that. They were supposed to exist on air and 'good vibes' or whatever. I mean, they didn't *eat*. My sister *loved* that. She was all set to run off and join them when she found out it was all a crock of shit. My sister is seriously weird," he said.

"Does your sister have an eating disorder?" Brooke asked.

"My sister has a mental disorder, I think. She thinks food is out to get her."

I would have laughed, but Brooke said seriously, "How sad. Has she gotten any help?"

"She saw a shrink years ago—we all did, actually, when my parents got divorced—but if it did any good, it was never obvious to me. Anyway, Dad's sort of scared of her now. Plus, he admires her for it, in a way. He says she has very exacting standards."

Brooke snorted. "Your father seems to go for people who have exacting standards," she said.

Uh-oh. Their voices lowered conspiratorially. Oh, well, I suppose it was a bonding of sorts. I waited a decent interval before I stepped inside. "I'm back," I said cheerily. "Croissants and coffee all around."

After he left, Brooke said to me, "You were right about Patrick. He's very smart and very perceptive, don't you think?"

"Very," I said gravely.

Her eyes had a faraway look. "I think all he needs is just the *tiniest* little push."

CHAPTER 31

In addition to its toll on my peace of mind, my conscience, my sleep, and even my appetite, my secret life was starting to affect my friendships as well. I'd never realized how important sharing confidences was as a cornerstone to female relationships until I started withholding information.

"So how are you getting along with Jack?" Kay asked me over coffee. One advantage of my diminished client base was that I could take time off from the office, even during the week.

"Okay, I guess." Even to my own ears, I sounded as spiritless as Patrick. I stirred my coffee with a spoon, wondering how little I could get away with saying. I probably should have avoided getting together at all, but I'd already turned her down twice.

"How lovely and passionate," Kay murmured, watching me over the lip of her cup.

I laughed. "Sorry," I said. "I guess I don't feel much like talking about it."

"Well, okay," Kay said doubtfully. "It's just that I'm a little concerned about you, because last time you mentioned that you were thinking of . . . you know."

Leaving him. The words hung there unspoken.

"You seemed so disappointed," she added.

Disappointed, yes. "I was—I am—pretty tired," I said. "That's a big part of it. There's a lot going on." I wondered if I should tell her how much effort it was taking to try to fix everything in my life that had gone wrong.

"What are you thinking about?" Kay asked me. "You looked a million miles away."

About three thousand, to be exact, in some future New York City with Alexei. I shook my head.

"Christ, Lynn, I hate to see you like this," Kay said. "I can tell you don't want to talk about it, but maybe you should see someone. It's not good to keep things bottled up."

I smiled. "I wonder why people always say that," I said. "Sometimes *not* telling is the most generous thing you can do."

"For the other person maybe, but not for yourself," she insisted. "Anyway, do you think it would help you to come to the group again?"

"Not just now, thanks. Maybe later."

"Okay," she said, giving up. "I'll drop it for the moment." She took a sip of her coffee. "So how are the wedding plans coming, if that's not too touchy a subject?"

I grimaced involuntarily.

"That bad?" she asked happily.

"They've booked the Moulin Winery for the reception," I said.

She whistled. "My God! That costs a fortune!" she said authoritatively. Kay knew how much everything cost.

"Tell me about it," I said. The Napa Valley was world famous, but in truth the Bay Area was dotted with wineries. There were wineries in the coastal hills, in the valleys, and on the flat. There probably would have been wineries in the marshes if someone could have figured out how to make grapes grow among the reeds. Wine was everywhere, and wineries ranged from the funky "fill your own bottle" type en route to Half Moon Bay to the charming "bring your picnic lunch" Mirassou Vineyards in San Jose. Meredith had eschewed funky and gone beyond charm in favor of a French-style château in the Napa-Sonoma area that represented the pinnacle of style, exclusivity, and expense. I'd seen tackier places in the Loire Valley.

"I thought she didn't drink," Kay said. I'd confided a lot of details about Meredith's food aversions in the early days of my marriage, when each revelation was a fresh source of amazement.

"She doesn't," I said.

"Then isn't a winery an odd sort of choice for the reception?"

I smiled grimly. "Janet drinks," I said. "And Janet wants a very big show."

"Well, she'll certainly get it at Moulin." Kay shook her head. "It's beautiful, though. They have lots of society weddings there."

"Yes, society. That's the trouble."

She laughed. "You say the word as if it were 'small-pox.' It's not that bad."

"It's not bad at all," I said. "It's just not me."

"Is it Jack?" she asked slyly.

Once I would have answered, *Of course not,* and been certain I was right. "I don't think so," I said, less certainly. "But who ever really knows anyone else?" Marriage was full of contradictions, I thought. On the one hand, you end up knowing more than you should about the other person, and on the other there were things that could surprise you after fifty years. I had to take the fifty-year part on faith, though. I wasn't likely to find out firsthand.

"Well, that's for sure," Kay said vehemently. "I—"

My cell phone rang.

Kay, ever the real-estate agent, gestured magnanimously with her hand. "Go ahead. Take it."

"Hello?" I said. I kept my face impassive, in case it was Alexei.

"Lynn? It's me. Patrick."

"What's wrong?" I asked, knowing he wouldn't have called me otherwise. "Is it your dad?"

"No. Not Dad," he said. "It's your cat. You'd better come to the vet's."

"I'M REALLY SORRY, LYNN," Patrick said when I walked into the veterinary emergency clinic. "He was behind the wheel of the car when I backed out. I just didn't see him. I'm really sorry."

He looked so distraught that I swallowed hard and said, "I know you didn't mean it, Patrick. Is he dead?"

He touched my shoulder. "No, but he got hit in the head. I told them to do whatever they could to save him. I hope that's okay."

"Sure," I said, hoping it was. "Thank you for bringing him here."

He looked down. "I know you love him," he said, surprisingly. "And I know I wasn't always cool about him when I moved in, but I didn't want him to get hurt."

"I know that," I said.

"He used to sleep on my bed sometimes," he said, like a little boy.

I forbore asking what had happened to his allergy to cats. "They get to you," I said.

"Yeah," he agreed.

DR. STEELE, the proverbial woman in white, introduced herself as a specialist in veterinary ophthalmology. "There's good news and bad news," she said. "The good news is, I think he's going to be okay."

I let out my breath. "And the bad news?"

"We had to remove one of his eyes. I'm sorry—it was too badly damaged."

Patrick's eyes filled with tears. He turned away.

"Cats do very well with one eye," Dr. Steele said. "They're amazing animals. We've stitched the socket shut, and the hair will grow over it. After a while he won't even notice it's not there."

Ha, but at least he was alive. Although she was a

very attractive young blonde, Dr. Steele had a no-nonsense style that was highly reassuring, at least while delivering news like that. I tried not to shudder.

"How should we take care of him?" I asked.

"Just keep him quiet for a few days. I'll give you some antibiotic pills. He's got a collar on to keep him from scratching at the stitches."

Eeuuw. "Thank you, Doctor," I said, getting a grip.

"Oh, and he might bleed from his nose a little bit," she said. "But don't worry. Unless there's lots of blood, it doesn't mean a thing."

"Right," I said hoarsely.

"Carrie will bring him out in a few minutes," she said. "She'll get you his antibiotic and check you out."

Carrie was adding up numbers on the bill with the zeal of an Enron accountant, but she stopped and smiled warmly. "I've got seven cats," she said. "He'll be okay."

I smiled back. "Thank you," I said.

She handed me the bill.

I stopped smiling. "Seven hundred dollars?" I said, my voice squeaking a little. Maybe those flying fingers had punched in a few wrong keys.

"As operations go, it's not that expensive," she said kindly. "I gave you a discount."

Patrick made a strangled sound. "I'll help pay for it," he said. "Out of my first paycheck."

"Don't be silly," I said.

"What will Dad say?"

"Not a thing," I told him, getting out my checkbook.

* * *

BREWER EMERGED looking like a cross between Little Bo Peep and Freddy Krueger. The plastic collar encircled his head like an oversize bonnet, and the hairless skin surrounding the puckered, sewn-up socket was raw and pink against his black fur. The stitches stuck out from his eyelids in stiff little spikes. The sight might have given Stephen King nightmares.

Patrick and I looked at each other in dismay.

"It'll get better soon," Carrie said encouragingly. "You'll see. The hair grows in really fast."

"Maybe we should get him an eye patch, so he could be the Hathaway Cat," I said, attempting a feeble joke.

Very feeble. They both looked at me blankly. I hate it when some cultural reference reminds you how far you've descended into geezerdom.

"Never mind," I said.

"I think he's peed in his carrier," Patrick observed.

PATRICK VOLUNTEERED TO RIDE HOME with me to keep an eye on the cat, just in case. I assured him it wouldn't be necessary. "He's fallen asleep again," I said. "Take a look."

"I'd just feel better about it," he insisted. "Please let me."

"Of course, if you want."

"I feel so bad about this," he said.

"Shit happens," I told him. "And anyway, you saved his life. Thank you for that."

His look lightened a bit. "I'm glad you can still thank me after you saw the bill," he said.

"Not to mention his face," I said.

He laughed, a little. "I was afraid to say that," he said. "But it is pretty awful, isn't it?"

"Ghastly," I agreed.

"I guess love really is blind," he said.

"Not blind," I told him. "Just sort of selective about the focus."

We drove along in silence for a minute or two. "As long as you're here . . . ," I said.

"Yes, what? Anything," he said.

"I'm wondering if I could stop in at the office and pick up a file on the way home. I don't think the cat will wake up and start yowling, but in any case it will just take a minute. I was having coffee with a friend when you called, so I haven't been back all afternoon."

"Sure, I'll stay in the car with him," Patrick said bravely.

"I'll be right back," I said.

THE LIGHT WAS OFF IN THE OFFICE, so at first I didn't see Brooke sitting at the desk in the dark. I threw the switch, and she put a hand to her face, blinking. I wondered if she'd been dozing.

"Sorry," I said. "I didn't know you'd still be here."

She looked at me. "He's dead," she said tonelessly.

I am ashamed to remember that when she said that, I assumed she'd somehow heard about Brewer's accident from Patrick. No other explanation occurred to me. "No he isn't," I said. "He's fine. Well, not fine, but not dead. He's out in the car."

Her eyes widened. "Who is?" she whispered.

"Brewer."

She looked blank.

"My cat," I said, feeling my face start to flush. "Isn't that what you meant?"

She shook her head. "I didn't know about your cat," she said, speaking in the careful voice people use to address the patently addled. "It's Harrison."

"Harrison?" I parroted, my mind rebelling at the obvious implication.

She nodded. "It's Harrison who's dead."

CHAPTER 32

Jennifer Grady, Harrison's daughter, wanted the services to be strictly private. "Just family," she said, in response to my inquiries. "I don't want any incidents."

"Incidents?"

"I'm sure I don't have to remind *you*," she said, a touch waspishly, "that he was in trouble with the law." I hoped she was just distraught and therefore more than usually abrupt.

"No, you don't have to remind me," I said, holding on to my temper. "But I don't think you have to worry about anyone trashing his funeral. Besides, how many family members are there?"

She cleared her throat. "Just me, for the moment. I'm trying to convince my aunt and some of the others."

"How sad," I gasped involuntarily.

"I don't really want to get into it, but my father didn't exactly endear himself to the rest of the family when he left my mother," she said.

I'd always thought Harrison's wife had left him, but

naturally I didn't say so. "And where are you going to have the service?" I asked.

"Mem Chu," she said, without a trace of embarrassment. Mem Chu, or Memorial Church, was the gilded, neo-Byzantine chapel on the Stanford campus. Like all the other memorials to Leland Junior erected by his parents, modesty and restraint were very little in evidence. (Campus folklore held that the grieving parents had preserved little Leland's last breakfast in the Stanford Museum, but no one I knew had ever actually seen it. Still, you had to believe that "nothing in his life became him like the leaving it" definitely applied to Junior. How many other fifteen-year-olds were responsible for the founding of a major university?)

"Well, surely that's big enough to hold a few more people," I said. In fact, it was big enough to gratify the most ambitious mourner, which had, after all, been the founders' intention. "Some of the people who used to work in your father's office would really like to come to the service, and I'm sure there must be others."

"How very odd," she said, "after what he did."

"I guess we made our peace with that," I said. Professional peccadilloes were obviously easier to forgive than personal slights. "More or less anyway. And he is, not to put too fine a point upon it, dead."

"That he is," she agreed. "I'll think about it and let you know."

"I'm so sorry for your loss," I told her.

*   *   *

BROOKE EXERCISED MASTERFUL SELF-RESTRAINT and didn't upbraid me for failing to believe that Harrison was really dying. His death reminded me of one of those macabre cemetery jokes where the tombstone reads "I told you I was sick." Actually, he'd told me he *wasn't,* but maybe that was just to ward off pity. In his place I would have done the same. On the other hand, maybe he'd deliberately misled me because he knew how bad I'd feel when I found out the truth, paying me back for not believing him in the first place. Who knows? But why had Brooke spotted the truth when I hadn't?

Maybe I'd have to admit that I'd been the teeniest bit wrong about her after all.

HARRISON'S MEMORIAL SERVICE, when it did take place, was a sad tribute to a life gone wrong only at its end. Despite the years he had lived in the area, none of the expected attendees—the business and professional associates and community leaders—showed up. The splendid setting notwithstanding, there were only a handful of mourners outside the family, including a few clients from better days, Jack (reluctantly) and me, Ronnie Sanchez, Harrison's longtime secretary (now retired), Brooke, and (surprise!) Patrick.

"They're friends," I whispered, in response to Jack's startled query. "I introduced them, remember?"

"She looks . . . formidable," Jack whispered back. "Do you think he can handle it?"

"I think she wants to shape him up," I said. "If I

were you, I'd let her. Look at Patrick. Does he look like he minds?"

"Actually, no," Jack said, with a smile. He touched my hand briefly. "The Hughes men can always use a good woman to help shape them up."

My eyes welled, and he squeezed my wrist. "We'll talk later," he said.

Harrison's chief apologist was a man from AA, who attested to the encouragement and kindness he'd shown at meetings. "Even though he was"—he cleared his throat in anticipation of a touchy subject—"*forced* to come, at least initially. Even when he knew he was dying," he said.

The head of the admissions office at Stanford related how Harrison had served as a community adviser to the admissions committee, a "tireless advocate on behalf of poor students, the sort of student he said he had once been himself."

Harrison's daughter, who bore him little resemblance in any respect, looked somewhat startled at this, the only emotion I saw her display. I wondered what was going through her mind. I suspected that Jennifer was one of those people who bury their feelings under a superefficient exterior. I wondered what Harrison had done to hurt her so much, to make her afraid of her emotions even at her father's funeral. What I was thinking was how little you really ever knew about anyone else. If Harrison had been there, I would have liked to ask him why he took me on, whether he'd seen in me a means of rescue instead of just a way to shift his problems onto somebody else. I'd have liked to ask him if he thought I'd repaid his initial leap of faith. On the whole I thought he would. I hadn't saved Grady & Bartlett, but I'd cleaned up the problems he'd left behind and served the clients well. Not a bad legacy, that.

"What are you going to do with . . . ah . . . the remains?" I asked Jennifer after the service. I assumed, from the absence of a coffin, that he'd been cremated.

She rubbed the bridge of her nose with her hand. She looked tired and strained. "Why do you ask?" she said.

"I was just wondering if you were planning to scatter his ashes near Lake Garda," I said.

"What?"

"I mean, he always used to talk about how much Lago di Garda meant to him," I added.

She stared at me. "Lake Garda? In Italy?"

"Yes. I gather he went there with your mother years ago."

"Good God," she said, sounding surprised. "They did go there on vacation before they got divorced. My mother said it was the most dreadful two weeks she'd ever spent in her life. It rained every day, and the electricity kept going out in the hotel, so there wasn't even a light to read by. Mother said she was all for getting on the first plane home."

"Why didn't she?" I asked.

"I don't know," she said.

*   *   *

"I'M GLAD THAT'S OVER," I said to Jack on the way home. "I didn't expect to feel it that much."

We were driving down Campus Drive, through the eucalyptus groves and undeveloped land that was Stanford's most attractive feature. I had mixed feelings about the campus; it was a wonderful school, but I'd gone there when it was at its worst—when people were hurling things at each other and burning professors' life work in orgies of self-righteous protest—and I couldn't help remembering that, despite all the elevated talk of Principles, it wasn't even safe to leave your laundry on the communal clothesline lest someone with an overdeveloped notion of entitlement come along and rip you off.

Jack smiled. "You do have your attachments," he said, braking for a group of bicyclists crossing University Avenue.

He meant my *inexplicable* attachments, but it cost me a pang anyway. "I suppose," I said. "But I can't help feeling sorry about it. And look how few people showed up."

"If the Ice Maiden was responsible for inviting them, I'm not surprised," he said. "And anyway, don't lose sight of the fact that he brought this on himself."

"I'm not," I said.

I expected him to drop it then, but he added, "People are going to do what they're going to do, and tearing yourself up over what is essentially the other person's responsibility is pointless."

He sounded angry.

"Are we talking about Harrison?" I asked him.

"What else?" he said. He kept his eyes forward, on the road.

"I guess I'm just sad at the way things turned out for him," I offered. "It's such a waste."

He didn't answer me. "Do you want to stop and get a coffee on the way home?" he asked after a moment. "We can talk."

"No one's home," I said. "Patrick's gone out with Brooke. Unless you're expecting someone?"

He shook his head. "I'd rather . . . just stop for coffee, I guess." He meant he wanted to talk in neutral territory.

I tried not to flinch. "Sure," I said. "That'd be fine."

I ORDERED THE SWEETEST, most calorie-laden drink on the board, a beverage somewhere between coffee and cheesecake. Stress generally afflicts people with loss of appetite, but I am a firm believer in the restorative powers of sugar and chocolate. Not to mention whipped cream. Now that Dr. Atkins was in vogue again, I didn't have to feel guilty about the cream at least.

Jack ordered black coffee. "Wouldn't you like a maraschino cherry to top it off?" he asked, eyeing my concoction with something akin to astonishment.

"Maraschino cherries are retro," I said. "Like pedal pushers. Nobody younger than we are even knows what they are."

"How . . . deflating," Jack said with a smile.

I shrugged. "Well, good riddance. And anyway, their turn will come."

Jack said, "That's what I've always liked about you, Lynn. You take such a vengeful view of fate."

I laughed. "You mean you think I believe everybody will get what he deserves in the end?"

"Well, don't you?"

"Not at all," I said, licking whipped cream from my spoon, waiting for the ax to fall.

"Can you tell me . . . ," he said after a moment, "what it is you want?"

I looked at him, wondering whether I should answer what I thought he was really asking or temporize. "I'm not really sure," I said.

He leaned forward and touched my hand. "What I want is what I've wanted all along," he said. "I want to share the rest of my life with you. I want us—all of us, Merry and Patrick and, I guess, Justin—to be a family. Isn't that what you want?"

I took a deep breath and let it out slowly. "I'm not really sure," I repeated. "I thought it was."

He sat back in his chair, looking shaken. "Oh," he said. "What are you saying?"

"I'm not saying anything," I said. Not yet.

"Of course you are," he said.

"I guess I'm not really sure how I do fit into the family, Jack," I said finally. "It's a pretty tight circle, and a lot of the time I'm on the outside looking in."

"I know you think I haven't been very good at setting boundaries," Jack said. "With Meredith and

Patrick, with Janet . . ." He looked at me. "But I've always been on your side. Always."

"Fair enough," I said, as evenly as I could manage. Under the circumstances I could hardly let him shoulder all the responsibility for what had gone wrong between us. "I'm not blaming you."

"Aren't you?"

"I knew you had other . . . obligations when I married you," I said. "The past doesn't just disappear, even if you'd like it to."

"That statement tells me quite a bit," he said.

"It wasn't intended to," I told him. "Please don't read something into this that isn't there."

"It's difficult not to, when I'm not sure exactly what the problem is," he said.

"It isn't that I don't care about you," I said.

"Do you know how desperately sad that sounds?" he asked.

I looked into my cup. "I'm sorry," I said. "I'm not trying to hurt you." I tried to take another sip of coffee, but it wouldn't go past the lump in my throat. "You're the kindest man I ever met, Jack." It was true. Even with his secretary, he defied the "no man is a hero to his valet" rule. "I don't want that to change."

"So where does this leave us?" he asked eventually.

I shook my head. "I don't know. I need some time to figure it out. Can we just put things on hold for a bit?"

He frowned. "I love you, Lynn," he said. "I want this to work. I'm willing to make changes, if that's what you think you need. If we have to leave here—"

"I—" I started to protest.

He waved his hand to silence me. "I know you've suggested it, and I shut you down. What I'm saying is, I'm not ruling anything out," he said.

"That's very generous, Jack," I said, because it was true. I knew how he felt about leaving. "Thank you."

"Don't thank me," he said, "not until you've heard the rest. What I'm not willing to live with is being put on probation while you make up your mind whether I'm—*we're*—what you want. At least not for long." He looked at me. "I'm drawing a line here. Can you understand that?"

We both had our lines and boundaries. The question was, could they intersect? "Yes," I told him. "I understand."

CHAPTER 33

Alexei's cell phone was turned off, and SLAC said he had called in sick three days in a row. On the fourth day, I picked up some soup at the deli (no, not borscht) and went to his guesthouse.

After the third knock, he called, "Who is it?"

"Florence Nightingale," I said through the door, before I had time to consider she might not be considered such a heroine to someone on the other side of the Crimean War. "I heard you were sick."

He opened the door about four inches. "Ms. Bartlett," he said. "How nice of you."

I stepped back from the door.

"My lawyer," he said, to someone behind him.

"A lawyer who makes house calls," said the other man, stepping forward and opening the door wider to give me an assessing look. He was large and blond and clean-cut and looked like a Russian in a James Bond movie—smart and dangerous. "How interesting." His voice was heavy with innuendo, which, under the circumstances, I could scarcely resent.

"There are a few of us left," I said, with as much dignity as I could muster.

Alexei smiled. He looked drawn and unshaven. "Dmitri Gregorivitch, this is my lawyer and my friend, Lynn Bartlett. Lynn, Dmitri is a former colleague." He did not, I noticed, offer his colleague's last name in addition to the patronymic, probably so I couldn't run home and look him up on the Internet and find out he was last year's Nobel Prize winner.

"Aren't you going to invite her in?" Dmitri asked. He added something in Russian, which, naturally, I didn't get.

"Speak English, Dima," Alexei said.

He did not move aside, so I said, "I really should be going. I just wanted to bring you this soup." I offered him the sack.

"That's very kind of you," he said, in his stranger's voice.

"Why does Alexei need a lawyer?" Dmitri asked me. "Is he in some kind of trouble?"

I looked him in the eye. "I sincerely hope not," I said. I turned to Alexei. "We can talk later, when you are well."

"Yes," he said, "probably that would be best. I'll see you to your car."

Behind him Dmitri laid a hand on his shoulder.

"That won't be necessary," I said to Alexei. "I hope . . . you're feeling better soon and that your friend doesn't catch anything."

Alexei said nothing but smiled wanly.

Dmitri laughed. "It's not contagious," he said. "And there is a cure, never fear." He gave me the same assessing look he had greeted me with. "So nice to have met you, *Ms*. Bartlett."

TO BE A HEADHUNTER IN SILICON VALLEY, like being a venture capitalist, was to have lived beyond your glory days. Gone were the days when employers competed for workers with "zero drag" (no responsibilities, so they could work long hours and travel at a moment's notice) with the ferocity of would-be homeowners bidding for a house on the Peninsula under six hundred thousand. Now that so much of the Valley business had proved to be vapor, supply and demand had shifted again in favor of the employer, and headhunters had to scramble to find positions even for people who were not watching their client lists dwindle, their assets erode, and their hormones expire.

"I'm not going to bullshit you, Lynn," said Richard Gregory of Gregory Associates. We had known each other only one hour, but already he was administering verbal slaps on the back. "It's not going to be easy. Law firms aren't taking a lot of lateral hires right now."

"I've also thought about going as in-house immigration counsel to some big company," I offered.

He shook his head. "Well, I gotta tell ya, since nobody's hiring, there isn't a lot of immigration work," he said. "I'm going to be honest with you—I make most of my money these days placing people out of state."

"Look," I told him, "lots of people are in a panic because their visas are running out and they want to stay on. Permanently. I'm a specialist in helping them. There has to be a market for that."

He looked dubious but was apparently too polite to ask why, if there were such a big market, my practice wasn't making enough to support me. Or maybe he just didn't think of it.

"Anyway," I added, "I'm just exploring my options at this point."

"Options, right."

"And you'll keep this confidential, of course?"

He raised a finger to his lips theatrically. "Of course," he said. "I think I have a sense of what you're looking for. I'll check around." He raised an eyebrow. "Um . . ."

"Yes?"

"Would you be willing to relocate? I mean, I know you said you and your husband live here, but that would widen your options a lot, if you know what I mean."

I knew what he meant. I folded my hands into my lap. "I wouldn't rule it out," I told him.

"Atta girl," he said. "I'll call you in a few days and let you know how things are looking."

"I'M SORRY," Alexei said when he called two days later. "I couldn't help it."

"Who is he?" I asked.

He was silent a moment. "A colleague. A former colleague. Really."

"A colleague from the Soviet Union," I said.

"Yes."

"He was sent, wasn't he? To pressure you to go back?"

"Yes," he said finally.

"I see."

"I won't," he said.

"Can they force you? Do they have leverage?"

"No," he said, but I thought I heard uncertainty in his voice.

"Alexei?"

"Yes?"

"I think you should get an attorney."

"What a great idea," he said. I could hear his smile.

"I'm serious. A criminal attorney. You should be prepared in case they try to pin something illegal on you to force your hand."

"I'll consider it," he said.

"Also," I said carefully, "although I'm ashamed to admit that this is even a possibility, it's not beyond the realm of imagination that you could be thrown into a detention camp somewhere without any rights, if somebody here gets the idea you might be a terrorist."

"American gulag?" he asked.

"It's not funny," I told him.

"I know it isn't," he sighed. He hesitated. "Can you come?"

My throat closed, and I couldn't answer him. "I can't," I said at last.

"I understand," he said.

No, he didn't. "I want to," I said. "You know how much. But I can't, not until I'm clear in my mind what I'm going to do. If I saw you . . ."

"You don't have to explain, Lynn. Really."

"You know that I—"

"Yes," he said. "I know."

CHAPTER 34

In the end it wasn't Richard Gregory who called me about a job but Nora Larimer, one of the founding partners of Elson Larimer. I was so used to thinking of Elson Larimer as the Goliath to my David that at first I misunderstood who was calling, nor, when the caller identified herself for the second time, did I perceive exactly what it was she wanted.

"Am I under a misapprehension?" she asked, sounding amused. "You did ask Gregory Associates to explore some career-change possibilities for you, didn't you?"

"Yes, yes I did," I said, recovering my wits.

"Well, if you're not totally averse to the idea of joining Elson Larimer, perhaps we could meet for lunch?"

At that point I was not totally averse to joining the Oakland Raiders, although I doubt they would have had me. I said I thought it would be very interesting to meet her.

"Meet *us,*" she said. "Barbara Elson will be there, too."

I was flattered and said so.

"Barbara and I," she said crisply, "believe in handling these things ourselves. We find we get much better people that way, and in the end everyone wastes far less time. At all events, are you free for lunch on Friday? The Clift Hotel?"

I didn't even pretend to check my calendar. I said I'd be there.

THE CLIFT HOTEL used to be the embodiment of Old San Francisco snobbishness, the sort of place where, if you were a man, you got thrown out if your hair was too long or you weren't wearing a coat and tie. In the moneyed and less contentious eighties, it was a beautiful, elegant place to stay and eat, minus the rules. In the dot-com era, the hotel had become a bastion of trendy exclusivity, where, in the words of one *L.A. Times* journalist, "Being accepted there is a confirmation of your stylishness." Of course, L.A. always has it in for San Francisco, but in this case I think the writer was right. "Accepted" was the key word. Forget "welcomed." You can't even find the place (on Geary Street) if you don't already know where it is, and the atmosphere is about as friendly as it is in one of those ultrachic boutiques that will only admit you by appointment.

Since I am the sort of person who usually gets seated next to the serving cart or, worse, the men's room in restaurants, it has been apparent to me for some time that I do not transmit the kind of hipness

that maître d's, waiters, or concierges instinctively recognize. Maybe if such people rushed to kiss my hand,
I'd feel otherwise, but I hope not. I think that the desire
to demonstrate your superiority to the rest of mankind
for whatever reason is a natural human trait but not a
very likable one, and I don't think it should be pan-
dered to. Since an awful lot of human enterprises—
from Madison Avenue to MENSA—exist precisely
because of this tendency, I don't expect to be listened
to anytime soon.

Meanwhile, although the Clift's restaurant was
leaching money at an alarming rate (many of the hip
young dot-commers having moved back in with their
moms), it was still a lovely spot for lunch, if you go for
a sleek, intimidating look reminiscent of the world's
most expensive safari. The food was "Chino Latino"
and the prices sky-high.

I had never met either Barbara Elson or Nora
Larimer, but I recognized them even before the maître
d' conducted me to their table.

They were laughing. It was the discreet, don't-
notice-me laugh of the middle-aged woman, but it was
genuine, a joke shared by friends who know each other
well. I relaxed a little. They might be high-powered attorneys in expensive suits, but at least they liked each
other. A good sign, on the whole.

We shook hands all around.

"I'll cut right to the chase," Nora said, sounding exactly like the chase-cutting sort of lawyer she was re-
puted to be. "We know you're desperate."

I laughed. I probably shouldn't have, but I couldn't help it. It was so unexpected. "What happened to 'would you like to order?' " I asked.

"Would you like to order?" Barbara Elson said, looking concerned. I wondered if this was a good cop/bad cop routine they'd perfected.

"Yes, I would," I said, studying the menu. "What's the lobster boniato mash?" I asked the waiter.

"White sweet potato and lobster chunks. It's a side dish," he sniffed.

"Nevertheless, that's what I want," I said. I felt reckless and festive all at once. The desperation comment had liberated me from pretense, not to mention hope. What did I have to lose?

They ordered more conventionally, and we all sat back. I waited for my desperation to seep back into the conversation.

It didn't take long.

"So where were we?" Nora said. Her eyes were a very vivid blue that pinned you with their gaze.

"You know I'm desperate," I offered pleasantly.

Her mouth twitched. "Oh, yes."

"Is it really as bad as that?" Barbara asked sympathetically.

"Probably," I agreed. "If you know anything at all about me, you'll know that Harrison Grady's problems wreaked havoc with my client base."

"Yet you went to his funeral," Nora said.

"How did you know that?" I asked.

"I was there, too," she said. "We were friends a long

time ago." She sighed. "You wouldn't have seen me," she said, reading my mind. "I sat in the back."

I shrugged. "Then you understand," I told her.

"He didn't wreck *my* career," she said pointedly.

"No," I agreed.

She nodded, as if she'd satisfied herself on some particular point I hadn't yet grasped. I waited.

"Well," she said, "Barbara and I are very impressed with your work."

"Thank you," I said.

"I'm not just saying that," she said, a little sternly. "I've reviewed some of your extraordinary-ability petitions." She consulted some notes she had put on the table. "Most recently you did one for SLAC, didn't you? A Dr. Strela?"

I'd almost forgotten that SLAC had asked Elson Larimer to review the petition. I nodded. "I should probably tell you that Dr. Strela has a very strong case, but there are some complications you don't know about. He might not get approved."

They both nodded. The ways of the INS were mysterious and unpredictable.

"Anyway," I added, "it's how you handle the weaker cases that counts, don't you think?"

Barbara, the good cop, smiled. "Absolutely."

The waiter brought our lunches. The mashed sweet potatoes and lobster alone made the entire trip—the drive in traffic, the scramble to find a parking place, the interview jitters—worth it.

"How is it?" Nora asked.

I sought the right adjectives. "Magnificent," I said. "Ethereal."

She smiled. "I like women who aren't afraid to eat," she said. "So, Lynn, do you think you might be interested in joining our firm?"

I swallowed carefully. "I know it's said that beggars can't be choosers, but I couldn't answer that without knowing the terms."

She nodded curtly. "All that would have to be worked out, of course. I'm not offering you an equity partnership, at least not right away. We'd have to see how your client list grows. But we're very interested in expanding our extraordinary-ability practice, and you seem to fit the bill. If that doesn't interest you, tell me right now, and we'll drop this discussion altogether."

"Keep talking," I said.

"We're planning to increase the practice in the Bay Area," Barbara said, "but we would also like to open an office in Southern California. That would be an exceptional opportunity for the right person."

"Where?" I asked.

"That's negotiable," Nora said. "Also, we have a small office on the East Coast that we're hoping to build up."

"In New York City?" I asked, my voice rising. The odor of brimstone filled the air, and Nora didn't even know what she was tempting me with.

"Of course," she said with some asperity. "Hackensack was full up."

Barbara laughed, so I did, too.

"Also," she said, "if you want to bring any of your associates along, we'd be willing to consider them as well."

"There is just the one," I ventured, wondering what they would make of Brooke.

"Is he competent?"

That required either a very long answer or an inadequate one. I chose inadequate. "With some reservations, yes, she is."

"We'd do our own screening in any case," Nora said. "But your recommendation would carry the most weight." She set her napkin beside her plate. "Those are some options," she said. "Think it over. If you want to take it further, we can hammer out the details."

"I will," I said, scarcely able to get the words out fast enough. "I'll definitely think it over."

"Good," she said, "I'll get the check."

"Thank you," I said. "Thank you very much."

CHAPTER 35

I was wondering . . . ," Meredith began. Her voice
sounded uncharacteristically reticent.

I was sitting at my desk in a state of total self-
absorption, frozen by the possibilities Elson Larimer
had offered me. I could go to New York with Alexei. I
could stay here. I could go back to Southern California.
To be offered what you wished for most—choice—was
profoundly unsettling. If I left with Alexei, I could start
over. I could reinvent my life one more time. I knew
that part of his charm was that he, too, in headhunter-
speak, had "zero drag"—no inconvenient attachments,
at least not here. A blank slate, the projection of my
yearnings. Unfortunately, he filled a void in me I didn't
even know I'd had until he filled it. How was I going to
go on without repeating the mistakes of the past?

If I left with Alexei, I would ruin everything I had with
Jack. Even battered and damaged, we already had a story,
a shared history, a family life. But if I stayed, things
would have to change. The marriage would have a chance

only if there were two of us at the center of it, and if that meant the kids had to "go lower," as they say in Jane Austen novels, it also certainly meant I had to give up Alexei. When you've felt that much for somebody, you don't rip him out of your heart without a lot of scars. If I'd been a character in a Graham Greene novel, I would have done the decent thing and killed myself before I hurt anyone, which I was bound to do, maybe myself most of all.

Meredith's call shook me out of my reverie, if that's the right word for it. "Yes?" I said. "Sorry. You caught me daydreaming."

"Oh," she said, as if this were an alien concept.

She didn't continue, so I asked, "How are you? How are the wedding plans going?" It was all I could think of to say.

"Fine," she said. "Everything is under control."

That was such a typically Meredith statement that I almost laughed. "That's great," I said, mastering the impulse.

"Actually, that's what I wanted to talk to you about. I want you to know . . ." She hesitated.

"Yes?"

"That I'm very grateful to you and Dad for putting on the wedding." The words came out as if she'd squeezed them out of a toothpaste tube, from the bottom up. I assumed that Jack had suggested that such a statement should be forthcoming, but I didn't care. At least it was something.

"It's our pleasure," I said. Not a sincere sentiment exactly, but a necessary one.

"Also . . ."

"Also?"

"A friend of my . . . of Mom's is giving me a shower. I was wondering if you'd like to come."

Now I was sure Jack had put her up to it. "I take it it's not a surprise or anything like that?" I asked. I could just imagine Janet's naked dismay when I showed up at her daughter's party. One bad turn did not deserve another.

"I don't like surprises," she said.

"No, I suppose not. I guess what I mean is, does your mother know you're inviting me? Is it all right with her?"

"It's my shower," she said authoritatively.

"Yes, but it's your mother, too. She has feelings, and they ought to be taken into consideration. If she doesn't know already, ask her if she minds. If not, then I'd be glad to come. If she'd rather I didn't show up, then I won't. No hard feelings."

"She won't mind, but I'll ask if you insist," she said.

"I insist," I said.

"She won't thank you for it," she pointed out.

"She doesn't have to," I said.

She paused. I thought the conversation was as difficult for her as it was for me, so I was just about to thank her for calling and hang up. "By the way . . . ," she said, before I could. "I'm really sorry about your cat. Patrick told me."

"He's okay," I told her. "The hair is growing in, and he's gotten all kinds of treats and sympathy since the accident. He seems to be enjoying himself."

"That's good," she said. "I love animals."

"*Do* you?" I tried unsuccessfully to keep the incredulous note out of my voice.

"Of course," she said. "I always . . . Mom would never let us get a pet."

"Because Patrick was allergic?" I suggested.

She made a derisive sound that in anyone less controlled would have been a snort. "Anyway," she said eventually, "that's mostly why I became a vegetarian. At age ten," she added proudly. "Ask Dad."

I said I believed her. On the basis of our acquaintance so far, I could just imagine her determination as a ten-year-old child, confounding her parents and upsetting everyone's menu plans. In a way I sort of admired it, at least before things got out of hand. My parents never let me have a pet either, and now I'd turned dotty about an elderly, one-eyed cat.

"I'll be in touch," she said.

"DID YOU," I asked Jack carefully after dinner, "say something to Meredith about thanking me for the wedding?" We were sitting on the couch watching the DVD of *I, Claudius*. Despite having seen it at least three times, I didn't get tired of watching it again, and tag lines from the episodes—"People *really* are despicable"—had worked themselves into our household vocabulary. It is probably a sign of age to prefer watching what you've already seen to trying something new, choosing comfort over excitement, Hawaii over Nepal. Still, the pleasures of re-viewing—like rereading—are underrated. Particularly when you share them with somebody else. Even something as small as a shared reaction to a TV program reinforced the concept of *us*.

"Why do you ask?" he said, not taking his eyes off the screen. Livia had just warned Tiberius not to eat the figs. She'd poisoned them, in order to get rid of her husband, Augustus Caesar. "Nobody would eat the figs," Jack said, before I could answer. "Figs are inedible."

"I like figs," I said. "And so did Augustus. That's the point. He thought he was safe eating them, and he wasn't. And you're evading the question. I'm asking because Meredith called me today."

"That was nice of her," he said blandly.

"Yes, it was," I agreed.

He sighed and hit the "stop" button. "Then why pursue it? Isn't it enough that she called?"

I had my answer. "It's okay," I said. "I'm glad you did, at least I think so. It just led me to think of something else."

"I thought," Jack said quietly, "that it was time she started treating you like family."

My fingernails dug into my palm. "Thank you for that," I said. "As long as you feel that way, there's something I want to ask you."

"What?" he asked.

"I want you to let me pay half of our contribution to the wedding." He started to shake his head, but I forestalled him. "I know we've discussed it before, but this is important to me. I've thought about it a lot. Please let me."

He looked at me. "If you're feeling guilty over wanting out of this relationship, you don't have to pay me off," he said.

It was a moment before I could speak. "I haven't said . . . ," I protested. "And anyway, that isn't it. Oh, Jack, you know it isn't."

"Tell me," he said.

The thoughts tumbled around in my head. That I wanted to be treated as a partner, not a guest. That I wanted a tangible investment in the family. That expiation, however much I denied it to him, was a distinct possibility. I could give up my money if I didn't have to give up my life.

I did not, at that moment, know which, if any, was the truth. Did I want to stay, or did I just want to feel less guilty if I left, like someone who had paid off her debts? I thought I knew, but I wasn't sure. "I can't tell you," I said. "Not right now anyway. But if we're to go on, I have to have a stake in this marriage. You and Meredith and Patrick and even Janet have to know I have a stake in it, too. And you know I'm not just talking about money."

"I've just been trying to protect you," he said. "I didn't think you should be penalized because Meredith and Janet are envisioning some extravaganza worthy of—"

"Madonna meets Michael Jackson?"

He laughed. "I was thinking more of Liz Taylor and

Elvis, but that will do. Anyway, why should you have to pay for it?"

"Because we got married, Jack. That should mean we share things, even things we don't agree with or even *on*. Protecting me means shutting me out. Surely you can see that?"

He looked at me. "You said *if* we're to go on."

"Yes."

"What if we don't?"

He wanted a definitive answer, and I couldn't give him one. I tried to imagine what the Anne Boleyn Society would advise at this point. Claire "Doctor" Billings would no doubt remind me that second marriages with children from previous marriages have a 50 percent higher chance of failing than do second marriages without children. Kay would tell me to consider the bargain I had made and decide whether I still wanted to live up to it. Lorraine would say . . .

Lorraine would say, had said, *There's always something you can do*.

"I just know that it's important to me," I said. "Can't that be enough for right now?"

"All right," he said, after a moment.

"Thank you," I said.

He smiled sadly. "Isn't it supposed to be the other way around?"

I couldn't answer him.

"There's something I've been thinking about, too," he said eventually.

I straightened at his tone. Even though I wanted to

get past this, one way or the other, it took all my courage to ask, "What's that?"

He looked out the window into the dark. "I think that if . . . I think we should definitely sell the house and move somewhere else."

I did not rush to ask—insincerely—*Why?* or *Why now?* I waited.

"I've thought it over," he said, "and I was wrong to refuse when you suggested it before. All this"—he gestured, palms up, around the room—"was my life, not yours. I didn't think how hard it would be, just stepping into the tableau like that. Meredith, Patrick, Janet—all of it. I was so eager for things to work out that I didn't want to see that they weren't working." He looked at me. "I'm sorry," he said.

One of the things I had always liked about Jack, in addition to his willingness to apologize (an unusual quality in a man, as I'm sure I don't need to mention) was his eye for the perfect metaphor. Stepping into a tableau—the interlude during the scene when all the performers onstage freeze in position and then resume action just as before—was exactly what it had been like. My eyes filled. "Oh, Jack," I said.

"I hope it's not too late," he said.

"I don't think moving would make you happy," I told him. "Your life has always been here."

"My life is with you," he said. "I have other commitments, but the one to you comes first. Besides, you can't deny that it might be a good idea to move a little farther away from Janet."

I had to smile.

He sighed. "And the kids, too; I admit that. They're probably too dependent on me. It might do them good to have to make it on their own."

I thought it unlikely that any distance between the Bay Area and wherever we moved would stop their importunings for financial help, but at least they were showing promising signs of independence. "I'd never want you to cut them off or anything like that, Jack. I hope you know that. But a little space between us and them while we worked things out might be . . . helpful." I smiled. "At least till you have grandchildren. The thing is, though," I added seriously, "it's a leap into the unknown. Sometimes the unknown can be negative as well as positive." What if, once we were alone together, we found out there wasn't any *us* anymore?

"I love you. I'm willing to take the chance if you are," he said. He understood what I was afraid of. "It still wouldn't obligate you, if we decide there's nothing to hold us together. You'd be free—you are free— to do what you think is best for you. But I'd like to give it a try."

"Oh, Jack," I said again.

"You don't have to say anything now. I just wanted you to know it's on the table." He said more matter-of-factly, "I can continue in a consulting role in the business from a distance, but it's going to be a long time—if ever—before the company is profitable, and I'm thinking I need to start practicing law again. My former law firm has approached me about opening an office in San Diego to capitalize on the biotechnology business. It's a hot area. You liked living there once— maybe you'd like to start up a practice again."

I wanted to say something, but he held up his hand. "Also," he said, "we'll get a small fortune for the house. We could pay off the tax liability without borrowing and still have enough for a nice condo or something like that."

"It would mean burning your—our—bridges financially," I said. "Once we've sold, we couldn't realistically afford to come back, not with housing prices the way they are."

"Yes," he said. "I know."

Like Cortés, I thought, and I remembered thinking the same thing when Jack asked me to marry him and my life with him was still an unimaginable, unpredictable shape. Remembering that, and realizing just what burning bridges would really mean, made my eyes fill again.

"We can talk later," Jack said.

I nodded. "There's time," I said.

He looked at me. "I thought we'd have the rest of our lives," he said.

CHAPTER 36

Alexei's approval notice from the Vermont Service Center arrived on a Tuesday morning, a clear, beautiful late-summer day so fresh and unpolluted you could almost imagine the Peninsula full of fruit trees again. I had checked the INS phone update line the day before and learned the news, but until the papers arrived, I didn't want to say anything. He might still have trouble with his adjustment of status, but the first hurdle—the big one—had been cleared. He was safe, at least for the moment. I turned the papers over and over in my hands, deciding what to say.

The professor and his wife had planted citrus trees in big terra-cotta pots in the courtyard outside Alexei's guesthouse. It must have been lovely in the spring. I sat down on a wrought-iron bench across from his door. The windows to the main house were shuttered, the occupants not, apparently, at home. I would not be observed. I sat waiting, letting the afternoon sun warm me, letting sensation crowd out thought. I closed my eyes.

"Lynn? Are you all right?" Alexei's voice roused me. "You said it was important," he said.

I tried to smile. "It is," I said.

"I came as fast as I could," he said. He moved to unlock the door. "Come in," he said.

I stood up and followed him into the guesthouse. He regarded me with concern. "Can I get you anything? You look pale."

"Just some water," I said. "Please."

He handed it to me, and I sat on the edge of the bed. He sat in a chair, facing me. Behind him there were open boxes, half-full of books. "You're packing," I observed.

He looked at me with a clear, penetrating gaze. "I have to be ready," he said. "For whatever happens."

My mouth was very dry. I swallowed some water and lifted the approval notice from my case. "Congratulations," I said, handing it to him.

He read it without changing expression. "What happens now?" he asked after a moment.

"We withdraw the appeal to the earlier denial. Don't leave the country—that's important. We'll apply for adjustment of status and see what happens." I looked at him. "Did you contact a criminal attorney, as I suggested?"

"Not yet," he said.

"Well, we can hope you won't need one, but you don't want to be unprepared, so don't put it off. In the meantime you're free to leave SLAC and move to New York and start your life there."

He handed the paper back to me. "That's very good work, Lynn."

I took a deep breath. "I can't go with you." I looked away. It was out. It was done. It could never be unsaid.

"I know," he said.

I looked at him. "You knew?"

"You haven't called, you don't write except for terse little updates on my case. Of course I knew," he said. "We've always known it would come to this, haven't we?" He lifted his hand to touch me, but I drew back.

"Please don't," I said. "I don't think I can do this if you touch me."

"It's all right," he said. "I've told you, there's no need to explain. I understand."

"How can you?" I asked. "I didn't know myself what I had to do."

He shook his head, as if I were a naive child. "I have to confess that I lied to you," he said.

"About what?"

He gave a small smile. "I have read *Anna Karenina*."

"So have I," I said. I was parched, with the taste of dust in my throat. I pulled myself together. "I should be going," I said.

He stood. "All right."

"I'll give you the name of someone in New York to see you through your adjustment of status after you get there," I told him. "It might be better to use someone local." I caught his look and added, "I would have done that anyway. Truthfully."

"All right," he said again. "I trust you."

"Thank you for making this . . ."

"Easy?" he asked, with a trace of bitterness.

"No," I told him. "Not easy." I looked at him. "You know it's not." I tried not to think of him all alone again. "Will you be okay?" I asked.

He smiled. "Of course."

I stood.

He came with me to the door, but I didn't look back. I heard it close behind me. I glanced up, half expecting that the day had clouded over, like some ominous foreshadowing in a Victorian novel. Instead it was still bright and lovely.

I would miss such days when we moved away, I thought. The breeze off the bay had its own special quality. I would have to tell Jack that. It seemed as good a way as any to start the rest of my life.

CHAPTER 37

It was almost dark by the time I got home, and the porch light was already on. I stood outside for a moment, schooling my face and heart into eagerness to return. Nothing less would be enough.

I opened the door. "I'm home," I called.

"In here," Jack answered. "In the kitchen."

Patrick was sitting at the kitchen table, holding the cat in his lap. Brooke was sitting next to him. "I've ordered Thai," Jack said. "Brooke's staying for dinner."

They all looked at me, gauging my reaction.

I smiled. "That's great," I said. "As a matter of fact, I'm really glad you're here, Brooke. I have some interesting news that could affect you, too. Remember our rival, Elson Larimer? Well . . ."

AFTER A SUITABLE INTERVAL OF SILENCE, I nerved myself to call Alexei with the name of a New York attorney who could handle his adjustment of status. I left messages on his voice mail at work, which he didn't return. I sent e-mails, which bounced back. His cell phone was off. On the fifth try, my call to SLAC was routed to the central switchboard.

"I'm afraid Dr. Strela is no longer with us," the receptionist said.

I gripped the receiver. "Do you know where he can be reached?" I asked. "Has he gone to Cooper Livingston?"

"I'm afraid I don't have that information," she said. "He's no longer in our database. I hope," she added, sounding a little more human, "that it was nothing important?"

How could I answer that? "No," I said. "I suppose not."

I tried the cell phone, and I even tried Cooper Livingston, but to no avail. He'd disappeared.

I was apprehensive, but there was little I could do without risk. He was a grown man and, as I had made perfectly clear, nothing to do with me. I would have to wait till he called me.

AT THE END OF THE WEEK, I was sitting in my office staring at the paperwork for the handful of H-1s that constituted the remaining legal work of Grady & Bartlett. After I finished them, there was nothing standing in the way of moving back to Southern California to open the La Jolla office of Elson Larimer. I would have to find someplace to live until we found a condo or a house we could afford on the proceeds of the sale of the house in Los Altos. We wouldn't move permanently until after the wedding. Jack had requested that, and naturally I'd agreed.

"You're going *where?*" Kay asked in horrified accents when I told her the news. She made it sound as if we were proposing to move to Greater Mogadishu. "What are you planning to do, set up shop over a tanning parlor?"

"No, a surf store," I told her.

"You'll have to get a face-lift," she said, immune to sarcasm. "Everyone gets them down there. They have to, because they get so wrinkled from the tanning."

"I'm a card-carrying member of the cosmetic underclass," I protested. "And I'm not giving up my Birkenstocks either."

She snorted. "You never wore Birkenstocks a day in your life."

"My symbolic Birkenstocks, then. Really, Kay, you sound ridiculous. It's a lovely place. They have bookstores and opera and theater and all the things we have here. And so far they don't have a dot-com hangover. That's one thing I won't be missing."

"So . . . um, is Jack okay with this?" she asked.

"I'd say he's moderately enthusiastic," I replied. "It's a big change for him."

"I'll say. He'll never wear anything but shorts again."

"Kay—"

"And will you be joining the Southern California branch of the Anne Boleyn Society if I can find you one?" she asked lightly.

I smiled into the phone. "Probably. Jack and I still

have some things to work out. It's not going to be easy. But I really think this is going to be good for all of us."

"Not for me," she said.

"Well," I began.

She picked up on my tone. "You'll be selling the house, then?" she asked.

"Yes," I said. "And the listing—"

"Yes?" she asked breathlessly.

"—is yours," I said.

"You're a peach, Lynn," she said. "Or should I make that an orange?"

MY CONCENTRATION WAS INTERRUPTED WHEN, like something out of a B movie, a shadow fell across my desk. I looked up, startled.

"Sorry if I frightened you," Dmitri said. He stood in front of my desk, arms folded, in a way that made me remember nervously that I was alone. "The door was open."

"Where is Alexei?" I asked him, getting straight to the point.

"I think you know where he is," he said.

I said nothing.

He sighed and consulted his watch. "I would imagine," he said carefully, "that at this very moment he is preparing for bed in Moscow. May I sit?"

I made a gesture indicating an invitation somewhere between *Be my guest* and *How can I stop you?* He sat.

"I'm not the enemy, you know," he said.

He could have fooled me. "Oh, really? What are you, then?"

"I am a patriot," he said. "I am also Alexei's friend."

"How can you say that? He didn't want to go back. You know he didn't."

"I know he was torn. But you must accept that no one forced him. It was his choice. Nothing anyone else said or did could make him do what he didn't want to do."

"I have only your word for that," I said. I didn't want to think what my own part in Alexei's decision might have been.

"You have a lot more than that," Dmitri said. "You know his character."

"Your government pressured him," I protested.

He shrugged.

"You know how he felt before, that the situation was hopeless?"

"I know about his breakdown," he said.

"What will he do, feeling that way?" I asked.

"The best he can," he said, "as we all have to. Besides—and I tell you this as Alexei's friend—the feelings of one person are nothing next to the magnitude of the need for his services."

"Even if it destroys his life?" I demanded.

"Yes," he said, "even then. But it won't. Times are better now, and Alexei is brilliant. But I'm sure you know that already."

"Yes," I said. "I know that."

"Cheer up," he said. "Alexei's taking a very important position. He will have a great deal of honor, and he has friends and family in Russia. He even has a wife, as you probably know. Here he was alone."

Not alone, I thought. But I remembered the half-packed boxes and the photo albums, and I knew he was right. I'd probably always known, down deep, that Alexei would go back, as he had known before I did that I'd stay with Jack.

He gave me a shrewd look. "You have your friends and your own family, don't you?"

"Of course."

"I imagine you are also the sort of person to honor your commitments, so I think, in the end, you will understand what Alexei has done."

"I'll try," I said. It was all I could think of.

He took out his wallet. "Alexei asked me to give you this," he said. He handed me a check for the remainder of my bill. I took it and folded it and put it in the drawer.

"And this," he said, passing me one of my own cards—Grady & Bartlett, on which someone had circled my name in pen. "He said you once gave this to a friend of his. You'd know which one."

I smiled, my eyes swimming a little, remembering David Peh's encounter with Repo Man on the night of Jack's party. "I know which one," I said. I turned the card over. On the back Alexei—or someone—had written a Web address. "Thank you," I said. "What will you do now?" I asked him.

"Go home," he said, with an answering smile. "Eventually."

WHEN HE HAD GONE, I turned on the computer and typed in the address. After a moment, the screen filled with tiny print. I scanned the page for text among the formulas and read:

> Particles that have interacted at some point retain a type of connection and can be entangled with each other in pairs in a process called correlation. No matter how great the distance between the correlated particles, they will remain entangled as long as they are isolated.

It was a definition of quantum entanglement.

CHAPTER 38

Meredith's shower was catered by a trendy restaurant whose cuisine was described as "haute vegan." Ever since the success of Roxanne's demonstrated a demand for raw food, an increasing number of caterers offered uncooked organic fruits, nuts, and vegetables. Fortunately, the "nothing heated to more than 118 degrees" rule meant that wine was technically raw and therefore permissible. Meredith wouldn't drink it because "Alcohol kills your brain cells," but the rest of us were grateful.

We sat on the patio with plates on our laps, sampling celeriac puree and almond-milk cheese and feeling virtuous and purified between sips of wine. *Sunset* magazine, the journal of western good living that originated on the Peninsula, had once done a feature on the hostess's house, with its glassed-in patio room and tropical landscaping around the pool. Kay had told me that if *Sunset* features your house, it's an automatic 10 percent added to the asking price. If you get into more exalted publications like *Architectural Digest* or *House & Garden,* the percentage goes up even more.

The hostess was a friend of Jack and Janet's from earlier days, someone I'd met in a casual way at one or two dinner parties when we were first married. She introduced me to the other guests—three teacher friends of Meredith's from her school, Justin's sister and mother, a cousin of Janet's, and a number of middle-aged women who were clearly there because of their relationship to the parents of the bride or groom. There was no one who looked or sounded Italian, so Valerio's faction was patently underrepresented. I felt doubly virtuous and took another sip of wine.

Janet and I nodded graciously to each other across the room. I assumed that would be it, since she was a costar of this production and mine was just a cameo role, so I was surprised when she came and sat down next to me, shoving her chair into the fronds of a gigantic tree fern.

"I'll move over," I said, and I did.

"Thank you for coming," she said.

I considered thanking her for approving my invitation, but I assumed that was understood, so I settled for, "I wouldn't have missed it."

She leaned forward conspiratorially and said, "What can you tell me about this girl Patrick is seeing?"

"Brooke?"

She nodded.

I tried not to roll my eyes or in any way indicate that

Brooke wouldn't be perfect daughter-in-law material, although I couldn't imagine what she and Janet would make of each other if it ever came to that. The thought made me smile. "She's very . . . cheerful," I said carefully. "Very competent. Full of plans," I added.

"Not like Patrick," Janet observed.

I was not touching that one. I went on smiling, as if I didn't hear.

Janet sighed. "I suppose she might be good for him. He certainly seems crazy about her. I hope I'll get to meet her before the wedding."

"I'm sure you will," I said, giving way to a less-than-noble enjoyment of the fact that there was something I knew about that Janet didn't.

We both looked at Meredith, who appeared to be trying to explain the green-papaya salad to her future mother-in-law. Justin's mother, down from L.A., looked like Edith Bunker might have if she'd gotten an updated hairdo and wore pants. She seemed very proud of Justin and couldn't help touching his muscled arm or shoulder at frequent intervals. Justin's sister was overweight and peevish-looking. Of course I didn't share any of these observations, but Janet was not so reticent.

"Merry's going to have trouble with that woman," she said sotto voce. "She's already making problems about the guest list for the wedding. I have a feeling this is only the beginning."

I watched Justin's mother pick at her salad with undisguised horror. "Thanksgiving should be interesting," I murmured.

Janet looked at me and then laughed. "Thanksgiving is the ultimate test of any relationship. If you can survive each other's families, you can survive anything."

I was tempted to respond to that one, too, but I gave it a pass and shrugged.

"Valerio and I are getting a divorce," she said.

I sat up straighter. "I'm so sorry," I said. I meant it, for a number of reasons.

"It's all right," she said. "I've been alone before." She looked at me. "It's probably just as well you and Jack are moving away," she said.

"Yes," I said candidly.

She sighed and looked back across the patio at Meredith and her future relations. "You never really know what you're getting into, do you?"

Before I could answer, the photographer came up, attracted by our conversational pose. "Can I get the mothers?" he asked.

I started to move out of the way, until I realized he was referring to me. I sneaked a look at Janet, who looked startled but amused.

"Well, why not?" I asked.

JANET MOVED OVER TO HELP MEREDITH record the gifts and enact the traditional shower ritual of saving all the bows into one big ribbon bouquet. There were tedious rules about not breaking the ribbons and what you're supposed to do with the bouquet, but it had been so long since I'd been to a shower that I didn't remember what they were. Justin's mother took up a position on Meredith's other side, in her rightful place of honor. The two mothers were tense and brittle, but Meredith was oblivious. She was having fun. She was actually giggling. She opened my food dehydrator and blew me a kiss across the patio.

I waved back and smiled. "You're welcome," I said. We were both trying hard.

I looked at her with her bouquet and realized that Janet was right. You don't know what you're getting into. You might think you're marrying one person, but when you get to the end of the aisle, there's a whole throng waiting, like a gathering of ghosts. Parents, children, friends, pets—they're all part of the package. It's surprising that you should need to be reminded of that, but sometimes the most obvious things are the least apparent.

"Could I get all the family over here for one more picture?" the photographer called. Meredith and Janet and Justin's mother and sister were lining up at the pool's edge.

This time I stood up without checking for a reaction. Commitment is a journey, not a destination. I took a step toward them.

EUROPRESS INTERNATIONAL: Unnamed sources in the Russian Ministry for Atomic Energy (Minatom) today confirmed reports that a major nuclear disaster—potentially on the scale of Chernobyl—has been averted. Sources said that the leak in the aging Doubinski reactor was spotted and sealed in time owing to new review measures and the quick action of a nuclear-response team dispatched by Moscow. The response teams are an innovation resulting from the recent reshuffling of Minatom and the appointment of Dr. Alexei Strela, at one time a physicist at the Stanford Linear Accelerator facility in California, as Director of Ecology and Safety. Minatom had no official comment.

The perils and absurdities of life and love,
California-style, from the phenomenal

CATHERINE TODD

SECRET LIVES OF SECOND WIVES

0-06-095347-0•$7.50 US•$9.99 Can

After waiting more than a decade for the "right" man to come along, attorney Lynn Bartlett said "Yes!" as soon as kind, clever Jack Hughes proposed.

EXIT STRATEGIES

0-06-000878-4•$7.50 US•$9.99 Can

Becky Weston had a comfortable, enviable life until the money vanished after her husband divorced her for a much younger trophy wife. And when her ex dies, leaving the purse strings in the greedy hands of Mrs. Number Two, Becky is truly left out in the cold.

STAYING COOL

0-380-78775-X•$6.99 US•$9.99 Can

With a successful business to run, an elderly mother gradually losing her focus, and a teenage daughter about to spread her wings, Ellen Santiago Laws is the last person who should be taking unnecessary risks.

MAKING WAVES

0-380-78773-3•$6.99 US•$9.99 Can

What's a loyal forty-year-old California housewife supposed to do when her hot-shot lawyer husband tells her he wants a divorce? If she's Caroline James, she holds her panic at bay with a makeover and a massage.

Available wherever books are sold
or please call 1-800-331-3761 to order.

www.AuthorTracker.com

CTO 0304